Stranger in My Arms

Stranger in My Arms

ROCHELLE
ALERS

ARABESQUE®

STRANGER IN MY ARMS

ISBN-13: 978-0-373-83008-4
ISBN-10:   0-373-83008-4

www.kimanipress.com

Printed in U.S.A.

Dear Reader

You were introduced to ex-CIA field operative Merrick Grayslake in *No Compromise* and again when he stepped on stage in *Renegade* to exchange vows with Alexandra Cole.

Merrick is back, this time in his own role as an enigmatic hero in *Stranger in My Arms,* and to take his final bow in Book #12 in the ongoing Hideaway legacy.

If you want to know the events that led to Merrick and Alex's courtship, then I invite you to join these unforgettable characters in a sensual romance where their love could put them at the greatest risk of all.

Yours in Romance,
Rochelle Alers

PART ONE

Friends

Chapter 1

Three knocks on the bedroom door in rapid succession stopped Alexandra Cole as she prepared to slip her feet into a pair of three-inch, silk-covered, midnight-blue pumps.

A frown furrowed her forehead as she stood up. This was the second interruption that had thwarted her getting dressed for her cousin's wedding.

The first time it was Ana who, in the full throes of PMS, had experienced a temporary meltdown when she couldn't zip up the dress she'd chosen to wear for the New Year's Eve ceremony. She and Ana were the same height, five-three, but Alex outweighed her younger sister by a mere five pounds. The crisis was resolved when she offered Ana one of the two dresses she'd brought with her.

"Who is it?" she called out.

"Jason."

Alex rolled her eyes. Now it was her younger brother. "What's the matter, little brother? Do you need me to tie your tie?"

"Very funny, Alex," he drawled sarcastically from the other side of the door. "I came to tell you that one of your loser ex-boyfriends just showed up uninvited, and Uncle Martin's security people won't let him in. What do you want to do?"

Crossing the carpeted bedroom on bare feet, she opened the door. Jason Cole stood before her in a dark blue suit, white shirt and white silk tie. It wasn't often that she saw him in a suit, but Alex had to admit that her twenty-four-year-old brother cut a very handsome figure in tailored attire.

Jason was the quintessential Cole male: over six feet, olive coloring, black curly hair and a dimpled smile. And in keeping with a family ritual that dated back to the marriage of their grandparents from which the prospective groom was exempt, any male who claimed Cole blood affected light-colored neckwear.

"Who is he?"

Jason lifted sweeping black eyebrows. "The message was, 'Tell her Donald is here.'"

Her large clear gold-brown eyes narrowed. "Donald," Alex repeated. She knew two Donalds. One who'd been her study partner in undergraduate school and another she'd dated only twice before she handed him his walking papers. "Did he leave his last name?"

Crossing his arms over his chest, Jason shook his head. "He also said, and I quote, 'She'll know who I am,' end quote."

Realization dawned. He had to be Donald Easton. "That arrogant SOB," she whispered. "Tell them to let him in and have him wait for me by the refreshment tent."

A sardonic smile parted Jason's lips. "If you want, Gabe and I can give him a blanket party."

Her brow furrowed. "What are you talking about?"

"We'll throw a blanket over his head, then kick his ass. And I'm willing to bet that if he wasn't getting married in an hour Michael would also want to get his licks in."

Alex stomped a bare foot. "Stop it, Jason! There will be no brawling tonight or any other night. Donald Easton has a problem with the word *no*. I'll take care of him."

"Are you sure, Alex?"

Forcing a dimpled smile, she patted her brother's arm. "Yes, I'm sure. Now go so I can finish dressing."

Jason flashed a wolfish grin so reminiscent of their father's. "Okay. By the way, you look great."

"Thanks."

Alex closed the door and crossed the expansive bedroom she shared with Ana and two other female cousins whenever they gathered in West Palm Beach.

Slipping her feet into her shoes, she wondered why a man she hadn't seen in nearly a year had come from Virginia to see her. Unfortunately she'd told Donald that she always celebrated Christmas and New Year's in Florida with her extended family; it was apparent he wanted to surprise her.

Well, the surprise would be on him because she had no intention of resuming what had been doomed from the start.

A member of Martin Cole's private security detail took a glance at the SUV with West Virginia plates and entered the number into his PDA. Smiling, he nodded at the man behind the wheel.

"We'll park your vehicle for you, Mr. Grayslake." He gestured to a parking attendant before returning his attention to Merrick Grayslake. "Once you walk through the gates and make a right someone will escort you to the Japanese garden."

Merrick nodded. "Thank you."

Reaching for the suit jacket resting on the passenger-side

seat, he got out of his vehicle, slipped his arms into the sleeves, then as directed made his way through a set of iron gates that protected the property that made up the Cole family West Palm Beach compound.

He hadn't taken more than half a dozen steps when he spied a small camera attached to the upper branches of a tree. Security personnel and surveillance equipment monitored everyone entering or leaving the property.

He'd left Bolivar, West Virginia, at dawn, stopping twice to refuel and stretch his legs. The drive south had taken longer than expected because of bumper-to-bumper holiday traffic along I-95. It was New Year's Eve and motorists were heading either home or to clubs or restaurants where they'd ring in the coming year with their families and/or friends.

At thirty-five, Merrick Grayslake had lost count of the number of countries where he'd welcomed in a new year. Whether in Central or South America, the Middle East, Southeast Asia, or in his last assignment as a CIA covert field operative—Afghanistan—for him it had become just another uneventful holiday.

Now, for the first time in more than two years, he wouldn't be alone or engaged in an undercover mission when the clock struck midnight. It had taken the wedding of Michael Kirkland, a man who'd saved his life, for Merrick to temporarily forsake his reclusive way of life and leave what had become his sanctuary, a modest two-story home near the Allegheny Mountains.

He'd checked into a local hotel and asked the front desk for an eight-thirty wake-up call. His head had barely touched the pillow when the ringing telephone woke him from a deep, dreamless sleep. He'd drunk a pint of water from the wet bar to offset dehydration before he readied himself to attend a New Year's Eve wedding.

When U.S. Army captain Michael Kirkland had come to him to solicit his help in protecting his social worker fiancée, Merrick experienced a long-forgotten shiver of excitement that always preceded a new covert mission. But the feeling was short-lived. He'd helped Michael identify Stanley Willoughby, the man behind a conspiracy to kill Jolene Walker; he'd remained in the Washington, D.C., area for several weeks following the arrest and subsequent indictment of the D.C. power broker before returning to his adopted home state.

Merrick still didn't understand why he'd decided to put down roots in West Virginia, but there was something about the topography that suited his temperament. The panoramic views, the rugged splendor of the mountains, and the small towns that predated the Revolutionary War and still bore the scars of the Civil War had remained virtually untouched, architecturally, since the 1950s.

The slate path widened to a lush, manicured meadow where an enormous gauze-draped white tent protected cloth-covered tables from insects. A smaller tent, less than fifty feet away, doubled as a portable bar. The weather had cooperated: clear skies, full moon and nighttime temperatures in the low sixties. His pace slowed as he joined a small crowd milling around the entrance to a garden.

A young woman sporting a white blouse and black skirt approached him. As she came closer he saw the earpiece in her left ear; he found it ironic that whenever he left Bolivar his surveillance instincts kicked in to high gear. It was as if he went into hunter mode, watching, listening and mentally recording everything around him.

She flashed a professional smile. "Your name, sir?"

"Grayslake."

"Please follow me, Mr. Grayslake." She led him into a large tent in the middle of a Japanese-inspired garden;

organza-swathed chairs were lined up in precise rows like soldiers at a military parade. She indicated a chair with a Velcro tag bearing his name. "The bar is open for appetizers and liquid refreshment."

Merrick was grateful for the offer. He hadn't eaten anything in eighteen hours. "Thank you." Nodding to the woman, he went back the way he'd come.

The light from the full moon competed with strategically placed floodlights and thousands of tiny bulbs entwined in the branches of trees and lampposts. With the artificial illumination it could've been ten in the morning rather than ten at night.

Merrick had received an engraved invitation that read that Michael Blanchard Kirkland and Jolene Walker were scheduled to exchange vows at eleven, followed by a midnight reception dinner and a New Year's Day brunch.

He would remain in West Palm Beach for the wedding and reception. He'd decided to skip the brunch because his plans included spending a few days in Miami before heading down to the Keys. He hadn't told Rachel he was coming, praying she wouldn't seek retribution because he hadn't kept his vow to keep in touch.

A hint of a rare smile played at the corners of Merrick's mouth as he neared the bar. He was never one to make resolutions, but the events of the past three months had forced him to rethink his monastic existence. Since reuniting with Michael Kirkland he'd socialized more than he had in years.

The sound of voices raised in anger caught his attention. As he turned around, his gaze caught and held the petite figure of a woman in a dark-colored dress with a revealing décolletage. Light reflected off the sparkle of diamonds in her ears, several delicate strands gracing her slender neck and in her dark hair. Merrick only saw her profile, but what he saw held him captive.

* * *

Alexandra glared at Donald. He'd downed one glass of champagne while holding another flute filled with the bubbly wine. She couldn't believe he'd come—unannounced—to her uncle's house and proceeded to get drunk.

"What are you doing here?" She didn't bother to disguise her annoyance.

Donald tilted the glass to his mouth and swallowed the imported champagne in one gulp. "What does it look like, Miss Alexandra Cole?" He spat out her name. "I came to ring in the New Year with my snobby, bitchy girlfriend."

She wrinkled her delicate nose in revulsion as the odor of something stronger than wine wafted into her nostrils. Donald Easton, the brilliant computer programmer, Donald the arrogant egotist yet always the consummate gentleman, had shown up at her family's estate drunk!

"I am not your girlfriend, Donald," she said, raising her voice above its normal tone. "I never was, never will be. Now I want you to leave."

"What if I don't want to leave?" he shouted. Those close enough to hear his outburst turned and stared at him.

"I think you should do as the lady says," warned a deep male voice filled with a lethal calmness that sent a chill over Alex despite the comfortable nighttime temperature.

She shifted to her right. A slender man with brilliant silver-gray eyes stood less than a foot away from her and Donald. Her gaze caught and held his; she was hard-pressed to pinpoint his age or ethnicity. His close-cropped hair was an odd shade of red-brown that complemented his khaki-brown coloring. His lean face, with smooth skin pulled taut over the elegant ridge of prominent cheekbones and the narrow bridge of his aquiline nose and firm mouth, hinted at a Native American bloodline.

Donald, weaving unsteadily in an attempt to maintain his balance, squinted at Merrick. "And who the hell are you?"

Merrick took a step and forcibly wrested the flutes from Donald. "You don't want to know." He handed the glasses to Alex. "Take care of these while I take care of your boyfriend." His request was a command. His right hand caught Donald's neck, fingers tightening on his carotid artery. "Let's go, buddy, while you're still able to breathe." He loosened his grip when Donald clawed at his hand.

"He's not my boyfriend," Alex said to the stranger's back as he led the interloper away.

Her hands were trembling when she placed the flutes on the bar. One of the bartenders came over to her. "May I get you something to drink, Miss Cole?"

"I'll have sparkling water." She asked for water when she needed something stronger to calm her jangled nerves. When she'd told Jason she would handle Donald she hadn't thought he would be intoxicated. The last thing she wanted was for her brothers to confront him when he was unable to defend himself. It would've been better for Donald if her uncle's security staff escorted him off the property than for her male relatives to get involved. She'd always teased them, saying even though they were trust-fund babies, they were a whit above thug status. They generally did not go looking for a fight, but none were willing to back down from one if a situation presented itself.

Jason was right about Donald being a loser, and it had taken her two dates to come to that realization. His insistent bragging about his accomplishments and a need to tell her how to live her life had been his undoing. However, Donald wasn't a man who took rejection lightly. After their second date she refused his telephone calls, text messages and letters that continued long after she'd left Virginia for Europe where she'd enrolled in an accelerated graduate program for a master's in art history with a concentration in European architecture and pre-Columbian art. She'd completed the first half of the program wherein she'd spent six months studying and traveling throughout France, Spain and Italy. And in another three weeks she would leave the States for Mexico City to complete her course and fieldwork for the program.

"Here you are, Miss Cole."

Alex accepted a goblet filled with ice and carbonated water. "Thank you." She took a sip, welcoming the chill bathing her throat as the man who'd come to her rescue returned. As he closed the distance between them she noticed, for the first time, his height. He was tall, as tall as her father and brothers.

However, there was something about the stranger that disturbed her more than Donald's unexpected appearance. She wasn't certain whether it'd been his eyes, the lethal calmness in his voice when he'd spoken to Donald or the speed with which he'd grabbed the man's throat. Everything about him radiated danger.

She forced a smile, dimples deepening as she extended her right hand. "I'd like to thank you, Mr…"

"Grayslake," he said, reaching for a hand that was swallowed up in his much larger one. "Merrick Grayslake."

Alex's smile did not slip. "Thank you, Mr. Grayslake, for diffusing what could've become somewhat embarrassing for my family."

Merrick gave her fingers a gentle squeeze before releasing them. He angled his head, his penetrating gaze taking in the perfection of her small, oval face in the bright light. Her eyes weren't as dark as he believed they would've been given her nut-brown coloring and inky-black hair, hair piled atop her head in sensual disarray and secured with jeweled hairpins. He fixed his gaze on her face rather than her petite, curvy body in a provocative halter dress with a generous front slit showing a liberal expanse of shapely legs. Her heels and upswept hair-style put the top of her head at his shoulder.

"Please call me Merrick." His voice was low, calming. "And whom do I have the pleasure of rescuing from the Big Bad Wolf?"

A soft laugh escaped her parted lips. "Alexandra Cole. But everyone calls me Alex."

Merrick's dark eyebrows lifted with this disclosure. "Well, because I'm not everyone, I hope you don't mind if I call you Ali. Alex is for a boy." And there was nothing about Alexandra Cole that even hinted of *boy*. Not with her curvaceous little body.

It was Alex's turned to lift her eyebrows. Over the years, she'd been called Alexa, Lexie and Zandra, but never Ali. "No, I don't mind." Merrick moved closer and she felt his heat, inhaled the haunting fragrance of his cologne that was the perfect complement to his natural body scent.

"I can think of a way where you can really thank me, Ali."

Alex went completely still. Merrick had gotten rid of one nuisance only to become one himself. "I don't think so, Mr. Grayslake. I don't date."

It was Merrick's turn to recoil from her unsolicited frank-ness. A shadow of annoyance crossed his face. "I wasn't going to ask you out, because like you I don't date."

She tilted her chin, the gesture obviously challenging. "Are you married?"

Merrick's impassive expression did not change. "No."

"Engaged?"

"No."

"Do you prefer men?"

He blinked once and forced back a smile. "No. And to put your mind at ease, I absolutely have no interest in you romantically."

A becoming blush darkened her face. Alex didn't know whether to be annoyed or embarrassed. Her quick tongue had gotten the better of her—yet again. She closed her eyes for several seconds as heat singed her cheeks. "I'm…I'm sorry, Merrick, but I—"

"It's all right, Ali," he interrupted. The smile he'd struggled to hide softened the angles in his rawboned face. "There's no need to apologize. I can assure you that I'm not like your boyfriend."

Her delicate jaw tightened when she clamped her teeth together. "Donald is *not* my boyfriend."

"That's not what he said."

"What did he say?"

"You were lovers."

Alex's eyes conveyed the fury racing through her. She should've let her brothers take care of the drunken liar. "He was never *my* boyfriend or *my* lover."

Merrick felt a strange numbed comfort with her disclosure; he'd thought Alex and Donald were having a lovers' spat. "Good for you."

"Why? Even though you're not interested in me romantically you think you'd be better for me than Donald?"

He was momentarily speechless in his surprise. Alex Cole was as outspoken as she was beautiful, a trait he wasn't used to in the women with whom he'd been involved.

"No. That's because I've never been a good boyfriend."

Alex took another sip of water, staring at Merrick over the rim of her goblet. "Do you realize you're an anomaly?"

"Why would you say that?"

"Most men would never admit to being less than perfect in the romance department."

"That's because some of them are either liars or fools."

"And you've been neither?"

Attractive lines fanned out around Merrick's luminous silver-gray eyes when a natural smile slipped under the iron-willed control he'd spent most of his life perfecting. "Wrong, Ali. I've been a fool a few times."

He'd become a king of fools when he'd trusted a woman whose duplicity had cost him a kidney and a career with the Central Intelligence Agency.

What he didn't tell Alex was that whenever he'd gone undercover he became a liar—someone with a fictitious background. He'd become an actor in a role wherein one slip would compromise his mission. His focus hadn't been the risk that he would forfeit his life, but completing the mission. And it was always the mission.

A server approached with a tray of appetizers. She handed Merrick a napkin and he took several puff pastries, offering them to Alex. She shook her head. "No, thank you. I'm saving my appetite for dinner."

"Speaking of saving, I'd like you to save me a dance."

His request surprised Alex. "You want to dance with me?"

Slowly, seductively, his silver gaze slid downward before it reversed itself. "Yes."

She felt a tingling in the pit of her stomach she found disturbing. Merrick Grayslake was disturbing to her in every way she didn't want. She would dance with the man, and after tomorrow she would never see him again.

"One dance," she crooned, flashing her enchanting dimpled smile. She wiggled her fingers. "I'll see you later."

Merrick stared at Alexandra Cole as she lifted the hem of her dress and walked out of the tent.

He'd come to West Palm Beach for a wedding and unwittingly found himself bewitched by a slip of a woman who just happened to be the groom's cousin.

Chapter 2

Alex spied her sister coming toward her. Her expression said it all: she'd recovered from her hissy fit. "That dress looks better on you than on me," she told Ana.

The black sheath dress with a squared neckline and wide bands crisscrossing her bare back was a perfect fit. The garment's hemline, ending inches above Ana's knees, and a pair of black silk sling backs showed off her strong, shapely legs. She'd recently cut her shoulder-length curly hair, and the pixie-cut style called to mind the gamine look affected by a young Audrey Hepburn. There was never a doubt that Alex and Ana were related. In fact, she and her sister looked more alike than Ana and her fraternal twin, Jason.

Ana looped her arm through Alex's and smiled. "Thanks. Come with me." She spun her around. "I've got a case of the munchies." PMS always triggered a craving for salt, alcohol or chocolate. She steered her older sister back to the tent.

"Quién es él?" she asked in Spanish, a language she and her siblings had learned from their bilingual parents.

"What you talking about?" Ana was notorious for talking in riddles.

"That guy over there staring at you."

Alex slowed her step. She wanted to tell her sister about Merrick and Donald Easton, but knowing Ana, the story that she had a stalker boyfriend would be on the lips of their family members before the stroke of midnight.

"His name is Merrick Grayslake, and he's a guest either of Michael or Jolene." He hadn't moved from where she'd left him.

"Damn-n-n-n-yum!" The expletive came out in five syllables. *"El es Caliente!"* Ana whispered, sotto voce.

"He'll do," Alex whispered back.

Leading Alex toward the bar, Ana stopped and placed the back of her hand to her sister's forehead. "Nope, you don't have a fever. Girl, is there something wrong with your eyes?"

She pushed Ana's hand away. "There's nothing wrong with my eyes. Just because I don't go buck wild over a good-looking man it doesn't mean there's something wrong with me either."

It wasn't that she hadn't found Merrick Grayslake attractive, because he was that and more. She thought him attractive, well groomed, confident and stunningly virile.

"So, you agree with me?"

"What about?"

"That he's hot."

"I'm too old to compartmentalize men as either hot or cold, Ana Juanita Cole."

Ana knew she'd hit a raw nerve because Alex had called her by her full name. Sucking her teeth, she signaled for a bartender. "And you're beginning to take life a bit too serious, Alexandra Ivonne Cole. Ever since you came back from Europe you've become someone I don't know or recognize. Lighten up, Alex, or you're going to turn into a bitter old woman."

Alex swallowed an angry retort. Ana wasn't the only one who'd mentioned that she'd changed. Perhaps it was because she'd matured while living abroad, that she had come into her own and knew what she wanted for her future.

Growing up as Alexandra Cole had afforded her a life of privilege. As a member of one of the wealthiest black families in the States, she and any woman who claimed the Cole name or blood were pampered and adored by their male counterparts and relatives. But as she matured she rebelled against the restriction that wouldn't let her travel like other young women who flew on commercial carriers, when she was forced to take the family-owned jet.

She'd lost count of the number of times she'd denied being "one of those Coles" when someone inquired about her name. Being the granddaughter of America's first black billionaire, the daughter of award-winning musician David Cole had distanced her from her contemporaries the moment she drew breath.

"I don't have time for a man."

"Yeah, right," Ana drawled. The two words dripped sarcasm. "You, Miss Party Animal, giving up men. I'm your sister, so spare me the melodrama."

Alex's expression stilled and grew serious. "I'm not going to argue with you, Ana. So spare me the lecture." She glanced over her shoulder. Merrick was gone.

Ana held up a hand in supplication. "Okay. No lectures. We're here to celebrate Michael and Jolene's wedding, and I intend to have a good time." She waved a bartender over, flashing a sensuous dimpled smile. "I'd like two apple martinis."

"I'm going to need some ID, miss."

Ana's smile was dazzling as she gawked at the delicious-looking Jesse Metcalf look-alike. "I can assure you that I am over the legal drinking age."

He winked at her. "You can't blame a guy for checking, beautiful."

Alex rolled her eyes upward. Her sister was at it again. She was a serial flirt. Ana flirted while she'd sworn off men—at least temporarily. After Alex finished her course work, earned her degree and secured a position as an architectural historian, then she would consider becoming involved with someone. At the present time that was not an option.

Ana handed Alex a glass with a pale green liquid. "Drink up and loosen up, sis." She touched her glass to Alex's.

Alex took a deep swallow of the icy-cold cocktail, feeling its potent properties immediately. Moaning softly, she closed her eyes. "Ahh-hh. That is good."

Taking a deep swallow of her drink, Ana inclined her head in agreement. "Ditto."

"Ladies, gentlemen, I'm going to ask you to take your seats. We'll be starting in less than fifteen minutes." The voice of the wedding planner, who was carrying a cordless microphone, was heard over the murmurs of those gathered under the tent.

Alex and Ana placed their glasses on the bar simultaneously. It had been a couple of years since they'd celebrated a family wedding, and whenever the Coles came together it was always a festive and momentous event.

Merrick ignored the young woman on his right. The psychologist, a coworker of Jolene Walker's, had talked incessantly without pausing to take a breath. He'd met her when Michael and Jolene hosted a dinner party at their Georgetown home. His expression reflected ennui while his gaze was averted less than ten feet away; his rapt attention was directed toward Alexandra Cole.

She sat next to a man, her head resting on his shoulder, and he assumed the man was her father. He didn't know what it was about the petite raven-haired, outspoken minx that fascinated him, yet knew realistically he couldn't uncover what it was in a few hours. One thing he was certain of, it wasn't lust.

Lust was an emotion he'd learned to control with the onset of puberty. The realization that he could father a child reopened a wound that had festered, healed and reopened to fester again each time he was shuttled from one foster home to the next.

His libido was strong, healthy, but he'd learned to control his physical urges. Whether it was fasting, meditation or exercising to the point of exhaustion, he refused to succumb to lusting after a woman just to slake his sexual frustrations.

Merrick reluctantly tore his gaze from Alex to Jolene Walker as her father led her down the flower-strewn carpeted path where Michael waited along with his best man, Damon McDonald, to make her his wife.

"Doesn't Jolene look beautiful?" the young woman whispered reverently.

"Yes."

Merrick was back to offering monosyllabic responses. The woman hadn't lied. Michael had confided to him that Jolene was carrying his child; impending motherhood appeared to enhance Jolene's natural stunning beauty that had most men holding their breaths and taking a second look whenever she entered a room.

The ceremony seemed surreal to Merrick as images of other weddings he'd attended in the past came rushing back, superimposed over the one taking place before him. He recalled those of his foster care siblings, fellow marines he'd met in the corps and one during a covert mission. He'd been so deep undercover that the man whom the U.S. had targeted as a terrorist had asked Merrick to be his witness at an impromptu wedding ceremony.

Applause brought him out of his reverie. Fifteen minutes had passed. It was over. Michael and Jolene Kirkland were now husband and wife, and he'd emotionally distanced himself from the ritual. As long as he did not acknowledge weddings, births and funerals he was able to plan for the next day.

Abandoned at birth, and not knowing his mother, his father or what he was had left a gaping hole inside Merrick that left him feeling detached and empty. Standing with the other guests and family members, he applauded the newlyweds as they traversed the path to a position where they'd receive those who'd come to help celebrate their new life together.

Alex felt the muscles under the jacket of her father's arm tense up before relaxing, wondering whether he'd reacted to his son Gabriel's rich baritone voice singing "True Companion," his nephew exchanging vows with his bride or that it wasn't one of his own children getting married.

David Cole had endured the relentless teasing of his brothers, Martin and Joshua, that he would never become a grandfather because his four children appeared to shun relationships that would eventually end in marriage.

It wasn't that Alex did not want to marry. It was that she wasn't ready for it. She had plans, ones that did not include a husband and children at this time in her life.

She lifted from his shoulder. "Jolene looks beautiful," she whispered.

David nodded and smiled. "She does," he whispered back.

Alex glanced up at her father's profile. The diamond studs in his ears were a constant reminder that David Cole was the least traditional of the offspring of Samuel and Marguerite-Josefina Cole.

The faint scar running along his left cheek was also a constant reminder of the former musician's brush with death.

Her father, who as CEO of ColeDiz International, Ltd., met her mother during a business trip to Costa Rica. He'd traveled to the Central American country to negotiate the sale of a banana plantation and found himself hostage of a deranged government official. He'd escaped, resigned his position with the family-owned conglomerate and set up Serenity Records.

She never tired hearing the story of how her parents met and fell in love. When she was a child it had become her favorite fairy tale, one wherein she'd imagined herself a princess who waited for her prince to rescue her from an evil king.

Princesses, princes and fairy tales were a part of her childhood with indelible memories of a home filled with laughter, music, exotic food and stories of Serena Morris-Cole's life in Costa Rica.

"Alex, are you all right?"

Alex's eyelids fluttered wildly, as she seemed to come out of a trance. "I'm fine, Daddy."

Overhead light shimmered on David's close-cropped silver hair. He smiled at his wife and daughter. "I don't know about you two, but I'm ready to eat, drink and party until the sun comes up."

Serena's short, reddish-brown hair framed a face that belied her age. She smiled up at her husband. "Steady there, sport. Do I have to remind you that you're sixty-seven, not twenty-seven?"

Lowering his head, David brushed a kiss over her mouth. "If you'd met me when I was twenty-seven you never would've been able to keep up with me."

Alex walked ahead of her parents rather than listen to their banter. They had been married for more than thirty years and were still madly in love with each other. If and whenever she fell in love she wanted what her parents had—a love that promised forever.

As she waited in the receiving line, she spied Merrick with a blonde clinging possessively to his arm. The woman was so close to him they could've been joined at the hip. Merrick glanced up, his gaze meeting and fusing with Alex's. A beat later they both looked away.

Playa! He'd asked her for a dance when he'd come with a date. *Liar!* she continued with her mental tirade. He said that he didn't date. But what did he call the woman draped over him like a second skin?

She shook her head. That was why she didn't date; she could not afford to be distracted by romantic notions. And like her free-spirited parents, she planned to eat, drink and party until the sun came up.

Alex inched along in the receiving line until she stood face-to-face with her cousin and his wife. Rising on tiptoe she wound her arms around Michael's neck and pressed her cheek to his smooth brown jaw.

"Felicidades, primo."

Michael Kirkland's green eyes shimmered like priceless emeralds. "Thanks, Alex."

She moved to her right, standing in front of Jolene. Extending her arms, she gave her a gentle hug. The two women had met for the first time earlier that morning. "Congratulations, cousin."

Jolene, resplendent in a simple empire strapless sheath of crepe that shimmered like liquid through a lacy coat in an off-white shade, looked like a Shakespearean princess. Her short naturally curly hair was covered with a circlet of tiny white roses and baby's breath instead of a veil.

Jolene returned Alex's hug. "Thank you, Alex."

In lieu of wedding gifts, Jolene and Michael had requested donations be made to the Jeanine Walker Retreat House, a facility named for her late twin sister who'd died at the hands of an abusive husband. As executive director of the Sanctuary Counseling Center, a D.C.–based treatment center for victimized women, she'd dedicated the past five years of her life helping women empower themselves.

Alex admired her cousin's new wife because she was so focused. Although a year older, Jolene knew exactly what she wanted and where she wanted life to take her. Her board of directors' fund-raising efforts had generated enough money to begin building the retreat house for battered women and their children. She'd fallen in love, married Michael Kirkland and now she looked forward to becoming a mother the following summer.

"Can I get you something to eat or drink?" she asked Jolene when the new bride pressed a hand to her slightly rounded belly.

"Bless you, Alex," Jolene said in a hushed whisper. "Please bring me some water and a few shrimp puffs."

"I'll be right back."

She wove her way through the throng waiting to offer their best wishes to the new couple. Her steps slowed when she came face-to-face with a man she hadn't seen since the last Christmas holiday family gathering.

Reaching for his hand, she smiled up at him. "Come with me, Diego, while I get something for Jolene to eat."

"Hold up, Alex."

Tightening her grip on his large hand, she forcibly pulled him along as she quickened her pace. "Unless you want to see your cousin's bride faint in front of her family and guests, you'll help me."

"Is she sick?"

"No, she's pregnant."

Diego Cole-Thomas smiled, an expression that was as rare to those who knew him as it was to see snow in the desert. "It looks like Michael couldn't wait to become a daddy."

Ignoring his cynical remark, Alex asked, "When did you get in?"

When she'd questioned her aunt Nancy as to the whereabouts of her eldest grandson, her answer was "He's expected
at any moment." Any moment had come nearly twenty-four
hours later.

"The jet touched down an hour ago. I barely had time to
make it to my place to change before driving like a bat out of
hell to get here before midnight."

Alex asked a member of the catering staff to bring her
what Jolene had requested, then turned to stare up at her
elusive second cousin. Diego Samuel Cole-Thomas was being
groomed to take over as CEO of ColeDiz International, Ltd.
Women liked the thirty-five-year-old confirmed-bachelor
venture capitalist and he liked them back. However, whenever
one broached the topic of marriage Diego managed to extri-
cate himself from the relationship unscathed.

Looking at Diego was like seeing Samuel Claridge Cole
reincarnated. Not only did he look like his great-grandfather
but he'd also inherited his business acumen. Diego's genes
had reached back several generations wherein he'd inherited
Samuel's height, powerful build, lean angular face and large
deep-set eyes, dark eyes that glowed like polished onyx. If
women weren't drawn to the slight cleft in his strong chin,
then it was to his smooth sable-brown skin.

"Did you bring Lisa?"

Diego lifted thick, silky black eyebrows a fraction as he
shook his head. "No. We stopped seeing each other a couple
of months ago."

Alex shot him a skeptical look. "Is it because she mentioned the M word?"

His solemn expression didn't change. "No. It was by
mutual agreement. How are you doing with your hip-hop
boyfriend?"

A rush of heat stung Alex's cheeks. She and Duane Jackson

had dated each other exclusively for five months, then without warning he'd stopped calling. She'd left a message with his housekeeper at his Miami mansion, another voice-mail message on his cell phone before relegating him to her past when he failed to contact her.

"That's over."

"I thought you guys were serious."

Alex accepted a small plate wrapped in a napkin from a waitress. "When have you known me to get serious about a man?"

Diego inclined his head at the attractive young woman who handed him two bottles of chilled water. He fell in step with Alex as they made their way back to the garden. "It's time you got serious about someone."

She ignored his censuring assessment of her love life. "I'll get serious about a man when you do the same with a woman."

"It's not going to happen, Alex. Not when my father has been talking about retiring." Timothy Cole-Thomas had announced he planned to turn over the reins of ColeDiz to his son the day he celebrated his sixtieth birthday. And that would become a reality in another four months.

"And it's not going to happen for me until I complete my graduate studies."

Diego gave her a sidelong glance. "Does this mean I can expect to see my little cousin married in the very near future?"

Alex rolled her eyes at him. "You wish."

"No, Alex. Your parents wish."

"Careful. Don't go there, Diego," she warned quietly in defense of David and Serena Cole.

Diego knew he'd struck a nerve with Alex. She was fiercely loyal and supportive of her free-spirited parents who'd raised their four children in an environment reminiscent of the seventies hippie culture. Gabriel, Alexandra, Jason and Ana Cole had grown up independent, headstrong, tolerant, secure, artistically gifted, while marching to the beat of their individual drums.

He stole a quick glance at his petite cousin. Men were drawn to her because of her beauty and carefree attitude yet none were able to tame the wildness that surfaced when least expected. And, if one did, then he would be deemed more than special; he would be exceptional.

Chapter 3

A loud hiss preceded the explosion of color in the nighttime sky as pyrotechnics spelled out HAPPY NEW YEAR! to the surprise and joy of those gathered outside the large tent. Amid cheering, applause, hugs and kisses, Merrick watched the faces of those closest to him. Dressed in their evening finery, many who'd had more than a few predinner cocktails, they were enjoying themselves.

"Happy New Year," a woman whispered close to his ear before planting a kiss on his unsmiling mouth.

He went completely still as he stared at the stranger. The tall model-like woman smiled, flashing her porcelain veneers. Although beautiful, in typically plastic Hollywood fashion, she definitely wasn't his type.

"Same to you," he mumbled, reaching into the pocket of his trousers for a handkerchief. Moving into the tent, he wiped the bloodred lipstick off his mouth. He wasn't one for public displays of affection, especially when unsolicited.

He wouldn't have been as repulsed if Alexandra Cole had kissed him; however, he doubted whether she would've kissed him even if it was under the pretense that the holiday called for the ritual of exchanging kisses.

The pyrotechnics went on for another ten minutes much to the delight of the young children whose *oohs* and *aahs* turned to protests as they were led back to the house. Those sixteen and over were permitted to join their adult relatives in the frivolity that would go on for hours.

Merrick was directed to his table under the enormous tent set up with seating for two hundred; he and Alex weren't seated at the same table but she sat close enough for him to take furtive glances at her; he'd lost his chatty hanger-on who, to his relief, was seated at the opposite end of the tent. Even if he'd wanted to reply to the psychologist, she hadn't let him get a word in edgewise, and he wondered whether her clients were given the opportunity to talk in their sessions.

And if he hadn't been so taken with Alexandra Cole's natural beauty he would've taken notice of the exquisite centerpiece of white roses, hydrangea, paperwhites, poinsettias and dusty miller spilling over crystal vases, the flickering pillars under glass chimneys and the exquisite place settings with Royal Crown china in a Derby Panel Green pattern and Vera Wang sterling and crystal.

Prerecorded music featuring the works of Gershwin and Ellington provided a soothing background to muted conversations as silent, efficient waitstaff filled wine and water glasses. They served course after course of endive with crème fraîche and caviar, bowls of delicious oyster soup, Caesar salad with crisp pancetta and garlicky croutons, wild-mushroom lasagna, grilled salmon, filet mignon and chicken cordon bleu.

Merrick lost count of the number of different wines poured for each serving as he alternated exchanging pleasantries with the two women flanking him while surreptitiously stealing glances at the woman who, despite his declaration that he wasn't interested in her romantically, had ensnared him in an invisible web of curiosity.

She was a Cole, a member of one of the wealthiest African-American families, if not the wealthiest, and was related to the groom. She hadn't worn any rings and professed she didn't date, and therefore he assumed her single.

Had her declaration that she didn't date mean that she wasn't into men? A hint of a smile tipped the corners of his firm mouth.

He would just have to ask her.

Throughout dinner Alex took surreptitious glances at the table to her right. There was something mysterious yet frightening about Merrick Grayslake. She wasn't certain whether it was the timbre of his drawling voice that indicated that he had southern roots or that he hadn't raised his voice to Donald; there was no mistaking the cold warning. And when he'd reached for Donald's throat she'd thought for an instant that he was going to strangle the poor man.

Staring at him through her lashes, she bit down on her lower lip, holding her breath. He'd caught her staring. The seconds stretched into a full minute. He acknowledged her interest with a barely perceptible nod. The corners of her mouth curved upward as her lips parted in an inviting smile.

Merrick was hard-pressed not to return her smile, his silver-gray orbs darkening with an emotion he hadn't felt in a very long time. He'd lied to Alex and to himself. There was something about her that made him want to know her. Putting two fingers to his forehead, he gave her a mock salute. A lump formed in his throat when she went completely still, then turned away to say something to the man on her left. Her expression before she'd glanced away was one of demure innocence.

Was she? he mused. *No, she couldn't be,* he continued with his mental monologue. Pushing back from the table, he looped one leg over the opposite knee; he studied Alex with a curious intensity that was so foreign to him. She reminded him of a lump of coal that appeared cold until touched. At that moment he likened her to a dark fire.

Alex had promised him one dance, and he hoped the single interaction would be enough to put his mind at ease as to why he felt drawn to his friend's cousin.

His attention was redirected to the bridal table where the best man offered a toast to the newlyweds. Flutes of champagne were hoisted over and over with the various toasts from a very pregnant maid of honor and the parents of the couple. Jolene and Michael cut the first slice of a four-tiered double-chocolate wedding cake decorated in white-chocolate curls and topped with marzipan roses and leaves. Individual wedding cakes in airtight containers and decorated with dark green satin ribbon were given to each guest.

With the pomp and circumstance of the wedding behind them, the bride and groom left the tent for an area where a portable dance floor had been erected in an open meadow. A DJ, alternating with a five-piece band, was on board to provide nonstop music.

The music was going full tilt when Merrick found himself standing off to the side watching couples twirling to a remix of Red Carpet's "Alright," a dance hit he'd first heard in a club in Amsterdam. He couldn't take his eyes off Alex as she danced freestyle with Michael Kirkland, sans jacket and tie. Others on the dance floor moved back to watch their spectacular routine.

Carefully coiffed curls fell over Alex's forehead as Michael spun her around and around on her toes. Reaching for a glass of champagne from a passing waiter, Merrick's gaze never left the petite figure. Their dance ended in applause as Michael lifted Alex off her feet, kissing her cheek.

Alex, her face flushed, made her way through the crowd. Merrick took two long strides and thrust the flute at her. "I believe you could use this."

She went completely still, only her chest rising and falling from the vigorous exertion, and stared at Merrick as if seeing him for the first time. There was a pause before she took the glass. Raising it to her lips, she took one sip, then another.

"Thank you."

Merrick inclined his head. "You're quite welcome."

Resting a hand in the small of her back, he led her away from the crowd. He wanted to talk to Alex, but didn't want anyone to overhear what he wanted to say to her.

Her spine stiffened against his arm. "Where are you taking me?"

"Relax, Ali," he said, leaning closer.

"Why should I when you haven't answered my question?"

His hand moved up to her narrow waist. "I want to ask you something."

She gave him a sidelong glance. "I thought you wanted to dance, not talk."

"We'll dance later." Alex stopped suddenly, causing Merrick to plow into her. She would've lost her balance if his reflexes were slower. Wrapping both arms around her body, he pulled her against his length. "Careful."

His breath whispered over an ear, and she felt a shudder of awareness of the man cradling her to his hard, lean body, awareness that she'd found herself attracted to a stranger when there was no room in her life for romantic fantasies.

"You can let me go now." He dropped his arms and she pointed to a cushioned wrought-iron bench under a magnolia tree. "We can talk here."

Merrick waited for Alex to sit before he sat down beside her. She took another swallow of champagne, handing him the half-empty flute. Cradling the stem of the glass between his thumb and forefinger, he fixed his gaze on the pale sparkling wine. There was a comfortable silence, neither seemingly wanting to initiate conversation.

He shattered the silence and asked, "Are you into women?"

A soft gasp escaped Alex's parted lips when she processed his query. "What!"

"Do you prefer women to men?" Merrick asked, this time rephrasing his question.

She gave him a hostile glare. "No. Why would you ask me that?"

"Because you said you didn't date."

Her nostrils flared in anger. "Because I told you that I don't date you assume I'm into women?"

Merrick lifted his eyebrows. "There was always the possibility."

She met his challenging stare with one of her own. "The answer is no, Merrick. I am *not* into women."

Rising to his feet, Merrick extended his free hand. "I'm ready for that dance now."

Alex shook her head. "No, Merrick." She patted the cushion beside her. "Please sit down." Waiting until he retook his seat, she turned and stared at his distinctive profile. She was certain he could hear the runaway beating of her heart that echoed in her ears like a kettledrum. Ana was right. Merrick Grayslake was exotic and *caliente!*

"Why should my sexual preference matter to you when you're here with a woman? Could it be you were afraid I'm going to make a play for her? And if you are, then I must disappoint you because I'm not into threesomes."

Merrick turned and looked at Alex as if she'd just grown a third eye. "Are you always this outspoken?"

"Yes," she answered quickly.

More amused than insulted, he smiled at her face in the diffused artificial light. "I'm not here with a woman. The young lady you saw me with works with Jolene. We met at a party at Michael's house in Georgetown a few months back. I, too, am not into threesomes, or foursomes. I'm a very private person, and if by chance I sleep with a woman, then there will be only the two of us in bed. And I asked about your sexual preference because I thought the two of us could possibly become friends."

Her delicate jaw went slack. "Friends?"

He lifted a shoulder under his suit jacket. "Yes, Ali, friends. You don't date and neither do I, so I thought we could hang out together."

Alex sat there, somewhat shaken by the unpredictable man sitting next to her. He wanted them to become friends when all she wanted was to flee his presence and surround herself with her family who always made her feel safe and protected.

But what, she asked herself, did she have to fear from Merrick Grayslake? After all, she was a Cole and the Coles always protected their own.

"I don't believe that's going to be possible."

There came a pause. "Why not, Ali?"

"I'm leaving the States in three weeks to study art in Mexico City."

Merrick swirled the remains of the champagne in the flute, then put the glass to his mouth and drained the contents, savoring the taste of the premium wine on his palate.

Resting his right arm over the back of the bench, he stared

straight ahead. Alex's declaration that she was leaving the country gave him conflicting emotions. He'd found her vaguely disturbing and exciting at the same time. He couldn't say she was his type, because he'd found himself attracted to all women irrespective of their race, nationality or culture. Perhaps it was because he didn't know who or what he was that permitted him to be more open-minded and accepting of others.

"Are you an artist?"

"No. I'm an architectural historian."

"What made you select art as a career?"

She lifted her shoulders under the revealing dress, bringing Merrick's gaze to rest on her exposed throat and neckline. "I've always loved museums. Whereas other children wanted to visit theme and amusement parks, for me it was museums and art galleries."

Looping one leg over the other in one continuous graceful motion, Merrick smiled. "I know absolutely nothing about art."

Shifting on the bench to face Merrick, Alex saw a flash from his incredibly perfect white teeth. Why hadn't she noticed them before? However, she knew the answer even before the question was formed in her head. It was the first time she'd seen him smile, and the gesture transformed his face, softening the sharp angles to make him even more breathtakingly attractive.

"Don't tell me you wouldn't recognize Leonardo da Vinci's *Mona Lisa*."

His smile grew wider. "That's the only exception."

"What about van Gogh?"

"Isn't he the one who cut off his right ear?"

"It was the left," Alex correctly softly.

"See? I told you I know nothing about art. How about giving me a crash course in art history?"

She felt him come closer when actually he hadn't moved. The smoldering flame she saw in his eyes startled her. Merrick

Grayslake spoke of friendship when everything in his gaze communicated the opposite.

"Not in three weeks." Her voice was barely a whisper.

Lids lowering over his penetrating eyes, Merrick stared at her lushly curved full lips. "I'm a quick study."

A tangible energy radiated from Merrick that drew Alex to him like a powerful magnet. He was maddeningly arrogant, but there was also something so soothing in his manner that she found herself unable to resist him.

It had been a long time since she'd been involved with a man, but that still did not explain why she'd felt as if her emotions were under attack; and she could not fathom what it was about the man a mere breath away who shattered her resolve to concentrate solely on her studies. She had three weeks, time in which she planned to visit with her parents and siblings before she returned to Virginia to close up her condo.

"Can you take a couple of weeks off from your job?"

Merrick was hard-pressed not to smile. "Yes. What do you have in mind?" He wanted to tell Alex that he didn't have a job or a career, and hadn't had one in two years. He had a government pension, albeit as a disability status, and the proceeds from shrewd investments permitted him a comfortable and uncomplicated lifestyle.

"I need you to come to D.C. Will that present a problem for you?"

"Not in the least. I live in West Virginia."

"Where do you live in West Virginia?" Excitement fired the gold in her clear brown eyes.

"Bolivar. It's a few miles south of Harper's Ferry."

"We're practically neighbors. I live in Arlington, Virginia."

They weren't neighbors, but it was close enough for Merrick to get to the Capitol District in a few hours. "How long have you lived in Virginia?"

"This coming March will be two years. I'm going to visit with my folks in Boca Raton for a week before I go back to D.C."

"When do you want to get together?"

"I should be back on the eighth. I have tickets for a showing that's also a fund-raiser on the ninth."

"That sounds good. I'm going to need a number where I can reach you so you can give me all the particulars."

"I'll give you my cell number. Do you have anything to write it down with?"

Merrick shook his head. "Tell it to me."

Resting a hand on one hip, Alex glared at him. "If you forget it, then don't blame me if we don't get together."

"I won't forget it. And if I do I'll call Michael and ask him."

Alex had her answer as to whose guest he was. And if he knew Michael, then there was no doubt Merrick Grayslake was either involved in the military or had ties to intelligence.

She recited her number, watching Merrick as he closed his eyes and mouthed the numbers. "Tickets to this event are as scarce as hen's teeth, so if I get one for you and you don't contact me, then there's going to be hell to pay, Merrick Grayslake."

His right hand moved up to caress the nape of her neck. Pressing his mouth to her ear, he repeated her number before reciting it backward. "Are you satisfied, Miss Alexandra Cole?"

Grinning, her mouth inches from his, she crooned, "I'm impressed."

Alex's soft, moist lips were a temptation, but Merrick knew she would never trust him if he suddenly took advantage of the situation and kissed her. He'd promised friendship, and that was what they would share until she decided otherwise.

"The score is now two for Grayslake, zero for Cole."

Vertical lines appeared between her eyes. "What are you talking about?"

Merrick's smile was toothpaste-ad dazzling white. "I earned a point when I rescued you from your annoying *stalker boyfriend,* and I just proved to you that I won't forget your number."

Pulling back and resting both hands on her hips in a challenging gesture, Alex narrowed her eyes. "*Oh-kay,*" she drawled. "You want this to be a competition? Bring it on, sport, because you're in for the fight of your life."

He sobered quickly. "Damn. You're a spunky little thing, aren't you?"

"Don't let my size fool you."

"One thing I'm not is a fool. I know enough not to mess over a Cole woman."

Her frown deepened. "How much do you know about my family?"

The seconds ticked off as they regarded each other like combatants. "A lot more than the average citizen," he replied cryptically.

A wave of apprehension swept through Alex, washing away her former bravado. "Who are you, Merrick? And what do you do?"

His impassive expression reminded her of a mask of stone. "I'm retired."

"Who did you work for?" Her normally sultry voice had dropped an octave.

There came another pause. "That's something you don't need to know."

Alex emitted an unladylike snort. "You want us to become friends, yet you don't trust me enough to tell me who you work for." She stood up, Merrick following suit. "Well, I just evened the score, Merrick. You don't have to tell me. Once Michael returns from his honeymoon I'll ask him."

Merrick knew when he was bested. He didn't want Michael

to know that he was seeing his cousin—not yet. "CIA," he said reluctantly.

Her mouth formed a perfect O with his disclosure. "You were with the Central Intelligence Agency?" He nodded. "Intelligence?" Merrick nodded again. She squinted up at him. "I see why you and Michael are friends." Her cousin, a West Point graduate, was a highly-trained army intelligence officer.

Merrick extended his free hand. "Are you ready to dance with me?"

Grasping his hand, Alex smiled up at him. "Yes."

Holding hands, they retraced their steps to where couples were swaying to the band playing Stevie Wonder's "You and I." Merrick wrapped his arm around Alex's waist, holding her close to his heart, and closed his eyes as she curved her arms under his shoulders. There was no need to concentrate on his footwork as they sank into each other's warmth, as if dancing together was something they'd done before. Before the last note faded, the DJ segued into the old-school ballad, P.M. Dawn's "I'd Die Without You."

Resting her cheek on her dance partner's shoulder, Alex closed her eyes and sang the words of the passionate love song. She lost herself in the strong arms, the sensual scent of his cologne and temporarily forgot her promise not to entertain notions of a romantic nature until she completed her education.

Going completely pliant in Merrick's embrace, she thought of a time when she'd lost her heart to a man who was undeserving of her love and trust. The song ended and they pulled apart.

Lowering his head, Merrick pressed a kiss to her cheek. "Thank you for the dance."

Easing out of his loose embrace, she gave him a dimpled smile. "Thank you for asking."

His gray eyes boring into her, Merrick inclined his head. "Good night, Ali."

Her arching raven eyebrows lifted. "Good night and Happy New Year."

Without another word, he turned and walked off the dance floor, leaving her staring at his broad shoulders until he blended into the crowd. She was in the same position when Jason reached for her hand.

"Come dance with me." He steered her to the middle of the dance floor as hip-hop blared from the powerful sound system. Raising her arms above her head, she snapped her fingers and lost herself in the driving rhythm of the infectious baseline beat. Her older brother, Gabriel, cut in, then Diego. After a while she lost count of the number of men she danced with as the hands on the clock made several revolutions. It was after four in the morning when she finally took off her shoes, walked across the carpet of grass and into the house that her grandfather had built for his wife before the Great Depression.

The twenty-four-room mansion designed in a Spanish revival style with barrel-tiled red roofs, a stucco facade and balconies shrouded in lush bougainvillea and sweeping French doors that opened onto broad expanses of terraces with spectacular water views was still one of the finest homes in West Palm Beach. The magnificent structure, set on twelve acres, was surrounded by tropical foliage, exotic gardens and the reflection of light off sparkling lake waters.

Alex always looked forward to coming to West Palm Beach for the week spanning Christmas and New Year's because it gave her the opportunity to reunite with her extended family and reconnect with her grandmother who'd celebrated her one hundred and third birthday December twenty-seventh.

She had the bedroom suite to herself, which meant she could linger in the shower. After cleansing the makeup from her face and brushing her teeth, she stepped into the shower stall.

Her eyelids were drooping when she pulled a nightgown over her head and slipped into one of the two queen-size beds. Alex was asleep within seconds of her head touching a down-filled pillow.

Chapter 4

Merrick checked out of his hotel, retrieved his truck from the parking lot and headed south. It was New Year's Day, the weekend, and he practically had I–95 to himself. An overcast sky had given way to bright sunlight, and when he entered downtown Miami the energy, passion, color and architectural treasures of the tropical city elicited a feeling of nostalgia. What was it, he asked himself, about Miami that made him feel as if he'd come home?

Slowing the SUV, he'd become the sightseer and tourist, driving past the harbor crowded with massive cruise ships and priceless pleasure boats. His sightseeing ended when he checked into a Miami Beach hotel. The view from his nineteenth-floor suite was spectacular. Opening the door to an armoire, he switched on the large-screen television to CNN. He'd planned to spend his time in Miami relaxing and soaking up the flavor of the city. Pulling a T-shirt over his head, he made his way in the direction of the bathroom.

After moving to Bolivar he'd discovered that he lost track of the days of the week; but that would change because of Alexandra Cole. Eight days—in another eight days he would call her to arrange a time when they would see each other again.

Stepping out of his jeans and underwear, Merrick recalled his interaction with Alex. He'd found her outspoken, opinionated and brutally honest, personality traits he hadn't encountered in any of the women in his past. She was a challenge, one he welcomed. Alex had promised him two weeks and he intended to make the most of their time together.

Merrick walked into a restaurant on Calle Ocho, Miami's Little Havana main thoroughfare. He took off a well-worn baseball cap and seated himself at a small table in the rear of the dining establishment. The mouthwatering aromas wafting from platters of food carried by the serving staff overwhelmed him. He'd opted not to order from the hotel kitchen because it'd been months since he'd eaten Caribbean cuisine.

Two months before, he'd become a lookout for Michael when he'd asked him to watch the building housing the Sanctuary Counseling Center. He'd set himself up in a vacant apartment across the street, bribing the building's superintendent to let him use the space under the pretense that he was a private detective hired by a foreign diplomat to watch his wife who'd abducted the two children the judge had placed in his custody. The greedy man barely glanced at his fake identification, accepting the one-hundred-dollar-a-day fee while offering to bring him lunch and dinner. The superintendent's wife was from the Dominican Republic, and Merrick spent three glorious days eating white rice, red beans, fried plantains, baked chicken and spaghetti with spareribs.

Picking up a plastic-covered menu, he studied the selections printed in English and Spanish. An attractive young waitress approached his table. "Are you ready to order?" she asked in accented English.

"Miro todavía," he said. *"Pero le agradecería una cerveza fría."*

The waitress's professionally arched eyebrows shot up. Not only was the gray-eyed man *guapo,* but he also spoke Spanish.

"Seguro." She flashed a sultry grin before walking away with an exaggerated sway of her hips. She took a bottle of beer from a freezer case, whispering to her girlfriend to take a look at the man in the light blue shirt seated in her section.

"El es guapo! But don't let Jorge see you flirting with him, Milagros," the other woman warned in English. "The two of you are practically engaged."

"Almost engaged, but not blind," Milagros whispered, winking at her best friend. She returned to her customer, placing the bottle of beer and a chilled glass on the table. She was the epitome of professionalism when she jotted down Merrick's order of black beans, white rice, baked chicken and an avocado salad.

Merrick lingered at the restaurant, eating, reading a Spanish-language newspaper and viewing a Spanish-language television station. It was as if he wanted to immerse himself in a language he'd learned from the Mexican housekeepers in the employ of his foster parents.

The foster parents were all cut from the same fabric: God-fearing folks who felt an obligation to take care of the less fortunate. They never stopped to think that the money they received from the state for their charges helped pay for luxury cars, state-of-the-art electronic equipment, expanding their already sprawling homes and vacationing in exotic getaways.

Forcing himself not to think of his troubled childhood, he paid the check, leaving a generous tip, and walked out of the restaurant. He put on his favorite New York Yankees cap, successfully concealing his dark auburn hair, and set off on foot to tour the area. He stopped at the Brigade 2506 Memorial that commemorated the exiled victims of the unsuccessful 1961 Bay of Pigs invasion of Cuba. The sun had set by the time he returned to pick up his vehicle and check back into his hotel room.

Unaccustomed to the heavy food and the winter heat he lay down on the bed in the air-conditioned room. Within seconds of closing his eyes, the face of Alex flooded his mind. Cursing under his breath, he sat up and reached for his cell phone on the nightstand. The only way he was going to exorcise her was to talk to her.

Merrick dialed her number as if it was something he did on a regular basis. It rang three times before he heard her greeting.

A smile crinkled the lines around his eyes. "I told you I wouldn't forget."

Her sultry laugh came through the tiny earpiece. "You're really full of yourself, aren't you? Are you trying to prove to me how smart you are, Mr. Former CIA Man?"

A bright smile spread over his face. "No and no. Right now I'm full of *arroz frijoles, pollo y aguacate*."

"You speak Spanish?"

"Sí, que tú hablas Español, también?"

"Yes. Both my parents speak the language. Who taught you?"

There was a pause before Merrick said, "That's a long story."

"I have all night, Merrick."

"All night for what, Ali?"

"To listen to you tell me about yourself."

"Why don't you wait until we see each other again?"

"Where are you?"

"I'm in Miami."

"That's one of my favorite cities. The architecture is spectacular."

"It is very colorful." Merrick wanted to tell Alex that she was spectacular but didn't want to come on too strong. "Now that I know you didn't give me the wrong number, I'll let you go."

"The wrong number!" she repeated. "If I hadn't wanted to give you my number, then we wouldn't be having this conversation."

He chuckled softly. "So, you do want to be my friend."

"Isn't that why I gave you my number?"

"No, Ali. You gave me your number because you promised to tutor me in art history."

"It's going to have to be an accelerated course."

"I told you before that I'm a quick study." What Merrick hadn't told Alex was that he had a photographic memory. He'd become known in the Marine Corps as "Lock and Load" because if he saw something or someone once, he was able to file the information away in his mind and recall it at will. This gift had served him well once he was recruited by the Central Intelligence Agency.

"I'm going to grade you."

"What can I expect if I get straight As?"

Alex laughed again. "I'll be certain to come up with something comparable to your final grade. How long are you going to be in Miami?"

"I plan to spend another day here. Then I'm heading down to the Keys."

"I've lived in Florida all my life yet I've never been to the Keys."

"Do you want to join me?"

"No."

"Why not?"

"Because I don't know you like *that*."

"Like what, Ali? Do you think I'd try to compromise you?"

"No. Of course not," she said much too quickly. "Maybe the next time I'll take you up on your offer."

"I'm going to hold you to that promise."

"I always keep my promises, Merrick."

"Good for you." He heard a signal that indicated Alex had another caller.

"Hold on, I have another call coming through." There was a momentary pause before she came back on the line. "I'm going to have to ring off now. I'll talk to you again on the eighth."

"Okay. Stay well and stay out of trouble." Her bubbly laughter floated into his ear. "Don't make me have to come to your rescue again," he teased.

"It's kind of nice having a personal knight in shining armor."

"I hate to tell you, but my armor's rusted and dented beyond repair."

"That doesn't matter. I'll still keep you, Sir Grayslake."

Merrick knew he had to end the call before he said something that would sabotage his fragile yet promising relationship with Alexandra Cole. "I'll call you on the eighth."

"Ciao, amigo," she said cheerfully.

"Hasta luego, Ali."

Merrick pressed a button, ending the connection. He was glad he'd called her. Hearing her voice and bubbly laugh was a reminder of what he could look forward to once he returned to West Virginia.

Merrick finally found Rachel Singletary's house without mishap. His vehicle's navigational system had never failed him. He turned down a narrow street that made up Key West. He found a parking spot in what he termed an alley, and walked the short distance to a one-story stucco structure painted a soft salmon pink and fronted by a wrought-iron fence protecting a flower garden overflowing with frangipani and bougainvillea.

Reaching over, he unlatched the gate at the same time the front door opened. Rachel stood in the doorway, an automatic handgun pressed to her jeans-covered thigh.

Merrick held up both hands. "I come in peace."

The network of tiny lines around the woman's dark eyes deepened when she recognized the tall man standing outside the gate. "Merrick! How the hell are you?"

He gestured to the firearm. "I'd be a lot better if you put that thing away."

Rachel waved him in. "It's all for show."

Merrick opened the gate as Rachel came forward to meet him. Looping an arm around her waist, he leaned over and kissed her cheek. "You look good, Rusty," he said, using her nickname.

"Not as good as you, Gray. To what do I owe the honor of you gracing me with your presence?" Rachel asked as she tucked the firearm into the waistband of her jeans under an oversize man-tailored shirt.

"I did promise to come and visit."

"That was two years ago." She moved aside as Merrick stepped into an expansive entryway.

"Better late than never," he quipped.

She closed and locked the front door. "Go onto the back porch where it's cooler."

He made his way through a living room filled with rattan pieces covered with colorful plush pillows and cushions in keeping with the tropical locale. A profusion of potted plants and palms brought the outdoors inside.

He stood on an enclosed porch, staring through the screen at the ocean. The view was awesome, humbling and peaceful. Living in a landlocked state definitely had its disadvantages. A low table held a television, a radio and a stack of recent bestselling books. It was obvious Rachel spent most of her time at the rear of her house.

"Sit down, Merrick."

He folded his length down to a cushioned love seat while Rachel sat on a chaise; he turned to stare at the middle-aged woman who at one time had been his supervisor in Langley, Virginia.

Twenty-five years his senior, she'd become his older sister, counselor and confidante. Tall and sturdily built, with even features, she'd teased him, saying they probably were related because both had red hair. The years had darkened the bright orange strands and added a liberal sprinkling of gray while the Florida sun had tanned her face wherein the liberal sprinkling of freckles blended with the added color.

Leaning to her right, she opened the door to a portable refrigerator and took out two bottles of beer. She offered one to Merrick. "I'm sorry I don't have anything stronger."

He waved a hand. "No, thank you."

"Don't tell me you've gone soft, Grayslake."

"A little," he admitted. "Being away from the action can do that."

Rachel twisted the cap off the bottle, put it to her mouth and took a long swallow. "You still could've been in the action if you hadn't cut and run like a candy-ass."

Merrick closed his eyes, shutting out the awesome sight of the sun setting over the ocean. "I didn't join the Company to sit behind a desk."

Rachel stared at the tall, slender man. "Neither did I, Merrick."

"But you did," he countered.

"That's something you wouldn't understand."

He opened his eyes, meeting her pain-filled gaze. "Understand what, Rusty?"

She shook her head. "Forget it."

Sitting up straighter, he rested his elbows on his knees. "What happened, Rachel?"

She avoided his stare, took another sip from her beer and stared through the screen at the large ball of orange sinking lower beyond the horizon. "After…" Her voice trailed off. "After someone—another agent who was very close to me, was captured and executed in Somalia, I requested desk duty."

Merrick knew no amount of pressure would get Rachel to divulge the name of the other agent. Even in death, the Company never identified its agents by name.

"You were in love with him." The query was a statement.

Rachel blinked back the tears. "My love for him knew no bounds. When I found out that he'd been killed I thought about taking my own life."

"Did he love you, Rachel?" Merrick asked in a hushed whisper. She nodded. "Why didn't you marry him?"

A cynical smile twisted her mouth. "I couldn't because he was already married. And in the twelve years we worked together I never asked that he leave his wife and children. I was willing to be his mistress and accept what little of himself he doled out to me." She took another deep swallow of the cold brew.

"My supervisor went ballistic when I requested desk duty, but there wasn't much he could do once I spoke to the Agency's psychiatrist and confessed to suicidal ideation. I'd been in the position as an intelligence research training specialist eight years when you enrolled in my class. I was the one who recommended you for my position once you returned from disability leave."

Merrick, hands sandwiched between his denim-covered knees, stared at the sisal rug covering the floor. "It wouldn't have worked. Not at that time in my life."

Rachel focused her gaze on the coarse reddish-brown hair

on Merrick's well-shaped head. She'd always thought his looks incredible. The contrast of his gray eyes in a khaki-brown face was startling and hypnotic. It was obvious he was a man of color, but it was impossible to identify his racial or ethnic group.

And not once during the time when she acted as facilitator for the intelligence training course had she ever seen him smile. She'd found it odd that he hadn't bothered to jot down notes like the other agents-in-training; her fear that he would flunk out was belied when his tests came back with perfect scores.

"What about now, Merrick?" she asked softly.

A half smile parted his lips. "It's something I could consider."

Her red eyebrows lifted with this disclosure. "Are you serious?"

His smile widened. "Just say I've been thinking about it."

"What brought on this epiphany?"

"I've been getting out more."

Rachel smiled. "Someone told me that you were holed up somewhere in West Virginia. Don't tell me that you met someone who has melted that lump of ice you call a heart."

Merrick sobered. "No. It had nothing to do with a woman." There was a moment of silence as the two regarded each other.

"How old are you now?" Rachel asked.

"Thirty-five."

"Are you married?"

"No."

"Do you have a girlfriend?"

"No."

"What about a lover?"

There was a pause before Merrick said, "No."

Rachel went completely still, her eyes boring into Merrick's. "Don't you have urges? I'm sixty and I still do."

"Do you do anything about them?" he asked, his expression deadpan.

"You better believe I do. I'm seeing somebody."

"Is it serious?"

"If you're asking whether I'll ever get married, then the answer is no. He's been divorced for fifteen years and has no intention of tying the knot again, and that's fine with me. I'm enjoying retirement. I get up when I want, and come and go whenever the whim hits me. I'm glad I got out when I did because it took a year of therapy to rid myself of the dreams that I was reliving every mission."

Merrick wanted to tell Rachel that he never experienced the disturbing images of his missions because he'd managed to become totally detached whenever he went undercover. He wasn't Merrick Grayslake but whoever and whatever his government wanted him to be.

Reaching across the space separating them, he patted Rachel's hand. "Would you mind sharing dinner with me tonight?"

She gave him a saucy grin. "Are you asking me out on a date?"

He winked at her. "Yes, I am, beautiful."

A rush of color darkened her face as she blushed like a young girl. "Keep talking like that and I'm going to tell my boyfriend."

Rising to his feet, Merrick offered her his hand, and pulled her up effortlessly. "Tell him," he teased. "I bet he can't beat me up."

Rachel smiled, tilting her head back to meet his teasing gaze. "He's got at least forty pounds on you."

Merrick kissed her cheek. "The bigger they are the harder they fall."

She patted his shoulder. "You're right about that. I know a little seafood place that's within walking distance. It's not fancy but the food is wonderful."

"That sounds great."

"How long do you plan to hang out in the Keys?"

"No more than four days."

"Where are you staying?" Rachel asked over her shoulder as she led Merrick off the porch.

"I've checked into the Marquesa." The Marquesa Hotel was an elegant restored home that dated back to 1884.

"Check out tomorrow and come stay with me. I have an extra bedroom."

"I can't do that, Rusty."

"Yes, you can."

"What about your boyfriend?"

"He's bound to be a little jealous, but he'll get over it once I tell him you're celibate."

Wrapping an arm around Rachel's neck, Merrick pulled her close. "You should know you're taking a risk inviting a sex-starved man to sleep under the same roof with you."

Rachel returned the hug, her arm going around his slim waist. "I made my reputation at the Company being a risk taker."

Merrick knew she was right. Rachel Singletary had become one of the best female agents in CIA history. But she'd lost her edge because she'd fallen in love with the wrong man while he'd almost lost his life because he'd trusted the wrong woman.

Chapter 5

Her head and body swathed in thick, thirsty towels, Alex walked out of the bathroom adjoining her bedroom suite to the ringing of her cell phone. Quickening her pace, she stubbed her toes on a leg of the nightstand as she reached for the tiny instrument.

"Dammit!" she hissed between clenched teeth as she activated the Talk button.

"I can always call back another time," came what now had become a familiar male voice.

Hopping on one foot, she sat down on the padded bench at the foot of her bed. The ColeDiz jet had touched down at Washington National Airport at three that morning, but it was close to dawn when she'd finally crawled into bed.

"No! Please don't, Merrick." Her little toe throbbed like a raw nerve.

"What's the matter?"

She registered genuine concern in the deep, drawling voice. "I just jammed my toe on a piece of furniture."

"Will you require medical attention?"

She smiled for the first time. "I doubt it. I want to thank you, Merrick."

"For what, Ali?"

"You said you'd call and you did. Most men I meet are such liars and dogs that I can't stand them. Are we still on for tomorrow?" she asked without pausing to take a breath.

"That depends on the weather. Have you looked out the window?"

"No. What's going on?"

"It's been snowing for hours."

Pushing off the bed and limping to the window, Alex opened the shutters covering the floor-to-ceiling windows. The roadway and cars parked along the street were covered with snow. Her mouth turned down in a frown. She didn't know why, but she'd spent the week looking forward to seeing Merrick Grayslake again. And if he was stuck in the mountains, then there was the possibility he would be snowed in.

"Is it snowing in West Virginia?"

"I wouldn't know because I'm in Arlington."

"When did you get here?"

"Yesterday afternoon. I'm at the Hyatt."

"You're within walking distance of my condo." She gave him her address. "How would you like to share dinner with me?"

"Is this a date, Ali?"

"Yes. Does it bother you that a woman asked you before you could ask her?"

"Not in the least. I like a woman who knows what she wants."

"It's not about what I want. I just thought that we'd begin your lessons earlier than planned." She didn't want to give

Merrick the impression that there would be more between them than friendship.

"That sounds good to me. What time should I arrive?"

Alex glanced at the clock on the nightstand. It was almost one o'clock. "Make it between five and six."

"What do you like to drink?"

"Don't worry about beverages. I have everything." She had a Sub-Zero Refrigerator with a compartment for chilling wines. "Is there anything you don't eat?"

"No."

"If that's the case, then I'll see you later." She ended the call without giving Merrick the opportunity to ring off.

Alex knew she had to wipe away the dust from the floors and tables that had gathered during her absence and shop for groceries to replace those she'd thrown away before she left for Florida. Turning away from the window, she returned to the bathroom to complete her toilette.

Merrick stomped on the thick straw mat outside the door to the three-story Federal-style building, shaking the snow off his boots as he rang the bell for Alex's apartment.

"Yes?" came her sultry voice through the building's intercom.

He leaned closer. "Merrick."

"Come on up." A buzzing sound disengaged the lock to the outer door.

He pushed it open with his shoulder, and heat enveloped him like a warm, comforting blanket. The mailbox in the vestibule bearing Alex's name indicated she lived on the second floor. Cradling a bag to his sheepskin-lined leather bomber jacket, he climbed the staircase to her floor.

Walking the four blocks had become a challenge. The falling snow had increased in intensity, and meteorologists were predicting more than a foot before tapering off later that night. A district-wide snow emergency was in full effect wherein government office buildings had closed at two and all nonessential vehicles were ordered to stay off major thoroughfares.

Merrick smiled as he stepped off the last stair. The unique voice of Tina Turner greeted him as the door to Alex's apartment opened and she stood there, an inviting smile tilting the corners of her mouth. Her curly hair fell around her face in sensual disarray, raven strands grazing her delicate jaw and the nape of her neck.

She looked younger and more fragile than she had a week ago. Today she hadn't bothered to put on any makeup, and in a long-sleeved cotton tee, body-hugging jeans and sock-covered feet she appeared barely out of her teens.

He handed her the bag filled with a bouquet of colorful calla lilies. "I decided to bring a little something to brighten up the table."

Alex met his gaze. The moisture from melting snow coated the strands of his close-cropped hair, and she wondered why he hadn't worn a hat. "They're beautiful, Merrick. Thank you so much. Please come in," she urged as he took off his gloves, shoving them into his jacket pocket, then bent over to untie his Timberland boots.

"I don't want to track snow over your floors."

An exquisite oriental runner in the foyer covered a highly-polished wood floor. Leaning against the door frame, he removed his boots, leaving them on the mat outside the door. Then he took off the waist-length jacket and hung it on a mahogany coat tree. Despite the frigid, snowy weather, the inviting space was imbued with a tropical mood, with a stunning French-Regency console table with Martinique-style carvings and a gilded Louis XV–inspired mirror. The table cradled a vase of fresh white roses and peonies and two hardcover books about the Mayans and ancient African art.

Alex pretended interest in the exquisite flowers wrapped in cellophane rather than stare at the man who'd unknowingly occupied her waking thoughts the past week. Why, she mused, hadn't she remembered Merrick's towering height or broad shoulders? A charcoal-gray crewneck sweater and black corduroy slacks made him appear larger, more formidable.

"You must be freezing. Come and sit by the fire."

She turned and retraced her steps to the living room, Merrick following, where a fire blazed behind a decorative screen. The fire and the pair of candles on the mantel were the only sources of illumination. Pressing a wall switch, she turned on two table lamps.

Moving closer to the fireplace, Merrick held his hands near the heat. The light from candles under chimneys on either end of the marble mantel flickered over the photographs of Alex's many relatives. And judging from the various group and individual family photos the Coles were definitely prolific.

Alex watched Merrick as he studied the framed photos of her relatives. "I'll be back as soon as I put the flowers in water." Seemingly as if in a trance, he turned and stared at her. "Can I get you something hot to drink?"

"I'd like that, thank you."

"Would you like chocolate or a hot toddy?"

"I prefer the toddy."

Alex smiled. "Good. I just brewed a pitcher before you got here."

Feeling as gauche as a schoolgirl on her first date, she left the living room as Tina Turner's "I Can't Stand the Rain" flowed from wireless speakers concealed throughout her condo. How was she going to maintain a friendship with

Merrick Grayslake when everything about him radiated un-abashed male sensuality?

Walking into her gourmet kitchen, she opened a cabinet and reached for a vase. She arranged the lilies in the vase, filled it with water, then removed a glass pitcher of cider brewed with mulling spices from the refrigerator. Pouring a generous amount into a saucepan, she put it on a stovetop burner to heat.

Merrick's sock-covered feet were silent as he made his way out of the living room with mahogany furniture reminiscent of pieces he'd seen in West Indian homes that had once belonged to wealthy European merchants and planters. Rich motifs of stylized carved pineapples and palm fronds deco-rated the legs of tables and chairs. A gleaming black concert piano was positioned in an alcove with a vaulted ceiling.

He entered a formal dining room with a table set for two. Prisms of light from a chandelier fired the facets in crystal stemware at the place settings.

Leaving the dining room he walked into the kitchen, stopping short when he saw Alex placing cinnamon sticks in two large mugs as she gyrated to "Nutbush City Limits." Crossing his arms over his chest, he leaned against the entrance to the enormous stainless-steel kitchen filled with the mouthwatering aroma of roasting meat, watching her as she closed her eyes, snapped her fingers and danced to the catchy tune. A smile touched his mouth when he remembered her dancing with Michael.

The selection ended and he put his hands together, ap-plauding. "Bravo."

Alex spun around, her face flaming with embarrassment. Merrick had caught her pretending she was an Ikette. She'd spent her teenage years wishing she were a backup dancer for Tina Turner.

Recovering quickly, she bowed from the waist. "Thank you, thank you, thank you," she drawled, blowing kisses to an imaginary audience.

He lifted a dark eyebrow. "You missed your calling. You should've become a dancer."

Alex emitted an audible sigh. "That was never going to happen. My mother made me take dance lessons, and when the kids went to the right I went to the left. The instructor thought there was something wrong with me because I couldn't follow the steps she'd choreographed and eventually expelled me from class. I never told anyone, but Madame H pulled me aside after my first lesson and lectured me sternly about showing up the other little girls. That ignited an unde-clared war and I did everything I could to make her life a living hell."

Merrick, lowering his arms, straightened. "Remind me to never cross you."

She affected an attractive moue, wrinkling her nose. "It wasn't often that I was a horrible little girl, but there was something about Madame H that pulled me over to the dark side." She pantomimed leaning to her left, limp fingertips grazing her forehead in dramatic fashion.

Shaking his head and smothering a laugh, Merrick found it hard not to respond to Alex's theatrics. Everything about her was young, fresh, uninhibited and spontaneous.

"Are you always this bubbly?"

She sobered, meeting his questioning gaze. "Don't you mean silly?"

He shook his head. "No, Ali. I meant exactly what I said. Bubbly."

Alex returned to the stove and poured the warm liquid into the mugs. "It comes in spurts," she said truthfully. "There are times when I'm as serious as a heart attack, but most times

I'm pretty loose." She didn't want to think of her family's assessment that she'd changed since she'd begun her graduate studies.

Merrick moved closer, inhaling the fragrant scent of cinnamon, cloves and orange wafting from the mugs. He was pleased that she felt comfortable enough with him to be *loose,* because he was more than aware that he'd made some people uneasy whenever he was in their presence.

"Are you concerned as to how people perceive you?" he asked.

"No," she said without hesitation. "And even if I was there's nothing I could do about it. There was a time in my life when I changed myself completely to please someone, and in the end I hated myself for it." She extended her arms. "What you see is what you get. Take it or lump it."

Merrick wanted to tell Alex that he would take it—take all of her just as she was. "I like what I see, Alexandra Cole."

She curtsied as if she were royalty. "Thank you, Merrick Grayslake." Her head came up as she straightened. "And I like what I see."

Resting his elbows on the cooking island, he impaled her with a penetrating stare. "What do you see, Ali?"

Boldly, unflinchingly, Alex met his stare, noticing things about Merrick that she'd missed New Year's Eve. There was a minute scar on his left cheek, a slight bump on the bridge of his aquiline nose as if it had sustained an injury and a hint of blue in his gray eyes. What she'd remembered was the shape of his mouth, a perfect masculine mouth with firm lips, and the close-cropped hair that was more red than brown.

She smiled. "I see a man who I look forward to calling a friend."

Merrick's eyebrows flickered. "I thought we were already friends." Reaching for one of the mugs, he waited for Alex to take hers. He raised his mug in a salute before taking a sip of the warm spicy beverage.

Alex sipped her toddy while she replayed Merrick's statement: *I thought we were already friends.* To her, friends supported, protected and comforted one another in the good and not-so-good times. A friend would be someone she could confide in and trust with her innermost secrets. And she wondered if Merrick Grayslake would and could become her friend in the true sense of the word. Only time would tell.

Setting down her mug, she handed him the vase of lilies. "Would you please put this on the dining-room table?"

"Sure."

Alex smiled when he left to do her bidding. Unknowingly, Merrick had just passed the first test. His expression hadn't changed, nor had he hesitated when she'd asked him to do something for her.

Merrick removed the fireplace screen, stoked the burning embers with a poker, then added another piece of wood on the grate. The flames caught and he replaced the screen; the sweet redolent aroma reminded him of the wood-burning stoves in his West Virginia home, a home where for the past two years he'd become a recluse, venturing out only to shop for food. Weeks would go by before he refueled his sport-utility vehicle.

At thirty-three he'd dropped out of sight as if he'd never existed, and it wasn't until Michael Kirkland came to see him that he was jerked back into the reality that there was another world outside Bolivar, West Virginia. In the past three months he'd visited D.C., Georgetown, West Palm Beach, Miami, Key West and now Arlington, Virginia.

But when he returned home after visiting with Rachel he'd been tempted to settle back into what was now a comfortable and secure routine of waking up at dawn and walking several miles in the cold mountain air before returning home to spend the day reading, chopping wood or watching television.

However, his plan to reconnect with Alexandra Cole thwarted the inclination to fall back into what was familiar when he packed enough clothes for a two-week stay in the Capitol District. And he never questioned or second-guessed himself once he'd checked into the Hyatt.

Sharing dinner with Alex had become an enjoyable event. Her exquisite culinary skills were only surpassed by her delightful companionship. Dinner had begun with shrimp cocktail with a piquant cocktail sauce, a salad of endive stuffed with lump crabmeat, marinated pork tenderloin stuffed with spinach and corn bread. A pale blush wine had become the perfect complement to the differing flavors that had lingered on his palate.

He'd offered to help her clean up, but she'd refused with the excuse that she didn't like anyone in her kitchen. It was apparent she liked being in control.

Alex walked into the living room to find Merrick stretched out on the rug in front of the fire, his head cradled on folded arms. She smiled. He'd truly made himself at home.

Closing the distance between them, she lay down beside him. She didn't have time to catch her breath when he reached out and pulled her into an embrace. Shifting to her right, she rested her head on his shoulder as if it was something they'd done countless times before, feeling safe, protected in his arms. His warmth and the lingering scent from his cologne urged her closer.

"It's still snowing," she said softly. She'd turned on the under-the-counter television in the kitchen to the Weather Channel; the snow totals for the D.C. region had surpassed fourteen inches.

"We'll probably get two feet before it's over," Merrick drawled, not opening his eyes.

"I hope you're not thinking of trying to make it back to your hotel tonight."

He opened his eyes. "It's not that far."

"It's too far for you to walk in a blizzard, Merrick. I have a spare bedroom. You're about the same height as my brother Jason, so you won't have an excuse that you don't have anything to wear."

He chuckled softly. "You're the second woman within the span of a week who has invited me to stay with her."

Alex went completely still, her heart pounding a runaway rhythm as she held her breath until she felt her lungs burning. Had Merrick lied when he told her that he wasn't involved with a woman?

"You stayed with a woman in Florida?"

Tightening his hold around her waist, Merrick pulled her closer to his length. "It's not like that, Ali. Rachel's someone I used to work with. She threatened me with bodily harm if I didn't check out of a Key West hotel and stay with her."

Some of the tension left her. "What did she threaten to do? Shoot you?" He nodded. Tilting her chin, Alex stared up at Merrick staring down at her. "Would she have shot you?"

"Of course not. Why are you taking what I'm saying so seriously?"

Vertical lines appeared between her eyes. "It's just that I don't need some crazy-ass woman looking to cap me because she believes I'm hitting on her man."

"That will never happen because I'm not involved with anyone. Tell me how it was growing up a Cole," he asked, deftly changing the topic.

"That all depends on which Cole household you're talking about. I believe mine was the most unconventional. My uncle Martin is rather traditional, and so are his children. My aunts Nancy and Josephine were raised believing they were Afro-

Cuban royalty, so they passed their values down to their children and grandchildren. The Cole-Thomases and Wilsons have this air of entitlement that can really work my nerves. My uncle Joshua is quite conservative, but that comes from a career in the military.

"Perhaps it's because my dad opted for a career in music rather than devote his life to the family business that we were raised without the restrictions imposed on my other relatives. I remember Abuela lecturing Daddy that he was raising *'los animalitos pequeños.'* My mother took offense to her mother-in-law's reference to her children as little animals, and it took months before they declared a truce."

"What did your parents do that ticked off your grandmother?"

"We played music all day and half the night—loud. The house was always open to our friends for sleepovers and pool parties. And because Daddy had set up his own record company, there was an unending stream of popular and wannabe musicians coming to the in-home recording studio. It was cool to see them come to record a demo, and a year later see them on television in their own music video."

"It sounds as if you had a lot of fun."

"It was. Where did you grow up?" she asked Merrick.

"Texas."

"I knew it."

"What did you know?"

"I knew you were from the South."

"Southwest," he corrected softly.

"Texas is still the South. Where in Texas were you raised?"

"Dallas, Waco, San Antonio, McAllen, Lubbock, Corpus Christi. You name it, I've lived there."

Easing out of his loose embrace, Alex sat up. "Why did your family move around so much?"

The last CD had finished minutes before, and there was

only the sound from popping wood and showers of falling embers. Merrick lay on the rug, lifeless as a statue as he stared up at the shadows on the ceiling. He couldn't chide Alex for asking him about his past because he'd opened the door when he'd asked about her childhood.

"My family didn't move. I was the one who moved whenever social workers shuttled me from one foster home to the next. I stopped counting at six."

Alex rested a hand on his shoulder. "Where were your parents?"

He closed his eyes. "I don't know, Ali. I never knew my mother or father because I was abandoned at birth."

Feeling as if her breath had solidified in her throat, Alex was unable to form a response or comeback. Here she was running off at the mouth about the Coles while Merrick had been passed around like an inanimate object to whoever was willing to accept him.

Merrick sat up. For a long moment he studied Alex intently. "Aren't you going to say what all of the others have said?"

"What's that?"

"That you're sorry."

Her eyelids fluttered as she registered the coldness that'd crept into his voice, and she wondered whether he'd grown up listening to people pitying him for a turbulent child-hood. What about those who'd been presented with an opportunity to change his life, yet stood by and did nothing? However, there was something about the prideful man sitting inches from her that silently conveyed that he wouldn't accept her pity.

"You're wrong, Merrick. Who am I to pity you when something tells me you'd throw it back at me?"

The hard, gray eyes that shimmered like glacial ice softened as a smile touched his mobile mouth. "You're right, Ali. I don't want your pity. My past is exactly that—the past." He traced the outline of her cheek with a forefinger. "It's getting late, so I'd better be going before I'll be forced to accept your offer to spend the night." He rose to his feet, extending his hand and pulling her up with him.

Alex looked up at him. "I doubt if the fund-raiser will go off as planned tomorrow night."

Merrick nodded. "It's going to be a couple days before things are back to normal." Lowering his head, he pressed a kiss to Alex's cheek. "Thanks for dinner and for your company. I'll call you tomorrow."

Wrapping her arms around his waist, she rose on tiptoe and kissed his chin. "Thank you for coming."

She followed him to the foyer where he opened the door and retrieved his boots. Sitting down on a chair beside the table, he put them on. Reaching for his jacket, she held it out for Merrick as he slipped his arms into the sleeves.

He turned, they shared a smile, and then he was gone. Alex closed and locked the door behind him. She returned to the living room and extinguished the candles. She stood in front of the fireplace, staring at the dying embers and recalling the past four hours, when she'd shared the most pleasurable time with a man that she had in years.

What had surprised her was that she'd felt comfortable with Merrick until he revealed his childhood, and she didn't think she would ever forget his expression when he said he'd been abandoned at birth. He'd closed his eyes and his face had been totally void of emotion.

What abuses, she mused, had he suffered in his various foster homes? Had he gone hungry? Was he beaten?

She'd grown up with both parents loving her and she loving

them; they'd protected and spoiled her, and nothing had been beyond her reach. Merrick couldn't go back in time to right the wrongs, but she made a silent vow that she would become a friend on which he could rely.

Chapter 6

Merrick stood several inches behind Alex as she explained the significance of a piece of sculpture at the National Museum of African Art. It had taken Washingtonians two days to dig out from under twenty-two inches of snow while those in northern Virginia took longer with nearly twenty-eight inches of the frozen precipitation.

The fund-raiser to which Alex had purchased tickets had been rescheduled to the middle of February. They wouldn't attend because Alex would be out of the country and he'd planned to return to West Virginia the day before she was scheduled to leave for Mexico City. He stared at the raven curls secured in a ponytail rather than at the strange-looking pieces that were now part of a permanent collection.

Alex gestured toward an elaborately carved wooden staff. "This piece comes from the Yoruba culture of southwestern Nigeria. The staff is named for the god of thunder, Shango, and was carried by Shango cult members as a symbol of their office." She pointed to a sculpture of a mother and child. "Although the mother and child figures represent an archetypal Yoruba theme, the *oshe Shango* also displays several unique qualities, namely for its three-dimensional form, its contrast of hard geometric shapes and its smooth surface with detailed…"

Her voice trailed off. She turned and stared up at Merrick, who wasn't looking at the sculpture, but directly at her. "Merrick!" she hissed through her teeth.

He blinked, as if coming out of a trance. "What is it?" he asked softly.

"I'm talking a mile a minute and you're not listening."

Reaching for her hand, Merrick led her away from the exhibit and over to a sitting area. "I've heard every word you've said. We've spent the past week together visiting every museum and gallery in this blasted city. I can tell you the portrait of Mary Cassatt painted by Edgar Degas hangs in the National Portrait Gallery. The Rhyton, a silver and gilt drinking cup dating from the fourth century A.D., probably of Iranian origin, is at the Arthur M. Sackler Gallery.

"*The Abandoned Doll* by Suzanne Valadon, who was also a model of Toulouse-Lautrec and Renoir and the mother of painter Maurice Utrillo, was renowned in her own right. This painting is evocative of the theme that brings drama and psychological truth to the universal rite of passage when the mother tells her pubescent daughter about the physical changes in her body. The doll on the floor symbolizes that the daughter must leave her childhood behind in order to embrace womanhood." He leaned closer and whispered in her ear, "If you take me to another museum I'm going to go ape shit, Alexandra Cole."

Clapping a hand over her mouth, Alex stared at Merrick as if he'd taken leave of his senses. She wasn't as stunned by his refusal to go to another museum as she was by his knowledge of what he'd observed and retained. Although she thought herself cogent in the art field, she still was hard-pressed to remember where every piece was housed.

Lowering her hand, she glared at him. "Where's the *Angel* by Abbot Henderson Thayer?"

"It's at the National Museum of American Art." He gave her a Cheshire cat grin. "Now can I have my A?"

Her thunderous expression softened. "Why didn't you say something?"

He pressed his mouth to her ear. "I didn't because I didn't want to hurt your feelings. Please, pretty please, give me my A, teacher."

Merrick continued to astound Alex with his mercurial personality. Most times he exhibited a staidness that made her uncomfortable, but then without warning he would soften, exhibiting a teasing quality that allowed her to lower her defenses, wherein she wanted him to become more than a friend.

Wrapping her arm around his waist, she rested her head against his shoulder. "You passed, Merrick."

"What's my final grade?"

She gave him a sidelong glance. "A."

"Let's go somewhere and celebrate?"

"Where do you want to go?" Alex asked. For the past eight days he'd driven to her place, where they planned their itinerary for the day. Three nights they ate at his hotel's restaurant, and she'd returned the favor and cooked for him again.

"Anyplace where I don't have to whisper. You're leaving the States in five days, and I'm going back to Bolivar where the only thing I'm going to hear is the sound of my own breathing."

"You should get a pet."

"I don't want a pet."

"Then get a girlfriend."

"I have a girlfriend," he crooned, catching her earlobe between his teeth, "but she's going to Mexico City."

Unexpected warmth eddied through Alex. The soft nip of his teeth on her ear and his moist breath flowing into it heated her blood rushing to nether regions, triggering a pulsing between her legs.

In five days she would leave the States and Merrick. They'd spent practically every day together walking the snowy streets of Washington, D.C., touring museums and art galleries and drinking lattes at Starbucks. They'd become friends and formed a comfortable camaraderie without the likelihood of a physical involvement. And there were times when she wanted to do more with Merrick than hold hands or exchange a chaste kiss.

Merrick released her ear. "What are you thinking about?"

"How do you know I'm thinking?"

"You're not saying anything."

She gasped. "Oh, no, you didn't!"

"Don't get your cute little nose out of joint, because I've never known you to be at a loss for words."

"You haven't known me that long, Merrick."

"That may be true, but even if we were together for the next thirty years I'd never know the real Alexandra. I'm willing to bet there are things about your father your mother doesn't know, and vice versa."

"You're probably right. Everyone has secrets."

Running a finger down the length of her delicate nose, Merrick replaced it with a soft kiss. "I have a secret."

She smiled. "Do you want to tell me about it?"

"I want you to spend the next four days with me at my place. I'll have you back in Virginia in time for you to make your flight."

Alex was totally bewildered at his request. Just when she was beginning to relax and feel comfortable with Merrick he changed the rules. He'd invited her to join him in the Keys and she'd refused, saying perhaps the next time. This invitation had become the next time.

"I told you before that I'd never put you in a compromising position," he continued in the soft drawling voice that never failed to send a shiver throughout her body.

"And I told you that I always keep my promises," she countered. "What time are we leaving?"

Merrick exhaled as a tender smile softened the lean contours of his face. He didn't know why, but he felt as if he'd been holding his breath since he first spied Alexandra Cole.

He stood up and extended his hand. He wasn't disappointed when Alex placed her hand trustingly in his as he eased her to her feet. "I'll drop you home to pack before I go back to the hotel to check out. We're also going to have to stop along the way to buy groceries."

"We can clean out my refrigerator, because I plan to disconnect it before I leave."

Merrick didn't want to think of not seeing Alex for four months. He liked her effervescent, teasing personality and her natural beauty that prompted men to turn around and stare at her. Whether dressed casually in a pair of jeans and a pullover sweater or a dress that flattered her sexy petite body, she was perfect. It was the first time he'd found everything he could possibly want in one woman: intelligence, beauty and sensuality.

Reaching for her navy blue wool swing coat, he held it as she slipped into it. A minute later she repeated the gesture when he shrugged into his jacket. Hand in hand they walked out of the museum, unaware that the next four days would change them—forever.

Chapter 7

Snow flurries intensified until a steady snowfall forced Merrick to slow down to less than forty miles an hour. He'd hoped to reach Bolivar before nightfall, but the weather had conspired against him. He'd dropped Alex off at her condo, returned to the hotel, packed and checked out of the Hyatt, then stopped at a supermarket to pick up dairy items before driving back to get her. Alex was ready when he arrived, and ninety minutes after they'd agreed to spend the next four days in Bolivar they were on their way to the picturesque hamlet nestled in a valley less than three miles from the Allegheny Mountains.

Alex glanced out the side window, watching the topography change the farther they ventured into West Virginia. Her ears popped with the higher elevation. There was enough light left to marvel at the natural splendor of the unspoiled, rugged wilderness that hadn't changed in more than a century.

"It looks so peaceful here," she said reverently.

Smiling, Merrick took a quick glance at his passenger before he returned his gaze to the winding road. "It is." It was quiet, remote, and if he didn't turn on a radio or the television he tended to lose track of the days of the week.

"What made you decide to move to West Virginia?"

Merrick knew he had to open up to Alex and reveal a little of his past or she would never trust him. And he wanted her to trust him because his feelings were changing, intensifying. He'd told her all he wanted was for them to be friends. She'd become his friend and unknowingly more. It was one thing to mouth the word and another to experience emotions that would shock her.

He wasn't certain when his feelings toward her had changed. One morning he woke from a disturbing dream that left him reeling from the sexual images and his own driving need to make love to Alexandra Cole. The harder he tried to ignore the truth, the more it nagged at him. His initial admission that he wasn't interested in her romantically, his vow not to become involved, was shattered completely when he'd asked her to come home with him.

"I suppose you could say I was running away," he said truthfully.

Alex shifted on her seat, turning to stare at Merrick's profile. His taut expression was one of pained tolerance. A shiver snaked its way down her body. Whenever she posed a question about his past she felt him withdraw from her. She turned away from the glum-faced man. The seconds ticked off, the increasing silence inside the vehicle deafening.

Merrick downshifted as he maneuvered around a sharp curve, a stretch of road locals referred to as Deadman's Curve. It veered sharply to the right, and then without warning the grade dropped off before the road veered left. Viewed from the air the road resembled a large undulating snake. A smile found its way through his closed expression with Alex's audible gasp.

Reaching over to his right, he caught her left hand and held it until she unclenched her fingers. "Relax, baby. I've driven this road enough to do it with my eyes closed."

"Please don't close your eyes, Merrick."

Not willing to avert his attention from the snow-covered roadway, he squeezed her fingers. "Don't worry, Ali. I'd never let anything happen to you."

"Promise?"

His smile widened. "Promise."

Alex alternated closing her eyes and holding her breath as Merrick navigated sharply to the right, then left as the wiper blades worked furiously to keep the windshield free of snow.

Half a mile later, Merrick left the paved roadway, maneuvering onto a narrow rutted path bordered on both sides with towering pine trees. Within minutes, the overgrowth of trees and shrubs gave way to an open meadow. The outline of a two-story house was visible in the steady beam of headlights. He slowed, coming to a complete stop under a carport.

"Aren't you going to park in the garage?" Alex pointed to a two-car garage about fifty feet from the house.

"There's no room. I'll show you what's in there tomorrow." He cut the engine, got out and came around to assist her.

Alex waited for Merrick to open her door; she extended her arms. He lifted her effortlessly, setting her on her feet. If it hadn't been for the truck's headlights and falling snow it would've been pitch-dark. There were no streetlamps or lights from nearby homes. Merrick lived in the middle of nowhere. He admitted moving to the wilderness because he'd been running away. Running away from what or whom?

Clutching his arm, she followed him up several steps to a porch; squinting, Alex tried seeing beyond the curtain of white but encountered eerie nothingness. All of her senses were heightened when she heard the distinctive sound of a lock opening followed by a soft beeping that was silenced when Merrick punched in a code for a security system. Within seconds light illuminated the first floor.

"Come in," Merrick urged. "You're letting out the heat."

She stomped the snow off her feet and walked into a living room with modern functional furniture. The saddle-tan leather sofa and love seat complemented the heavy oaken tables, giving the space a masculine feel. Polished pale pine floors and wide windows covered with bamboo blinds in a straw-yellow shade further enhanced an atmosphere of openness.

"It's wonderful." Her voice echoed awe.

Merrick stared at Alex, complete surprise on his face. "You like it?"

She smiled at him. "Of course I like it." Her smile faded as quickly as it'd appeared. "Why did you think I wouldn't?"

"I was under the impression you'd think it too rustic."

She rolled her eyes at him. "Where you live is rustic, not your home. Can I see the rest of it?"

"Sure. The kitchen is to your right and the pantry and laundry are off the back along with the family room. The bedrooms are upstairs in the loft."

Shrugging off her coat, she handed it to Merrick. "Can you please hang this up?"

He took her coat, snapping a smart salute. "Ma'am, yes, ma'am!"

"Show-off," she crooned as she made her way in the direction he'd indicated.

Merrick felt an overwhelming sense of pride that Alex liked his home. There were times when he felt it was much too large for one person, but he'd resisted sharing his life and home with a woman.

He'd never thought of himself as husband or father material because of his turbulent childhood. How could he know where he was going when he hadn't known who he was or where he'd come from?

He'd languished in a foundling hospital, then a group home, and at the age of four he was placed with his first foster family. He'd overheard the social worker tell his foster parents that a priest had found him wrapped in a blanket, umbilical cord still attached, under a pew in a South Texas church only five miles from the Mexican border. There was a bloodstained note tucked into the blanket that read: *Please take care of my son—Victoria Grayslake.* Father Merrick had cleaned and baptized the infant, giving him his first name before calling the authorities. Two days after his birth Merrick Grayslake became a ward of the state of Texas.

He didn't know what prompted him to bring Alex home with him, but with his rapidly changing feelings for her he didn't want to spend time analyzing everything he did. All he wanted to do was enjoy whatever time they had together before she left the country. He walked out of the house and returned to the truck to get their luggage and perishable foodstuffs.

Alex lay on the sofa, eyes closed and her head resting on Merrick's thigh. She'd toured his house, falling in love with the massive wood-burning stoves in the kitchen and family room. The second-story loft contained three large rooms. Merrick had claimed the largest as his bedroom. Another had been set up as a guest room and the third was filled with boxes and metal file cabinets. Whitewashed walls, wood floors covered with colorful rugs and fireplaces had turned his home into a perfect getaway retreat.

"Did you build this place?"

He combed his fingers through her mussed curls. "No. I

bought it for a fraction of its worth when the original owner died two days after he took possession. His widow, who never wanted to live here, said it was cursed. She moved out, leaving all of the furnishings, and never looked back."

Alex opened her eyes and stared up at him looking down at her. "I thought you'd decorated it."

"No. I wouldn't know where to begin. All that talk about fabrics and colors confuse the hell out of me."

"Where did you live before you moved here?"

"I rented the cottage on the property of someone I'd met in the Corps."

She smiled. "You were a marine?" Merrick nodded. Sitting up, she gave him a direct stare. "Were you really into that esprit de corps and *Semper fidelis* indoctrination?"

His luminous eyes widened until she could see their hoary depths. "Once a marine, always a marine."

Alex felt the chill of his words as acutely as if he'd struck her. The man with whom she'd found herself enthralled had morphed into a stranger, shedding his warmth like a reptile shedding its skin.

"No disrespect intended."

"And none taken," he countered quickly.

Pushing off the sofa, Alex knew it was time to retreat before she lost her temper and said something she wouldn't be able to retract. "Good night, Merrick."

He stood up and shoved his hands into the pockets of his jeans. "Good night, Ali."

Merrick felt as if he'd been punched in the gut when she headed toward the staircase. Why, he mused, did he keep pushing her away? Why, when it was the last thing he wanted to do?

Taking three long strides, he stopped her retreat, reaching for her upper arm and turning her around. His hands moved up to cradle her face. Slowly, methodically, his head came down and he took her mouth in a drugging, caressing kiss that told her wordlessly how much he wanted, how much he needed her.

Alex held on to Merrick's shirt like a drowning swimmer caught in a riptide. His warmth, his smell, the strength in his hard lean body seeped into her like water through a porous fabric, soaking and becoming one. Standing on tiptoe, she returned the kiss, her lips parting as delicious sensations raced from her mouth downward.

Merrick placed tiny kisses along the column of Alex's scented neck, his teeth nibbling softly at the base of her throat. Tightening his hold on her body, he lifted her off her feet until her head was level with his. He took her mouth again, devouring its softness. He'd tasted her, but instead of sating his hunger, it increased. If he could he would've devoured all of her.

He felt the flesh between his thighs stir and knew if he didn't stop what he'd begun he would do something he would regret for the rest of his life. Lowering Alex until her feet touched the floor, he pulled back. Passion had darkened her face and her eyes; he couldn't pull his gaze away from her slightly swollen mouth. A spurt of desire shot through his groin when he realized Alex was a woman who should be made love to—every day and every night. Her dark beauty smoldered with a sensuality that couldn't be learned or taught.

A hint of a smile tilted the corners of his mouth. "Good night, Ali."

Backing away, Alex wrinkled her nose. If they hadn't stopped when they did, there was no doubt they would end up in bed together. She wanted to arrive in Mexico City with memories of the two weeks she'd spent with her friend and not the few days she'd shared a bed with her lover.

"Good night, Merrick."

She turned and made her way up the staircase, feeling the

heat from the silver orbs on her back. When she reached the top, she turned and glanced down to find that Merrick hadn't moved. Even from this distance she could see the banked flames of desire in his expression.

Forcing herself to look away, she walked down the hallway until she reached her bedroom. Her hands and knees were trembling uncontrollably as she fell across the bed and pressed her face into the pillow.

She wanted him; she wanted Merrick Grayslake more than she'd ever wanted any man in her life. It was good that she was leaving the country, because to remain would prove disastrous to the plans she'd made for herself. And her plans did not include taking a lover or falling in love.

It was minutes after sunrise when Merrick walked into the kitchen. Alex sat on a tall stool at the cooking island, drinking coffee and concentrating intently on his handheld *New York Times* Sudoku. A smile crinkled the lines around his eyes as he crept silently across the room, swept her off the stool and lifted her high in the air. Bending slightly, he tossed her up like a rag doll and caught her.

Alex let out a bloodcurdling scream as her arms flailed wildly. "Stop, Merrick! Please put me down!"

Cradling her to his chest, Merrick settled her on the stool, his arms going around her body in a comforting gesture. "Good morning, baby."

Alex's right hand curled into a fist, her eyes narrowing. "Don't you dare good morning me!"

"You want to hit me?"

Baring her teeth, she glared at him. "I want to hurt you real bad, Merrick Grayslake, for scaring the hell out of me."

"Forgive me, sweetheart."

The endearment seemed to take the fight out of her. Within

a span of a minute Merrick had called her *baby* and *sweetheart*. What happened to friend?

Looping her free arm around his neck, Alex buried her face between his neck and shoulder and closed her eyes. He smelled of soap. Merrick had showered and shampooed his hair but hadn't shaved, and the dark stubble on his jaw and chin accentuated the masculinity he wore like a badge of honor.

She kissed the side of his strong neck. "I'll think about."

Merrick massaged her back over a sweatshirt. "Don't think too long, beautiful."

Alex eased back, giving him a long, penetrating stare. "What's going on between us, Merrick?"

He sobered, his expression closed. "What are you talking about?"

"Why are you calling me baby and sweetheart instead of Ali? And what happened to the pecks on the lips and cheeks? When you kissed me last night and I kissed you back, there was nothing friendly in what we shared." Reaching up, she smoothed down several wayward strands of damp hair over his ear. "What are we doing to each other, Merrick?"

Merrick cradled her head, his fingers massaging her scalp. "We are friends, Ali." He enunciated each word.

"But—"

"No buts, Ali," he said softly, interrupting her. "I like you—a lot—but I'm not going to take advantage of you. That's not my style."

Her gaze met and held his as she anchored her arms under his shoulders. "And I promise not to take advantage of you."

Merrick released her head, momentarily speechless in his surprise. "You're incredible," he whispered.

She gave him a saucy grin. "You just realized that?" she drawled without a modicum of modesty.

"Trash-talking will result in another beach-ball toss."

"You wouldn't."

Merrick nodded. "I would."

She pantomimed zipping her mouth and Merrick threw back his head and howled. Her laughter joined his as the unrestrained shared moment brought them closer together, cementing their friendship.

Alex was lost—lost in the splendor of the rugged countryside—and she'd lost track of the days, time. And she'd done what she'd prayed would not happen—she'd lost her heart to Merrick Grayslake.

Their relationship was uncomplicated and open. He hadn't tried to kiss her again, and for that Alex was grateful. Any display of affection would make her leaving more difficult.

They developed a comfortable routine of waking early and walking in the frigid morning air before returning to the house to prepare monstrous breakfasts. She cleaned the kitchen while he chopped enough wood to feed the gluttonous wood-burning stoves from the stack stored in a shed at the rear of the house. All the wood came from trees on the five-acre property. Merrick contracted to have trees felled and cut into large stumps. He claimed chopping firewood was his way of staying in shape.

The man she'd fallen in love with continued to mystify her when he opened the garage to reveal a functioning body shop with two classic cars he'd restored to their original state. One was a 1948 pickup and the other a 1952 station wagon with wood paneling. When she asked whether he planned to sell them he'd given her an incredulous look that spoke volumes, then said emphatically, "No."

He'd amassed an extensive reading and video library. Floor-to-ceiling shelves in the family room were packed tightly with fiction bestsellers and titles pertaining to history and military battles.

Most nights found them in the family room viewing movies. Alex preferred movies with foreign settings with romantic themes while Merrick liked sci-fi and action thrillers.

Fifteen minutes into *Man On Fire,* Merrick paused the DVD and stared at her. The film's theme dealt with the claim that every hour throughout Latin America someone was kidnapped and held for ransom. Alex belayed his fear that she would be a target of kidnappers because she'd enrolled in the *universidad* as Alexandra Morris. Her birth records listed her as Alexandra Ivonne Morris-Cole, and when she studied abroad transcripts listed her surname as Morris.

She was forced back to reality and what lay ahead of her when a call from Diego reminded Alex that he would accompany her on the flight to Mexico City before he continued on to Belize to meet with a consortium of banana growers.

The return drive to Arlington was accomplished in complete silence as she agonized over how was she going to leave Merrick now that she knew she was in love with him. And her love wasn't based on sex, because they hadn't slept together, and for that she was grateful. There was no way she wanted to confuse a physical connection with one that was emotional.

Merrick stood in the foyer with Alex, cradling her face in his hands. The eyes staring back at him were steady, trusting. He found himself at a loss when he longed to tell her how much he'd enjoyed their time together, how she'd managed to slip under the invisible wall he'd erected to keep all women at a distance, how much she'd changed him and how much he'd come to love her.

He loved everything about her, inside and out. He'd asked for friendship, got it, but wanted more. And the more was love. He wanted Alex to love him because he'd fallen in love with her.

"May I call you?" he asked.

Alex's lashes fluttered as she tried bringing her fragile emotions under control. "Of course you may. Call me at night because it's your voice I want to hear before I go to sleep."

"Are you living on campus?"

"No. I'm staying in a converted convent near the *universidad*." Her mood brightened. "Are you thinking of coming to visit me?"

Merrick's impassive expression did not change. "Do you want me to?"

A smile fired the gold in her large eyes. "Yes."

"It won't interfere with your studies?"

"As soon as I get my schedule I'll let you know when I have a break."

Lowering his chin, he lifted his dark, sweeping eyebrows. "I'll come to see you on one condition."

"I know," she said, laughing. "No museums."

He winked at her. "You learn fast."

"Not as fast as you," she countered. Moving closer, she wound her arms under his shoulders. "I'm going to miss you, friend."

Merrick dropped a kiss on her hair. Her curls reminded him of a field of wildflowers. "Hush, baby," he crooned. "I'll see you so much that you'll get sick of me."

"Never."

"Never say never, Ali."

Pulling back, she met his serious gaze. Like a chameleon he'd changed. Gone was the teasing man she'd come to look for, and in his place was the one who frightened her. Once again, he'd become a stranger.

She forced a smile she didn't feel. "I'll call you." Standing on tiptoe, she brushed her mouth over his compressed lips. *"Hasta luego."*

"Hasta luego," Merrick repeated. Turning on his heel, he opened the door, then closed it softly behind him.

Alex stood there for a full minute before she sat down on the chair next to the foyer table and closed her eyes. Everything she'd shared with Merrick Grayslake flooded her mind like frames of film: the night they lay in front of the fireplace and he told her how he'd been abandoned at birth, their trips to countless D.C. museums and art galleries that always ended with them drinking lattes at Starbucks. The nights she'd dressed up to share dinner with him at his hotel's restaurant, and the days and nights at the house in Bolivar where she'd learned to appreciate nature in all its wintry splendor.

What she didn't want to recall was the image of Merrick in a tank top and jeans chopping wood in the noonday sun. Each time he swung the ax, the muscles in his back and upper arms tightened and relaxed under the strenuous exertion. The first time she saw the shirt, wet from sweat, pasted to his body, it had excited her so much that she went inside the house until he completed the chore. The images returned in an erotic dream that left her aching with a desire that threatened to swallow her whole.

Opening her eyes, she came back to reality. Alex didn't know where her relationship with Merrick would lead, but she knew it had to be resolved. The two large pieces of luggage sitting in the foyer reminded her that in less than two hours she would be on her way to Mexico City. She stood up and made her way to her bedroom to exchange her boots, wool slacks and sweater for a cotton dress and sandals.

When she emerged she was ready for Mexico City *and* her destiny.

PART TWO

Lovers

Chapter 8

Alex found it hard to stay focused. She and the other students in her class had spent the past half hour staring at the image of an Olmec stone figure projected on the screen in the lecture hall.

The professor, a slight, middle-aged man with thinning black hair and a flair for the dramatic, had waxed eloquent about how the Olmec's "mother culture" inspired a series of successor cultures, including Maya settlements that began forming in the Mexican-Guatemala border region around 500 BC.

Move on and change the blasted slide! she fumed inwardly. They were a month into the new term and she'd learned more from reading than she had during her lectures. Alex was enthralled with Mexico's history and its people, but Professor Riviera was making it increasingly difficult for her to stay awake in his classes, and the downside was that she had him for three Mexican art courses.

Pretentious prig, she continued in her silent tirade, scowling.

"Señorita Morris, perhaps you can tell your fellow students the timeline for the rise and fall of the Olmec civilization."

Everyone's attention was directed to Alex as she glared at their professor. There was a pregnant silence as she composed her thoughts.

"Records show that the first Olmec settlements were established around 1500 BC. In 900 BC the Olmec city of San Lorenzo was destroyed and desecrated. Historians and archaeologists are unsure who or what led to the destruction and the Olmec civilization faded into obscurity."

Rivera smiled. "What else can you tell us about this culture?" he asked.

"They built ceremonial centers rather than cities, which suggests they were governed by a central authority. The Olmecs carved blocks of basalt into figures with massive heads like the one on the screen and other sculptures with stylized feline features. There is evidence they had ceramics, and digs have recovered jade figurines from this civilization."

Nodding his approval, the professor of design and art of ancient cultures, pressed his palms together. "*Bien dicho,* Señorita Morris. It appears you are quite serious in your endeavor to learn about Mexico's rich and colorful history."

Alex gave him a saccharine grin. "If I weren't, then I assure you I wouldn't be here."

"I told you he has the *hots* for you," whispered the student sitting next to her. Alex and Moira Morgan had formed a friendship within days of Alex settling into her room at the centuries-old converted convent she would call home for the semester. Moira, a tall, blond, thin Oklahoman, who spoke fluent Spanish, had ended a yearlong relationship with the son of a Texas oilman to study abroad. Alex cut her eyes at Moira. She'd come to Mexico to earn a degree, not form a relationship with her professor. Her mantra had become: once burned, twice shy.

"Señores y señoritas." Hernando Rivera addressed all women, whether married or single, as miss. "I would like to invite all of you to my home Saturday evening. A colleague has deigned to exhibit his private collection of art before donating it to several museums."

A chorus of groans and murmurs followed his announcement as a hand went up in the back of the lecture hall. *"Señor profesor, la asistencía es obligatoria?"*

Professor Rivera gave the young man an incredulous look. "What do you think, Señor Salinas?"

"Yes, it is," said the red-faced student, answering his own query.

"You all have my address and telephone number. I will expect everyone at eight." He held up a hand. "Before you ask, you may bring a guest."

The bell rang signaling the end of classes and Alex gathered her books. It was her last class for the day and week. At least it was before Rivera's mandate that everyone attend an impromptu gathering at his home.

She attended classes Monday through Thursday, cleaned her apartment, picked up her laundry and shopped for groceries on Friday, slept late on Saturday and either stayed home or went out with Moira and a few other classmates Saturday night. Sundays were set aside for attending mass and doing homework. She liked everything about Mexico, its people and the cuisine.

But she missed home *and* Merrick, but managed to stave off homesickness by staying busy. She alternated calling and writing her parents and exchanging telephone calls with Merrick.

He kept her updated on national news, while she told him about the political climate in Mexico. He disclosed he'd spent several days with Michael and Jolene, who'd returned rested and tanned from their Jamaican honeymoon, and it was only after their calls ended that she felt totally isolated. She'd become an alien in a foreign land.

The week before, she'd sent him a letter with postcards bearing the art of Mexican muralists Diego Rivera, David Siqueiros, José Orozco and her favorite Mexican artist, Frida Kahlo. She included a note that read: *You don't have to go to a museum or gallery to enjoy these.—AIM-C.*

"I've got better things to do with my Saturdays than look in Rivera's face," Alex mumbled as she slipped her books into a backpack.

"I've heard he hosts some wonderful get-togethers at his house," Moira said, gathering her own books.

"I still would rather pass."

A sardonic smile parted Moira's pale mouth. She never wore makeup during the week, but weekends transformed her into a siren when she replaced long skirts and dresses and wooden clogs with skintight garments and artfully applied makeup that highlighted her dark blue eyes in a tightly tanned face.

"We'll show up and eat his food and drink up all of his tequila, then leave. Someone on our floor said they're going to a club near the Zona Rosa where they play music from the States on Saturday nights."

"Who told you?" Alex asked as they made their way out of the lecture hall and down a hallway in the centuries-old building that had been dedicated to the study of Mexican art and architecture.

She hadn't bothered to make friends with the other students who had a habit of hanging out in one another's rooms. All of the rooms were equipped with a small utility kitchen, private bath and an expansive living/sleeping/dining area.

Alex cooked for herself during the week and took her meals at local restaurants on the weekend. With her dark hair and coloring, she was easily taken for a local; she wanted to blend in and not stand out as a foreigner. And it was not the first time that she was grateful her parents taught her Spanish.

"Umberto."

"Isn't he the one who's been hitting on you?" Moira blushed to the roots of her pale hair. *"Cuidado, chica. Umberto puede ser la causa del problema,"* Alex warned in Spanish.

She wanted to tell Moira that she'd heard rumors that the handsome art student was keeping count of the number of women he could sleep with before the school year ended.

"If there's going to be a problem, then it's going to be for Umberto because I have no intention of going to bed with him."

Alex gave her a sidelong glance. "I suppose you've heard about his exploits?"

"I saw him in action. I take that back. I saw him with his ass out. The first night I moved in I saw him leaving some-one's room, clothes in hand. His behind was beet-red as if he'd been paddled."

Alex wrinkled her nose. "Phew! It looks as if Casanova is a freak."

"He can get his freak on, but without me."

"I hear you."

The two women discussed an upcoming exam covering the Mayan calendar. They were still deep in conversation when they reached their student housing. They entered through an open courtyard that led to a smaller courtyard and the large decorative wrought-iron gate that protected the property from outsiders. Inserting a magnetic card into a slot a buzzing and green light deactivated the lock.

Alex pushed open the door, stepping into a lobby and waiting room. The difference between the outdoor heat and the cooler indoor temperature was almost fifteen degrees. Two-foot-thick adobe walls kept the heat at bay.

The young woman who manned the front desk waved to

Alex. "Miss Morris, there is someone waiting for you." All visitors had to wait to be announced.

"Who is it?"

"He's sitting over there." She pointed to her left.

Alex turned slowly to find a man, legs outstretched, sitting on a *butaca*, a leather sling chair; she couldn't see his face in the dimly lit space, but she recognized the hand resting on his thigh.

"Merrick." His name came out in a whisper. "Merrick!" she shouted when he came to his feet. Closing the distance between them, she launched herself at this chest, her arms gripping his neck.

"Baby," he crooned close to her ear. Wrapping his arms around her waist, he lifted her off her feet. The distinctive lines around his eyes deepened as he gave her a dazzling smile.

Alex brushed a kiss over his smiling mouth. "What are you doing here?"

He gave her a quick kiss. "I came to visit with my girlfriend."

She pressed her forehead to his, her lips caressing the bridge of his nose. "How did you find me?"

Merrick's gaze photographed every inch of her face, noting the changes. Her hair was longer, the Mexican sun had darkened her face to a rich, mocha brown and she'd replaced the diamond studs in her pierced lobes with a pair of large gold hoops. Alexandra Cole was beautiful *and* sexy.

"You put your return address on the letter you sent me with those blasted cards."

A sound of someone clearing their voice caught Alex's attention. "Please, put me down, Merrick."

He complied and she turned to find Moira staring at them, foot tapping and arms crossed under her breasts. Holding on to Merrick's hand, she led him over to her classmate.

Alex had to admit that a month's absence made him even more attractive. His close-cropped hair hugged his head like a cap, and it appeared as if he'd put on weight, because the hollows in his cheeks were less pronounced. Today he wore a lightweight gray jacket over a sky-blue shirt, open at the throat, that he hadn't bothered to tuck into the waistband of a pair of navy-blue slacks. Italian slip-ons had replaced his ubiquitous Timberland boots.

"Moira, this is my very good friend, Merrick Grayslake. Merrick, Moira Morgan."

Moira extended a limp wrist. "It's nice meeting you, Merrick."

He nodded, reaching for her fingers. "It's nice meeting you, too."

Moira shifted a leather book bag from one shoulder to the other. "I'm going to head up to my room and take siesta." She knew she was staring at Merrick longer than what would be termed polite, but he was drop-dead gorgeous. Reluctantly, she shifted her gaze to Alex. "I'll talk to you Saturday."

"Okay."

Alex looped her arm through Merrick's. Never had she been so glad to see someone. But she had to admit that he wasn't just someone. He was the man with whom she'd fallen in love.

"When did you get in?"

"I came in on the red-eye a little after three."

"You must be exhausted. Come on up to my room. We'll take siesta together."

Merrick followed Alex as she led him down a narrow hallway to a stone staircase that led to the second story. He was exhausted, having spent a restless two days deciding whether he should go to Mexico. But he also wanted to tell Alex that taking siesta together wasn't a very good idea.

Talking to Alex had only served to increase his longing for her. She hadn't given him her address and he knew he would never ask her for it; however, his dilemma was solved when he received the packet with the postcards. She'd indicated her return address and that presented the opportunity he needed to come and tell her what lay in his heart.

"The accommodations here are simple but comfortable," Alex explained as she opened the door to her room. *"Bienvenido."*

He stepped into the room, not seeing any of the furnishings. Reaching for Alex, he slipped the straps to her backpack off her shoulders, letting it slide to the floor, and closed the heavy oaken door with his foot. Lifting her off her feet, he crossed the room and sat her on the twin-size bed, his body following hers down. Flames of desire darkened his eyes; the silver had disappeared, and in its place was a shocking dark topaz blue.

Alex moved over and straddled Merrick's lap, her hands cradling his face, her fingertips tracing the contours of his cheekbones and jaw. "Why did you come, Merrick?"

"Isn't it obvious, sweetheart?"

Her gaze fused with his. "No. I've never been one to make assumptions."

Merrick closed his eyes, a thick fringe of lashes brushing the ridge of sculpted cheekbones. A knowing smile parted his lips. "I lied when I told you that I liked you." She gasped. He opened his eyes, meeting her questioning gaze. "The truth is I love you, Alexandra Cole. I kept telling myself that I wanted you as a friend, that we could be friends, but it just didn't work."

Her heart pounding a runaway rhythm thundered under her breasts as a rush of giddiness swept over Alex. He loved her! He loved her and she had fallen in love with him! But it was something she wouldn't tell him—not yet.

Biting down on her lower lip, she attempted to bring her fragile emotions into some semblance of order. She closed her eyes against his intense stare. "You love me, but your timing's wrong."

"What's wrong with it?"

"I have another four months before I return to the States. Long-distance relationships usually don't work."

"We'll make it work, Ali. I didn't wait thirty-five years for someone like you to come into my life to concern myself with a few months or miles."

A frown furrowed her forehead. "Do you realize how far it is between Mexico City and the East Coast of the United States?"

He smiled. "I know exactly how far it is. But distance doesn't matter if I have you here." Merrick placed his left hand over his heart.

A flood of tears shimmered in her gold eyes. "Don't do this to me, Merrick."

Burying his head against the side of her neck, he breathed a kiss under her ear. "Do what, baby?"

"Don't make me want you so much."

"Is that such a bad thing?"

She sniffled. "It is when I can't have you whenever I want you." Her hands curled into tight fists on his back.

Raising his head, Merrick saw her tortured expression. "Alexandra, please look at me." She opened her eyes. "I'm not going to put any pressure on you. We'll see each other whenever it's convenient for you."

"You don't mind waiting until June?"

"No. You're more than worth the wait."

Blinking through tears, she smiled at him. "Thank you, Merrick, for making it easier for me."

"Do you realize how easy it is for me to love you?"

Resting her head on his shoulder, she exhaled a soft sigh. "When you get to know me better you may change your mind."

"I doubt that," Merrick said.

"I've been known to go from nice girl into bitch mode in one point two seconds."

"That's your problem, not mine, because I don't argue or fight with women. So, if you go off, then don't count on me to entertain your tantrum."

Sitting up straighter, she stared directly at him. There was no trace of laughter or teasing in his solemn expression. "What would you do?"

"Walk away until you come to your senses. And stop trying to scare me off, because it's too late. I'm in this for the duration."

Alex's delicate jaw dropped before she recovered quickly. "What is your definition of duration?"

"Perpetuity."

"You can't be talking about marriage?" The query tumbled from her lips.

Merrick saw the rapidly beating pulse in Alex's throat. His gaze lowered to her heaving bosom under a simple white cotton blouse. Not only had he shocked her with his surprise visit, but his declaration that he wanted to spend the rest of his life with her had shaken the very foundation of her privileged existence.

There was a beat of silence before he said in an eerily quiet voice, "You mentioned the word, Ali, not me."

A rush of color suffused her cinnamon-brown face. "I'm not going to marry you, Merrick Grayslake, so you can forget about duration and perpetuity. I've spent the past ten years with my life in flux wherein I've studied, traveled and partied like a girl gone wild.

"My last year of high school I told my parents I wanted to put off going to college for a year because I needed a break from the books. My mother issued an ultimatum, go to college or get a job and move out of her house. And there was no job available to an eighteen-year-old that would pay me enough to afford me the lifestyle to which I'd become accustomed.

"Bowing to pressure, I applied to the Rhode Island School

of Design. They accepted me and I enrolled as a liberal arts major with a concentration in art and architectural history in their five-year degree program. Unfortunately I had an affair with one of my instructors in my sophomore year and…"

"What happened, Ali?" Merrick asked when she closed her eyes at the same time her words trailed off.

She opened her eyes. "I gave him my love and my innocence. Whenever I mentioned marriage he'd avoided talking about it before finally admitting he wasn't the marrying kind. That all changed when my parents came up to visit me. He did a one-eighty when he realized I was *one of those Coles*. He waited a week, then proposed, but at twenty-two I wasn't so in love that I didn't know that he was after my money. Once I told him that I wouldn't have control of my trust fund until my twenty-fifth birthday he dropped me like hot garbage.

"I graduated, secured a part-time position with a Boca Raton art gallery and during my free time partied like there was no tomorrow. I dated a lot of men but I refused to sleep with any of them. I saw them as someone with whom to pass the time. Then I met someone I believed was different from the others. We dated for five months.

"After this liaison I took a long hard look at myself, reassessing my life and what I wanted for *me*, not my parents, my brothers or my sister. I made the decision to return to school, and this time study abroad. Being on my own forced me to depend on Alexandra for everything, and I loved it." Her gold-brown eyes filled with a gentleness that made her appear angelic. "Like any normal woman I want marriage and children, but that can't happen now."

Merrick's arm tightened around her waist. "Are you finished with your soliloquy, Ali?" he asked in a soft voice she had to strain her ears to hear.

She blushed furiously. "Yes, I am."

"I've heard you and I remember everything you've ever told me. And I've told you that I would never pressure you to do what you don't want to do. There's no reason why we can't enjoy each other without marriage and children becoming part of the equation. And if we go from being friends to lovers, then I'll accept full responsibility for making certain you don't get pregnant."

Alex combed her fingers through her hair, holding the wayward curls off her forehead. She appreciated the fact that Merrick Grayslake hadn't tried to change her; he accepted her flaws and imperfections that permitted her to be Alex. Could she, she wondered, offer Merrick her heart? Would he be worthy of the love she'd guarded jealously since ending her first liaison?

Could she sleep with him and not want more?

Yes, whispered the silent voice in her head.

"I know I've been doing a lot of talking—"

"That you have," Merrick agreed, interrupting her.

Her hands came down and she hugged him. "Please don't interrupt me or I'll lose my nerve."

A small smile played at the corners of Merrick's mouth as he gave her a lazily seductive look. "Okay, baby."

"Do—do you think it's possible for us to stop being friends?"

Merrick's smile faded as he held his breath. "What do you want?"

"I want us to become lovers."

A powerful relief shook Merrick as his chest swelled with a peace he hadn't thought possible. Angling his head, he touched his mouth to Alex's, increasing the pressure until her lips parted while his hands explored the curve of her waist and hips.

"Get your clothes and books and pack a bag."

"Where am I going?" she asked between soft nibbling kisses.

"*We're* going to my hotel. There's no way two of us can sleep in this kiddie bed."

She laughed. "It's big enough for me."

"But I'm taller and bigger than you." He kissed the top of her head. "Let's go, *querida*."

Chapter 9

Alex walked over to the large window and opened it. Stepping out onto the balcony, she looked down onto a courtyard with a flowing fountain. A round table with two cushioned chairs near the wrought-iron enclosure provided the perfect setting for an early-morning breakfast or a late-night dinner.

Merrick had checked into a room at the Four Seasons Hotel containing all the amenities for work and relaxation. The spacious room was furnished with a king-size bed, desk, love seat, coffee table, flat-screen television, private bar and wireless high-speed Internet access. The full marble bathroom featured a garden tub, separate shower and water closet.

She felt the heat from his body as he came up behind her. Her slender hands covered the arms wrapped around her waist. "This place is spectacular. Do you always stay in upscale hotels?"

Merrick kissed the side of her neck. "Yes. There was a time

when all I could afford was seedy motels. The one time I woke with bedbug bites I vowed to sleep in my car rather than check in to another flophouse."

Turning slightly, she stared at him over her shoulder. "How long are you staying?"

"I'm checking out Monday."

Merrick wanted to tell Alex that he was scheduled to meet with a former supervisor at CIA headquarters in Langley, Virginia, to discuss the possibility of his returning to the Agency. He'd spent two years as a virtual recluse, but now he looked forward to reconnecting with the Agency and those whom at one time he'd regarded as his extended family.

"That gives us three days together."

"Four nights and three days," he corrected.

Closing her eyes, Alex leaned against the solid wall of his chest. She was certain Merrick felt the flutters from her heart, her tightening stomach muscles. "I'm going out Saturday night, but I don't know whether you'd want to come with me."

"Am I invited?"

She opened her eyes as a mischievous grin twisted her mouth. "You are if you don't mind viewing an art exhibit."

"Ali," he groaned. "What's up with you staring at paintings of dead people?"

"Are you going with me? If not, then I'll ask someone else."

Merrick's hands went to her flat belly. "That's not going to happen."

"What are you talking about?"

"I don't intend to share you with other men."

"Don't tell me you're jealous," she teased.

Splaying his fingers over her belly, Merrick pulled her closer. "No, Ali. I'm crazy."

Alex went completely still, her face clouding with uneasiness. His cold tone set alarm bells clanging within her, and she was suddenly anxious to put some distance between her and the man holding her to his heart. A warning voice whispered in her head that Merrick Grayslake was dangerous, that he would be a formidable opponent when confronted or crossed, that as a former CIA operative he'd probably committed unspeakable acts.

"Does this mean you're coming with me?"

"Yes, it does."

Merrick's fingers inched down Alex's blouse, easing the hem from the waistband of her slacks. He heard her soft inhalation of breath as he searched lower, under the delicate material of her panties. This time she gasped aloud when his hand cupped her mound. A knowing smile parted his lips as moisture bathed his fingertips.

Alex was ready for him, and he'd been ready for her. Unknowingly he had been the first time he saw her arguing with a man who hadn't wanted to let her go. Now he understood why the frustrated man had taken the risk and crashed a private event to see her.

Merrick found Alexandra Cole an anomaly. Assertive and confident, she spoke her mind. He'd come to admire her tenacity, her ambition and her friendly outgoing personality. But she was also hot-tempered and stubborn, negative psychological characteristics that did not detract from her overall strengths.

She wanted to complete her graduate studies, and he'd promised to support her during this endeavor. However, like most women, she wanted marriage and children—two things he was unable to offer her at this time in his life. What he would offer Alex was his love and protection. These were more than he'd been willing to give the women in his past.

His free arm tightened around her waist as he lifted her and backed off the balcony and reentered the bedroom. His hand still sandwiched between her thighs, Merrick sat down on the bed, bringing Alex to sit on his lap.

He pressed his mouth to the nape of her neck. "Are you ready to take siesta with me?"

Alex couldn't respond because she'd bitten down on her lower lip when the slight flutters grew stronger as Merrick's fingers worked their magic. She nodded like someone under the effects of a powerful narcotic.

"Yes-s-s." Her affirmation came out slurred as a long-forgotten passion rose quickly to engulf her in flames that refused to burn out.

Closing her eyes, Alex let her senses take over. It was as if she were viewing what was to take place between her and Merrick as a spectator rather than a participant. His fingers were deft, unfaltering when he released the tiny buttons on her blouse from their fastenings. She heard his breathing deepen as he viewed her breasts in a sheer white lace bra; his breathing became more labored with each article of clothing he removed.

She opened her eyes to find him kneeling over her, eyes shimmering like streaks of lightning, the nostrils of his aquiline nose flaring from the effort it took to control his respiration. No man had ever stared at her naked body with an expression mirroring awe and reverence. The heat pulsing between her legs spread throughout her body.

Merrick did not want to believe that clothes had artfully concealed a petite body so lushly curved that he feared spilling his passion before he joined his body with Alex's. High, firm breasts he'd only glimpsed on New Year's Eve were ardently displayed as they rose and fell over a narrow rib cage flaring out to a pair of rounded hips. Everything about her—the rich brown color that was evenly distributed over her body, the large gold-brown eyes that stared trustingly at him and the black shiny curls that were as wayward as the woman who claimed them—held him enthralled in a labyrinth of love and desire from which he never wanted to escape.

Moving off the bed, he removed his jacket and shirt, leaving them on the padded bench at the foot of the bed. His shoes, socks, slacks and underwear followed until he was completely naked. His footsteps were silent on the carpeted floor as he crossed the room, entered the bathroom and removed a condom from a small toiletry bag. He returned to the bedroom and slipped into bed with Alex, who'd turned on her side to face the window.

"Can you please close the window and pull the drapes?" Alex doubted whether the hotel guests across the courtyard could see into the room, but she'd never been one for public displays of affection.

Merrick kissed her shoulder. "Sure."

Her gaze narrowed when she saw the thin, pale scar running along the left side of his back. He'd told her that he had retired from the CIA, and she wondered if it was an injury that had ended his career, forcing him into early retirement.

Extending her arms, she smiled as Merrick made his way back to the bed. There was enough light coming through the opening in the patterned peach-and-gold draperies to make out his face, but not the other small scars on his body.

"Veo las huellas de mi amor, querido," she whispered as he took her into his arms.

Merrick wanted to tell Alex that she didn't have to ask him to make love to her. Alexandra Cole had bewitched him and unknowingly she possessed what it took to destroy him emotionally.

Supporting his weight on his elbows, he lowered his head and kissed her. Not a soul-searching, deep passionate kiss, but one better suited for a fragile newborn. He kissed her mouth, the hollow of her scented throat, the curve of her shoulders, venturing lower to her breasts. The flesh between his legs grew heavy, but he didn't, couldn't stop until he explored every inch of Alex's satiny skin. She smelled of fruit, flowers and spice.

Rachel Singletary had teased him because he'd opted to remain celibate, but she didn't know that he'd been waiting for the right woman. And he knew Alex was the right woman the first time they'd shared a dance, a kiss. Moving down the length of the large bed, he alternated kissing with flicking his tongue over her belly.

Alex's fingers curled into tight fists at her sides as she clenched her teeth. Moans of frustration mingled with the rising desire she was helpless to control. The mat of crisp dark hair covering Merrick's chest and his marauding mouth threatened to take her beyond herself. She wanted to kiss him the way he was kissing her, her lips and tongue tasting flesh in her journey to communicate wordlessly how much she loved and needed him.

Her breasts rose and fell heavily as the pulsing at the apex of her thighs increased. "Merrick!" Her hysteria was evident when she screamed his name. Reaching for his head, she attempted to capture his hair, but it was too short for her to secure a grip. He'd spread her legs and his hot breath had become a raging inferno that threatened to incinerate her—body and soul.

Merrick heard the desperate cry, inhaled her rising passion, knowing if he didn't take her now it would be over. Reversing his position, he reached for the condom, sat back on his heels and slipped it over his rigid flesh. It was for a brief moment, but he thought he saw fear and indecision in Alex's eyes as she watched him put on the latex sheath that would prevent an unplanned pregnancy. What he thought he'd glimpsed vanished as she extended her arms, welcoming him into her embrace and into her body.

Reaching for her hand, Merrick guided it to his sex. "Let's do this together."

Alex's tiny hand barely fit around his engorged tumescence as she positioned it to the entrance of her femininity. Merrick's hand covered hers as he eased himself into her body. Flames of desire rose quickly, overlapping her soft moans as he pushed into her; taut flesh stretched with each inch until he was fully sheathed. Then, in a rhythm that was as timeless as the beginning of creation, they offered each other all of themselves, holding nothing back.

Merrick established a slow, deliberate thrusting as Alex rose to meet him, pinpoints of gold in her eyes darkening with her rising ardor. Anchoring his hands under her hips, he held her fast, increasing the cadence, his hips moving with the velocity and power of a jackhammer. Her gasps and soft moans served to make the fire in his loins more intense.

He lost himself in the moment and the love flowing from the woman under him, not feeling the bite of her fingernails on his back. What he was aware of was the gurgling sounds coming from her throat that erupted into an unrestrained primal scream that sent him over a precipice wherein he surrendered all he had and was to the woman whom he knew he would love forever. They climaxed simultaneously, experiencing a free fall that made them one with each other.

They lay entwined, breathing heavily, waiting for their respiration to slow while enjoying the lingering pulsing sensations. Sated, they were loath to move. However, Merrick was forced to when he withdrew from Alex and went to discard the condom.

When he returned to the bed, he found her asleep, her face still flushed with passion. He lay beside her and within minutes Morpheus claimed him as they shared siesta for the first time.

* * *

Alex sat at a dressing table applying a coat of orange color to her lips. She and Merrick were scheduled to leave for Professor Rivera's soiree in fifteen minutes.

She hadn't made it a habit to wear makeup to the art institute, so she was certain the added color to her face and the dress would shock a few of her classmates. She'd decided to wear a minishift in a soft tangerine-orange with white orchids, reminiscent of a Japanese kimono with an empire waist and a halter top.

She'd come to the Four Seasons Hotel Thursday afternoon and left the hotel once to go to a nearby boutique and hair salon; she had her hair cut into a short and very becoming feathery style that flattered her round face.

She and Merrick shared brunch on the balcony outside their room that overlooked the courtyard and dined on exquisite Mediterranean cuisine at the hotel's elegant restaurant, Reforma 500. Earlier that afternoon she'd taken advantage of the services at the hotel's spa.

When she and Merrick weren't in bed sleeping or making love, she pulled out her books and studied for the upcoming exam. He'd surprised her when he offered to test her on her knowledge of the Mayans and their incredibly complex advanced society.

She'd asked him about the scar on his back and his response had been, *"Oh, that. It was an accident."* She didn't believe his glib explanation but decided not to pry. Their relationship was much too new to coerce each other to divulge what they deemed personal. And not once did Alex forget that what she shared with Merrick was tenuous at best. It was he who wanted a relationship that would go on for perpetuity, while she'd asked for right now.

It was ironic how she'd changed. At twenty-two she wanted

to marry her art history instructor, and now at twenty-nine she was willing to become a participant in a physical relationship that wouldn't result in a commitment.

Movement behind her caught her attention. She smiled when Merrick leaned over to press a kiss on the nape of her neck. He'd elected to wear a charcoal-gray suit in a tropical linen fabric with a pale gray finely woven shirt with a banded collar.

"You look and smell wonderful." She wore a perfume with sensual musk and woodsy notes.

Her smile widened. *"Gracias, mi querido."*

He straightened, unable to believe Alex could improve on perfection. Her short hairstyle and youthful-looking face made him feel as if he were robbing the cradle, when there was only a six-year difference in their ages.

She rose gracefully from the stool and reached for his hand. "I'm ready."

His gaze lingered on her smoky lids and lush mouth with the glistening lip color. There was a mysterious gleam in her eyes that made him want to strip her naked and take her back to bed. But he knew that wasn't possible because attendance at her professor's house was mandatory.

Merrick thought that after making love to her once he'd be able to rid himself of strong physical urges that came when he least expected. However, having her within arm's reach hadn't permitted him to exorcise the licentious images of what he wanted to do with Alexandra Cole.

What had shocked Merrick was that her libido matched his, and he wanted to demonstrate other positions and techniques, but decided to wait for another time; perhaps when he returned to Mexico she would feel more comfortable with other than traditional lovemaking.

Holding her hand, he led her out of the bathroom. She gathered her purse and a silk shawl in a pale shade that matched her silk-covered sling backs. They took the curving staircase instead of the elevator to the opulent lobby, not seeing the surreptitious glances directed at them.

The taxi Merrick had requested had arrived. He helped Alex into the vehicle, then ducked his head and sat beside her. He gave the driver the address before he settled back to enjoy the ride to Coyoacán and the delicate body beside him.

Hernando Rivera's home was in an area with a number of museums and art galleries and was within walking distance of the homes of several noted deceased inhabitants: Frida Kahlo, Diego Rivera and Russian revolutionary Leon Trotsky.

Alex walked into a brightly-lit courtyard while Merrick lingered behind to pay their driver. Long tables groaned with food and a portable bar was doing a brisk business, as evidenced by the number of people milling around holding glasses of tequila cocktails. Mariachi music blaring from hidden speakers added to the festive mood.

Moira came over to greet her. A black tank dress in a Lycra fabric hugged her lithe figure like a second skin while a pair of four-inch strappy sandals put her at the six-foot mark. Her pale hair was piled atop her head in tousled, sensual disarray.

"Where's your gorgeous friend?" she whispered.

Alex couldn't stop the wave of heat stealing across her face. "He'll be here."

Moira took a deep swallow of her drink. "Now he's someone I could get my freak on with." She'd had one too many margaritas to see Alex's scowl. "But I know he's off-limits, because I'd never make a play for a friend's man."

Forcing a smile that she definitely did not feel, Alex said, "That's good to know."

"Señorita Morris, I'm honored you've graced me with your presence."

Alex turned to find her host grinning at her. He'd forgone his conservative black suits for a white poet's shirt with matching linen slacks and tan sandals. She didn't know why, but he reminded her of cartoons in which the cat had swallowed a bird. "But, Professor Rivera, wasn't it you that said attendance is mandatory?"

He waved a hand, his dark gaze moving slowly from her face to her bare brown legs and her feet in the light-colored heels, then back again to her feathery hairstyle. "I always tell my students that, but there is no way I can enforce that rule. Field visits yes, my home no. Please come into the house to see the exhibit before you get something to eat and drink."

"Thank you, but I'd like to wait for my guest."

His black eyebrows lifted, reminding her of hash marks of birds in flight. "You came with someone?"

Alex wanted to laugh when she saw his stunned expression. "Yes, I did." The confirmation had barely left her lips when she detected the scent of Merrick's cologne. Turning, she smiled at him and extended her hand. "Darling, I'd like for you to meet Professor Rivera, who teaches design and art of ancient cultures. Professor Rivera, Merrick Grayslake. Merrick, Professor Hernando Rivera." The two men exchanged polite greetings and handshakes.

Hernando, having recovered from seeing Alexandra Morris in a dress that revealed more flesh than he'd ever seen on her, shifted his gaze to the tall man with her. "Grayslake," he said softly. "Are you Yaqui?"

A muscle jumped in Merrick's jaw. "I wouldn't know."

"You speak Mexican Spanish and your features are a blend of African, Yaqui and European. I suggest you explore your roots. I'm sure you didn't come to engage in an anthropological discussion. Come see the exhibit, then eat and drink."

Alex felt the muscles in Merrick's arm bunch up under his

jacket's sleeve. If her teacher had been able to identify Merrick's racial designation from looking at him, then there was no doubt he'd spoken the truth.

To say the professor was a brilliant art expert and anthropologist was an understatement. The first day of class he had everyone stand up and introduce themselves, and within minutes he'd identified their Spanish dialect. Alex had held her breath when he announced that based on her speech patterns and physical looks she was of African and Cuban ancestry. He'd astounded her with his accuracy, and in the following weeks Professor Rivera used his vast knowledge to subjugate *and* intimidate any student who attempted to challenge him.

Those who came to class unprepared were forced to undergo a tongue-lashing that usually went on for at least ten minutes before they were asked to leave and not return until they'd completed the assignment. The trustees of the *universidad* permitted Professor Hernando Rivera to conduct his classes like a despot because museums and art institutes the world over were vying for his attention.

They were shown into a room in Hernando's house that doubled as an art gallery. Alex couldn't believe the artifacts on display targeted for donations to local museums. There were fragile wooden, leather and clay masks from Puebla, Guerrero and Michoacan, a funerary mask from Teotihuacán and exquisite silver pieces from Oaxaca. The piece that captivated her was a Zapotec jade bat-god pendant. She thanked Hernando for permitting her to see the priceless artifacts, then returned to the courtyard with Merrick.

Smiling up at him, she noted his solemn expression. "It's over, darling."

He lifted his eyebrows as he met her amused gaze. "It really wasn't that bad. I believe hanging out with you has given me a healthy respect for art."

"Does this mean you're going with me to the museum tomorrow?"

"No, it doesn't. We have one more day together, and I don't intend to spend it in a museum."

She gave him a sidelong glance. "What have you planned?"

A knowing smile softened his firm mouth. "We're going to spend the day in bed."

Alex squeezed his hand. "You keep it up and I won't be able to walk."

Leaning down, he pressed his mouth to her ear. "I said nothing about making love, but if that's what you want I'm willing to accommodate you, because for some reason I can't get enough of you."

"Glotón."

"No lie," he drawled, grinning. "Now let's get something to eat and drink so that we can appear socially acceptable, then blow this joint."

Vertical lines appeared between her eyes. "I'm not ready to go back to the hotel."

Merrick gave her a long, penetrating look. "Where do you want to go?"

"The others are going to a club near the Zona Rosa. If you don't want to go, then I'll meet you back at the hotel."

"If you think I'm going to let you out of my sight looking like you do, then you're crazier than I am."

She glanced down at her dress. "What's wrong with the way I look?"

Pulling her closer, he dropped a kiss on her fragrant hair. "There's nothing wrong, baby. You look delicious."

She gave him her trademark dimpled smile. *"Gracias, mi amor."*

Merrick returned her smile. *"De nada, mi querida."*

Chapter 10

Merrick sat in the corner of a noisy, crowded club with flashing colored lights watching Alex dance. He'd begun drinking beer, but after the second bottle he switched to water. At first he'd found the pumping baseline beats infectious, but after three hours of nonstop music and the differing scents of cologne and perfume on sweaty bodies he was ready to find the nearest exit.

Resting an elbow on the small table, he cradled his chin on his fist. He hadn't flown to Mexico to see Alex and then share her with people she saw every day. But seeing her laughing and dancing tempered his selfishness because it was he, not some other man, who would share her passion.

Merrick had tried and failed to analyze what it was about Michael Kirkland's cousin that affected him wherein he was now willing to forsake his reclusive lifestyle to consider returning to the CIA as a bureaucrat. Instead of being briefed for covert missions he would become a trainer as an intelligence research training specialist. He'd had experience when he facilitated advanced training courses at Quantico for DEA agents. Yes, he would go back as an intelligence training specialist, secure his relationship with Alex and retire.

The driving rhythms slowed to a seductive ballad and Merrick stood up when he spied Alex coming in his direction. Reaching for her purse and shawl, he took several steps and curved an arm around her waist.

Her dewy face shimmered like brown velvet under the psychedelic lights. "Dance with me, Merrick."

He shook his head. "Not now, *querida*. We'll dance together at the hotel."

Her brow furrowed. "What's the matter?"

Pulling her closer, he shouldered his way through the throng on the dance floor. "The matter is I was ready to leave two hours ago."

"Why didn't you say something?"

"I didn't want to stop you from enjoying yourself, Ali."

"I enjoy myself even when I'm not dancing."

"What's going to happen once you start your career?"

"That shouldn't change anything. I'm not going to be working 24/7. Speaking of careers, I went online last week and applied for a position with the National Trust for Historic Preservation's northeast region. And if I'm hired, I'll be responsible for historic districts in New York, New Jersey, Vermont, Pennsylvania, Rhode Island, Connecticut, Delaware, Massachusetts and Maine."

Merrick noticed she hadn't mentioned any state south of Delaware. "Do you plan to relocate?"

"No. I like living in the D.C. area, and I love my condo. There may be a problem when I have to do the fieldwork."

"What, Ali?"

"There's a family mandate that I'm not permitted to take a commercial aircraft." She told him about how her uncle Martin's daughter had become a kidnapping victim forty years before, and since that time anyone who claimed Cole blood or married into the family was prohibited from flying on commercial carriers.

Merrick wanted to tell Alex that making arrangements to travel up and down the eastern seaboard was the least of her worries. Hadn't she realized she was a wealthy woman, and what would've become prohibitive for the normal working-class person was readily available to her?

"If you're hired, then how are you going to travel?"

"If I'm not able to secure a seat on the ColeDiz G4, then it will have to be a private jet. The money I spent on hiring private jets I could donate to my favorite charity."

They stepped out of the air-cooled club and into the unusually warm winter Mexico City heat that lingered even after the sun had set behind the mountains. All of the upscale shops were air-conditioned, but once anyone stepped outdoors onto the overpopulated streets with the smog and thermal inversion, many found breathing normally difficult.

Merrick startled Alex when he whistled sharply through his teeth for a taxi. A late-model colorful car skidded to the curb. The driver stepped out, rounded his vehicle and opened the door with the arrogant aplomb of any major city taxi driver. She got in, followed by Merrick. The driver closed the door and then took his seat behind the wheel.

"Ca dónde la, el señor?"

"The Four Seasons Hotel en el Paseo de la Reforma 500."

The driver took off in a burst of speed as Merrick settled against the leather seat, his arm going around Alex's shoulders. Minutes into the ride, she rested her head on his chest. Twenty-four hours. That was all they had left before he flew back to the States.

* * *

Alex shifted into a more comfortable position between Merrick's legs as an unconscious moan slipped past her lips; the cramping in her lower belly and a dull ache in her lower back were indicators that she would see her period in the next day or two.

"What's the matter, baby?" Merrick asked, his moist breath sweeping over her ear.

She moaned again. "Premenstrual cramps."

Merrick gently lifted the damp strands clinging to her scalp. They'd returned to the hotel and instead of Alex taking a bath and him a shower, she'd invited him to share the oversize tub.

"Is this the time of the month when you turn into a witch?"

Peering at him over her shoulder, Alex wrinkled her nose. "Don't tell me you've got sexist jokes."

Merrick's expression was one of unadulterated innocence. "No."

"Have you had a lot of experience with women who become viragos when they're PMSing?"

"Even if I have I'm not going to tell you."

Alex shifted until she straddled Merrick, the pulsing jets from the Jacuzzi adding to her buoyancy. Leaning forward, she pressed her breasts to his hair-matted chest. "Why won't you tell me?"

He stared at her under lowered lids. "I don't kiss and tell, Ali. The women in my past are just that—the past." He kissed the end of her nose. "That is a topic I will not discuss."

Alex affected a pout. "I told you about the men from my past."

"You told me not because I asked but because you wanted to. You know who and what you are, and because of that you're open and spontaneous, while I've lived my life speculating whether I'm African or Native American, and wondering if I father children whether they'll inherit a gene abnormality from an ancestor."

"What do you say you are?"

A wry smile touched his mouth. "I say African-American because unconsciously that's what I feel. And if my biological father is European or Native American, then I assume he'd slept with a black woman. Or it could be vice versa. You have a large family connected by blood and marriage, and because I don't know my parents I'll never know if I have a brother or sister, nieces or nephews."

Burying her face between his neck and shoulder, Alex closed her eyes. She felt the strong, steady pumping of his heart against her breasts. "Have you thought of trying to find your birth mother? There are Web sites and agencies set up to reconnect children with their birth parents. It shouldn't be too difficult for you because you know your mother's name."

"I did check a database for Virginia Gray or Grayslake and came up with more than nine thousand nationwide."

Alex opened her eyes and pulled back, meeting his intense stare. "Did you contact any of them?"

He nodded. "After the first thirty I decided to let it go. Each time I got a *'No, I'm not your mother'* I found myself overwhelmed with feelings of abandonment. It'd begun to affect my job performance, so I decided to let it go. Uncovering who my mother is or was is no longer a priority."

Looping her arms under Merrick's shoulders, Alex brushed a kiss over his mouth, feeling his pain as surely as if it was her own. It didn't matter who he was because he was the man with whom she'd fallen in love; he was the man she would love forever.

"I love you."

Merrick went completely still, certain Alex could feel the blood rushing through his veins. He was hot, then cold, confused, then clear-headed as her confession filled him with a sense of power, a strength that vanquished the lingering pain of abandonment that had become an emotional impediment to marriage and fatherhood.

"Let's get out of this tub," he said, recovering quickly.

Merrick anchored a hand along the shelf of the tub and came to his feet, bringing Alex up with him. He stepped out and reached for a bath sheet on a nearby table. Wrapping the velour fabric around her body, he lifted her gently from the bathtub and carried her into the bedroom, placing her on the bed.

None of his movements were rushed as he blotted the moisture from her satiny body, lingering over the curve of her breasts and hips. It no longer mattered that he would leave Mexico and Alex in a little more than twenty-four hours, because he had the rest of his life to share whatever he had and whatever he'd become with her.

Time seemed to slow down for Alex as she languished in the gentleness of her lover's touch. He dried the front of her body, turned her over and then repeated the action.

Then, without warning, his mouth replaced the towel, tracing a sensual path down the length of her spine, lingering at the indentation separating the globes of flesh defining her buttocks.

Heat, chills and undulating waves of ecstasy swept over her as she tried, and failed, to keep the moans from escaping her parted lips. His hands searched areas known only to her, his mouth exploring, and tantalizing, searching, savoring every hollow, dip and curve of her from head to toe.

Merrick couldn't get enough of Alex. His hands and mouth mapped every inch of flesh he could see and reach. Her smell, her essence, lingered in his nostrils and on his tongue. His passions rose quickly, and he released her, pausing to slip on a condom. It was as if time had stood still until he looped an arm around her waist; she knelt with her back to him as he pressed his groin to her buttocks. In one, sure motion, he eased his erection into her, both gasping from the unexpected joining of flesh against flesh, man against woman.

Merrick cupped her breasts, alternating squeezing with rubbing his thumbs over the pebble hardness of her distended nipples. The kneeling position allowed him deeper penetration, maximum pleasure. The sensual beauty of her naked limbs, her feminine fragrance mingling with the rising scent of their lovemaking threatened to take him over the edge where it would be over much too soon.

Withdrawing, he reversed their positions. Merrick lay on his back, arms anchored over his head, as Alex straddled him. He knew he would never get used to her sensual expression in the throes of lovemaking: flushed skin, dilated pupils, parted lips, flaring nostrils and heaving breasts. And her bubbly spontaneity out of bed became an uninhibited smoldering passion that stripped him raw wherein he was unable to hold anything back. Alexandra Cole claimed what he'd been unable to give anyone—all of himself.

Alex's gold-brown gaze met silver-gray. Her gaze inched down to the firm muscles under the brown arms in the diffused lamplight. Tufts of straight reddish hair grew out from his armpits, a lighter shade than the crisp, curling strands covering his chest that tapered down to a narrow line that spread out in an inverted triangle to coarser, tighter curls at his loins. Everything about her lover was a visual banquet. Merrick's deep drawling voice, powerful masculine presence and compelling, magnetic eyes held her captive in an abyss of loving and longing she never wanted to end.

Anchoring her palms on his shoulders, her gaze meeting and fusing with his, she lowered her body over his rigid flesh, making them one with each other. Simultaneous audible moans of satisfaction matched the rush of moisture bathing the pulsing area between her thighs.

The world as Alex knew it ceased to exist. All that mattered was the man offering her the most exquisite passion she'd ever known. What had begun as friendship was now a full-blown love affair, and she realized what she'd felt and shared with her art professor had not even come close to what she felt with Merrick. The pulsing grew stronger, becoming contractions that gripped his hardness before releasing it, then began again.

Heat rippled under Merrick's skin, became hotter, more intense each time he thrust upward. They had ceased to exist as individuals, separate entities. He was so attuned to the woman rising and falling over his throbbing erection that he felt the spasms that seized her, followed by a primordial scream that made hair stand up on the nape of his neck. Before the next spasm and Alex's next outburst of ecstasy, he had her on her back, feet anchored on his shoulders. He didn't want the pleasure to end—not yet. He wanted it to go on—forever, if possible. But it was not possible when he lowered his head, closed his eyes and enjoyed the most extreme physical gratification he'd ever experienced.

When it was all over he lowered her feet, then collapsed heavily on her smaller frame, waiting for his heart rate to return to a normal rhythm.

He loved her. He loved her more than anyone or anything.

Alex struggled to catch her breath as the pressure from Merrick's greater weight prevented her from moving. "What are you doing to me?" she whispered.

Breathing heavily, Merrick rolled off Alex and pulled her to his chest. "Loving you, baby. Loving you, *and* your life."

Chapter 11

CIA Headquarters...Langley, Virginia

A rare smile deepened the network of lines crisscrossing William Reid's weather-beaten face within seconds of the door closing behind a man who he'd believed he would never see again. His smile faded as one of the three telephones on his desk rang; reaching over, he picked up the receiver.

"Reid."

"Come to my office." The command was sharp, the caller's tone brusque, no-nonsense.

"I'm on my way."

Pushing back his chair and coming to his feet, he put on his suit jacket, left the office and made his way to one several doors away.

"He's expecting you," said the dour-faced woman who

guarded her boss's office like a Secret Service agent assigned to the presidential detail.

Carl Ashleigh stood by the door to his inner office. It wasn't often William saw the man wear a suit jacket unless he was scheduled to meet with the director.

"Let's go for a drive."

William, or Bill to the few friends he'd acquired since coming to the CIA from the FBI, followed his supervisor like an obedient puppy. It wasn't until they were seated in Ashleigh's gas-guzzling Yukon, maneuvering toward McLean, Virginia, that Ashleigh initiated conversation. He'd become used to the eccentric younger man who would order him to his office, then make him wait before granting him an audience.

"Is he coming back?"

William stared out the side window at the passing countryside. It was the first week in March, and winter appeared to have finally loosened its grip on northern Virginia.

"I assume you're talking about Grayslake."

High color suffused Carl's face, his pale blue eyes standing out in stark contrast. "Who the hell else do you think I'm talking about? Did he not spend the past two hours in your office?"

"Yes."

"What did he want?"

"He wants back in."

"What did you tell him?" Carl asked.

"I told him that he would have to go through the same protocol as if he were a new hire. He'd have to pass a physical, a psychological and of course obtain security clearance."

"What's he asking for?"

"Training."

Carl slowed the Yukon, turning onto a local road and coming to a complete stop behind a copse of pine trees; he left the engine running. Releasing his seat belt, he shifted on his seat and stared at William Reid. The man was only fifty-six but Carl thought of him as a dinosaur, a holdover from a past era with his military crew cut, cuffed trousers and wing-tipped footwear. William had given the Bureau fifteen years of fieldwork before transferring to the CIA as a desk jockey.

"Slow down his paperwork."

"What!" The single word exploded from William Reid's mouth.

The fingers of Carl's left hand drummed nervously on the steering wheel. "I want you to keep him on hold for a while."

William ran a hand over hair that looked like the bristles on a stiff brush. "How long is awhile?"

"Six months. Assign him to sniper training. With his background as a Marine Corps scout he'll do well there until we're ready for him."

William gave Carl a long, penetrating stare. "What's up?"

Carl's pale blue eyes narrowed, and he wondered how much he could tell his assistant without compromising the details of a joint meeting of agencies that included the FBI and the CIA. Biweekly meetings between the two directors, corresponding assistant directors and federal prosecutors had become akin to a world economic summit.

"We may need him for a special assignment."

"It can't be a field assignment," William insisted.

"I know that!" Carl said angrily.

William did not visibly react to his supervisor's outburst. "Grayslake is going to become suspicious if we take too long to approve his rehire or if he's assigned to something he hasn't requested."

Ashleigh stared out the windshield. "He wants back in, and that means he'll accept whatever we offer him. And if he makes it known that he's unhappy, then bust him down to a file clerk."

Carl hadn't been cleared to brief his assistant on Operation Backslap, but with Merrick Grayslake's possible return the initial strategy would have to be modified. Once Grayslake was given security clearance Reid would be briefed on an investigation certain to send elected officials scrambling to hire the best defense attorneys not only to salvage their political careers but to avoid going to prison.

William shook his head. "He's not going to go for that. If we lose him a second time, you and I know that he's never coming back."

"If you have a better plan, then you'd better tell me right here, right now."

The older man stared at his supervisor. "You know I don't have one."

Carl snapped his seat belt, put the vehicle in gear and maneuvered back onto the road back to Langley. The return drive was accomplished in complete silence, and when the two men returned to their offices both knew someone higher than them had determined Merrick Grayslake's destiny the moment his written request to return to the Company was received.

Merrick scrolled through his cell-phone directory and clicked on a name. "I'm in your neck of the woods," he said when hearing the deep-voiced greeting. "Can you spare me a few minutes?"

"Sure. What's up, Gray?"

"I'll tell you when I see you."

"I'll be here."

Merrick disconnected the call and shifted into a higher gear. Forty-five minutes later he parked his vehicle two blocks from Michael and Jolene Kirkland's house.

Making his way along the tree-lined streets in the D.C. suburb with opulent and historic colonial and Georgian-style homes, he recalled his meeting with Bill Reid. Merrick had been forthcoming when he revealed that he was more than ready to return to the CIA as a training specialist.

Turning a corner, he walked a block with only six structures in the charming cul-de-sac, most large, imposing, claiming spacious front lawns and, in the warmer weather, flowering shrubs. Michael's house stood apart from the others. Its simplicity was a Frank Lloyd Wright Japanese-inspired design. A broad sheltering roof with generous overhanging eaves and windows set with colorful geometric shapes radiated warmth, beckoning him closer. A waist-high slate wall was covered with a profusion of climbing vines. A gate made of iron pipe painted a Cherokee-red stood open, welcoming him.

Merrick strolled up the path, but as he walked up the six steps to the front door it opened and Michael Kirkland stood in the doorway, casually dressed in jeans and a black T-shirt.

He extended his hand, pulling Michael close in a strong embrace. "How's it going, Kirk?"

Michael Kirkland was an imposing figure. His exposed muscled arms were brown as berries. Tall, broad-shouldered and slim-hipped, former U.S. Army captain Michael Kirkland was as physically fit as he'd been when he graduated from the U.S. Military Academy at West Point a decade before. His face was as remarkable as the rest of him: close-cropped raven-black hair, clear green eyes that shimmered like precious gems in a sun-browned face. Men and women were drawn to his perfectly symmetrical features that were as delicate as a woman's.

Merrick's friend had resigned his commission and now taught classes in military law and military history at a private military school in northern Virginia. Merrick knew Michael's decision hadn't been an easy one, but now as a husband and prospective father he appeared content with the turn his life had taken.

Michael returned the rough embrace. "How long are you staying?"

Pulling back, Merrick shook his head. "I'm not. I plan to drive back to Bolivar tonight."

Lifting his sweeping black eyebrows, Michael stepped aside and beckoned Merrick into his home. "Come in. Don't tell me you've been holding out on me." Merrick walked into the living room of the two-story converted carriage house decorated with Asian and Southwest–themed furnishings.

Michael Kirkland stared at his friend, unable to believe the transformation. When he'd reconnected with Merrick six months ago, he'd found him long-haired, bearded and gaunt-looking. Not only had Merrick put on weight, but he always could've easily passed for a D.C. businessman or politician in his tailored suit, imported footwear and conservative haircut.

Merrick flashed a smile, not replying to Michael's accusation that he was hiding something from him. He followed Michael into a room that was an exact replica of a Japanese teahouse. Octagonal in shape, its walls were made entirely of screened-in glass windows. Two of the eight sides were open to take advantage of the crisp air. A low lacquered table, surrounded by large black and jade-green floor cushions, were set up in the middle of the room.

Merrick owed Michael his life from when he found him lying facedown in the street, bleeding from a gunshot wound to the abdomen. Doctors had repaired his spleen but were unable to save his left kidney. The police recorded the incident as a mugging, but Merrick knew he'd been set up, though he was unable to prove it.

"Where's Jolene?" he asked Michael.

Michael folded his tall frame down to the futon, motioning for Merrick to do the same. "She flew to Chicago to see her parents. And because she's at the end of her second trimester she said this will be her last trip until the baby comes."

Stretching out his legs, Merrick stared at an indoor pool built into a corner. The gurgling water created a soothing mood, trickling over rocks and pebbles concealed by a profusion of bamboo shoots and water lilies.

"Do you know what you're having?"

Michael shook his head. "No. I'd like to know, but Jolene wants to wait."

"Does this mean you do everything your wife wants?" Merrick teased.

"Hell, yeah," Michael said, smiling, "but within reason of course. I know enough when to advance and when to retreat."

"Marriage shouldn't be a military campaign, Michael."

The brilliant green eyes in a rich brown face glowed. "With Jolene and me there's never a military campaign. I give in to her because she's carrying *my* baby. Speaking of women, what's up with you, Gray? Do you have a little honey hidden away in your mountain retreat that has you running back to spend the night?"

Standing, Merrick removed his suit jacket, placing it over the arm of the futon and wondering how Michael would react if he told him that he was dating and sleeping with his first cousin.

Would he approve?

Disapprove?

Concluding his relationship with Alex was much too new and much too fragile, he decided not to say anything. "No," he answered truthfully. His *honey,* as Michael called her, was currently touring an archaeological site in Mexico's Yucatán Peninsula.

He missed her, missed her more than he thought he would miss a woman. And the missing had nothing to do with making love to her; that was something he could do with any woman. But Alexandra Cole had become much more to him than any woman.

Waking up with her beside him, their sharing meals together, taking long walks, discussing any- and everything were things he'd never experienced with a woman. Alex's spontaneity, her outgoing personality and her lust for life were refreshing changes because he tended to take life much too seriously.

"No, I don't," Merrick said, answering Michael's query. "But it is something I am considering."

Leaning back and crossing his arms over his chest, Michael gave Merrick a long, penetrating look. "Who is she?"

"I'd rather not say at this time."

Respecting his friend's right to privacy, Michael nodded. One thing he knew about Merrick Grayslake, and that was he was a very private person, and if he'd felt comfortable revealing the identity of the woman with whom he was involved, he wouldn't have hesitated telling him.

Michael glanced at his watch. It was after three. "Can you hang out long enough to have dinner with me?"

Merrick flashed a rare smile. "Sure."

"Do you want to go out or would you prefer me to throw something together?"

"We can eat here." Whatever Michael threw together was certain to equal or surpass any restaurant meal. Alex had revealed that it was a family tradition that all the men were taught to cook. The rationale was they would never have to depend on a woman to eat.

Michael pushed to his feet. "I'll take out a couple of steaks to defrost. When I come back, you can tell me why you left the mountains to talk to me. Do you want anything to drink while I'm up?"

"No, thanks."

* * *

"I'm going back to the Company," Merrick announced when Michael returned, his voice completely void of emotion.

Michael went completely still as an expression of shock froze his features. "You're kidding, aren't you?"

"No, I'm not."

"But why, Gray? I remember you telling me that you'd die a slow death if you had to sit behind a desk."

Merrick stared at the water spilling into the pool. "I'm dying a slow death living in Bolivar. I can go weeks without seeing or talking to another human being. I hadn't realized it, but you saved my life a second time when you asked me to protect Jolene, because I was on a fast track to self-destruction."

Looping one denim-covered leg over the opposite knee, Michael nodded slowly. "Can the church say amen?"

Merrick smiled and said, "Amen."

"To be truthful, Gray, you looked like the walking dead."

"Damn. Was I that bad?"

Michael smiled and said, "Hell, yeah." He sobered quickly. "Do you think you'll be able to adjust to not being in the field?"

"I don't have a choice. I gave the Corps ten years and the Company four, so my options are limited."

"They're not as limited as you think. You took advantage of your stint in the Corps to advance your education, and with your intelligence and Scout Sniper School training I could recommend you for a position at Leesburg Military."

Vertical lines appeared between Merrick's eyes. "Why the hard sell, Kirk?"

"I've been where you are now," Michael said. "I was mad as hell when I was transferred from intelligence to desk duty at the Pentagon, but during the four years, I used the transfer to my advantage when I went to law school. And when General Harry Cooper became more aggressive with his sexual advances, I knew I had to get out or forfeit my freedom for killing that little toad.

"I hated giving up my military career because it was all I knew. Twelve years of military school, West Point and then military intelligence. I'd hoped to become a lifer, but after I fell in love with Jolene I never regretted my decision to become a civilian. I teach courses I know and love, and the bonus is that I get to come home every night to my beautiful wife."

"What aren't you telling me?" Merrick asked, his expression a mask of stone.

Michael leaned closer. "If you have someone—a woman—then you can't think only of yourself, because even if you're not married to her you're still a couple."

"Come on, Michael. Spill it!"

"Even though you're going back it won't be as a civilian. You were trained as an operative, and you'll always be an operative."

Merrick's frown deepened. "You're talking in circles, friend."

Michael wanted to tell Merrick that the CIA would take him back if he had one arm and one leg because of his superior intelligence, an intelligence Merrick took for granted.

"Don't be surprised if you're called to sit in on a few Black Op meetings. Although you won't become an active participant, just being privy to what's going on in the strategy room will put you and your lady at risk."

"Are you trying to discourage me?"

"No, Gray. I just want you to know what you may have to face."

"I'll take your warning under advisement. I'll let..." Merrick's words trailed off when his cell phone rang. "Excuse me," he said to Michael as he reached for his jacket and the phone in the breast pocket. Alex's number came up on the display. Pressing a button, he put the tiny instrument to his ear. "Please hold on."

Michael noticed Merrick's expression softening as a gentle smile spread over his face. "I'm going to get something to drink," he announced, excusing himself.

Waiting until he was alone, Merrick said, "Hey, baby. How are you?"

"I'd be a whole lot better if I could see my boyfriend."

"Where are you?"

"I'm back in Mexico City."

"How would you like company this weekend?"

Her husky laugh came through the earpiece. "I was just going to ask you the same thing. Merrick?" she asked when he didn't respond.

"Yes, baby."

"I've made arrangements to come to the States. I'm flying into IAD."

"I'll meet you."

"No, Merrick. I've arranged for a driver to take me to Bolivar."

"When are you leaving?"

"Tomorrow morning."

"What time are you scheduled to touch down?"

"I was told around ten in the morning. I don't have to be back for a week."

Merrick could not stop the smile spreading across his face. "That's good. Ali?"

"What is it, Merrick?"

"I love you."

There came a swollen silence. "And I love you, too. Please hang up, Merrick, before I start bawling."

"I love you, I love you, I love you, Alexandra," he whispered, then disconnected the call.

For a brief second, the time it took to blink his eye, Merrick wanted what Michael had—marriage and impending father-hood. The moment of madness passed when he remembered who he was and Alex's declaration that she wasn't ready for marriage and children.

He'd existed in a state of suspended animation for two years, and then without warning Michael had come to his sanctuary to ask for his help. Leaving Bolivar and what had become his beloved woods and mountains forced Merrick to step outside himself to see how self-destructive he'd become.

He went for long walks, slept no more than three hours at a time, stopped cutting his hair and had grown a beard. He'd lost more than thirty pounds because there were days when one blended into the next and he couldn't remember when last he'd eaten.

Despite Michael's misgivings, he would go back to the CIA, rent an apartment in D.C., see Alex whenever possible and return to Bolivar to unwind on weekends.

Chapter 12

Alex stared out the window as her driver slowed down to less than ten miles an hour around the winding road. Biting down on her lower lip, she closed her eyes as the flutters in her belly increased, silently cursing Merrick for living in the middle of nowhere.

She'd berated herself over and over when she called Merrick to tell him that she was coming to visit him. She was going to spend the equivalent of an American spring break with a man who'd gotten under her skin like an annoying itch. She, Alexandra Cole, who'd earned a reputation of dating a different man every night, had found herself ensnared in a sensual trap from which there was no escape—and it wasn't that she wanted to escape.

There was still something about Merrick that frightened her and kept her off balance, yet it wasn't enough to stop her wanting to be with him. She'd also attempted to rationalize why she'd fallen in love with the enigmatic man, and wasn't able to come up with a plausible explanation except that Merrick Grayslake allowed Alexandra Cole to be Alexandra. Not once during the three hours they'd spent at the club in the Zona Rosa had he exhibited a modicum of jealousy when she'd danced with the other men, or attempted to flaunt his machismo with a display of control or ownership.

They'd started out as friends, and now were lovers. Neither of them wanted to get married, which meant their relationship would be smooth and undemanding.

Alex opened her eyes and exhaled an audible sigh. She didn't think she would ever get used to the dangerous curving stretch of roadway. A hint of a smile softened her mouth when the driver maneuvered onto the unpaved road that led to her lover's house. Her smile widened when she saw him standing on the porch in a pair of jeans and a pullover sweater, waiting for her.

Merrick was off the porch and opening the rear door to the town car within seconds of the driver shifting into Park, leaving the man with the task of removing Alex's luggage from the trunk.

He scooped her off the leather seat and cradled her to his chest. *"Estas tarde,"* he whispered. He'd expected her three hours before.

"La salida de Ciudad México estuvo demorada." Alex glared at him through her lashes. Her flight from Mexico City had been delayed several hours. "The important thing is that I'm here." Her explanation, though spoken softly, held a slight edge.

"I'm not keeping tabs on you, Ali. It's just that I thought something had happened to you." Bending slightly, he set her on her feet, one arm going around her waist. Reaching into the pocket of his jeans, he removed a large bill and pressed it into the driver's palm. "Thank you for keeping her safe."

The driver's head bobbed up and down like a buoy in a storm. "Thank you, sir." He nodded to Alex as if she were royalty. "Goodbye, miss."

She offered him her dimpled smile. "Goodbye." She stood with Merrick, watching the driver get into his car. They were in the same spot when the taillights disappeared from view. "I'd paid him, Merrick."

Pulling her closer, Merrick pressed a kiss on the top of Alex's hair. The last time he saw her, her short hair had afforded her a punk look. But now it was long enough to curl at the ends. The Mexican sun had darkened her face to an even nut-brown shade that fired the gold in her beautiful eyes.

"That's all right, baby."

Tilting her chin, Alex met his steady gaze. "I don't want you to throw your money away."

His expression changed, hardening, until his eyes glowed like flints of steel. "Do you think I can't afford to date you?"

Her delicate jaw dropped. "No, Merrick, it's not—"

"It's not what, Alexandra Cole? I wasn't a trust-fund baby, but I can assure you that I'm not a pauper either. So, if you think I'm going to pimp you, I suggest you call your driver and tell him—better yet, I'll drive you back to Arlington."

She stomped her booted foot. "Stop it, Merrick!"

"Stop what, Alexandra?"

Alex went completely still, her heart pounding painfully under her breasts. She'd flown back to the States to see Merrick when normally she would've gone to Florida to re-connect with her family.

"Stop putting words in my mouth," she countered slowly. "If I'd thought you were after my money, I never would have given you my number."

"Why did you give me your number?"

A rush of heat swept over her face, moving lower until she felt as if she were on fire. "Why are you asking me this now? Why not before we slept together?"

His hands came up and he held her shoulders in a firm grip. "I need to know how committed you are to our relationship."

Her eyes narrowed. "Are you afraid that I'm going to cheat on you with another man?"

Merrick shook his head. "Fidelity is not even remotely a concern."

"Then don't you dare question my feelings for you. Not when I've just spent thousands of dollars and flown thousands of miles to make my first booty call."

Merrick merely stared, complete surprise on his face, tongue-tied. "Is that what I am to you?" he asked, recovering his voice. "You see me as a booty call?"

"Huh-uh," Alex said flippantly. "Come inside and I'll prove it."

Pulling her close and lowering his head, Merrick captured her mouth in a burning kiss that buckled her knees. She sagged weakly against his body, shivers of desire and delight racking her limbs. The sensual assault on her mouth ended as quickly as it'd begun.

"We'll continue this after we come back, and then you'll see if I'm worth the money you spent for your so-called *booty call*."

Alex smiled, grabbing his hips. "You don't mind being a booty call?"

He chuckled. "I don't mind being *your* booty call."

Standing on tiptoe, she brushed a kiss over his mouth. She squeezed his firm buttocks. "I hereby stake my claim to this."

Merrick released her shoulders, his hand moving lower to cover her breasts over a soft wool sweater. Alex wasn't given time to react when one hand cupped the area between her legs. "And I stake my claim to these," he whispered and was hard-pressed not to laugh when an expression of pure shock froze Alex's delicate features. He leaned in closer. "Play with fire and you'll get burned, beautiful," he taunted.

A slow smile found its way across her face. "You're a bad, bad boy, Merrick Grayslake."

He lifted his eyebrows. "You think? You have no idea how very bad I can be."

"Bad boy, bad boy, what you gonna do? What you gonna do when *I* come for you?" she sang melodiously.

"Hey, you sound pretty good," he said, complimenting Alex on her singing. "You sing, dance and play the piano. What other gifts are you hiding from me?"

"That's it," she said, lifting her shoulders in a perfect Gallic shrug. "I sing and play the piano because I took lessons. You already know about my dance lessons."

Cradling her to his chest, Merrick rocked her back and forth. "What do you say we throw a party tonight?"

Alex stared up at him staring down at her. "What kind of party?"

"It will be private with just the two of us. We can begin with a wonderful dinner with drinks, then put on some mood music and dance for a while. And if we're not too tired we can retire to the bedroom where I'll show you just how much I've come to love you."

Her lids came down, hiding her innermost feelings from Merrick. Never in her wildest dreams did she think she would experience the peace and joy she felt at that moment. Merrick had become the answer to her dream of finding the perfect man. Under his steely stare, impassive expression and deep controlled voice he'd shown her another side of himself whenever he made love to her with a wild abandon that made her forget every man she'd ever known, a lovemaking that made her forget who she was when she discovered an ecstasy that took her to heights of passion she hadn't thought possible.

She'd chartered a private jet and car service to come to Bolivar, West Virginia, because not only did she love Merrick but she'd also missed his lovemaking.

Her eyelids fluttered as she struggled to bring her fragile emotions under control. Wrapping her arms around his waist and resting her cheek on his chest, she inhaled the familiar scent of his cologne that was the perfect complement to his body's natural fragrance.

"You don't ever have to tell me that you love me, *querido,* because I feel your love even when we're thousands of miles apart. Your face is the last thing I see when I close my eyes at night, and when I wake up it is you that I think about. I take your image with me when I go to class and I don't think I would've survived the two weeks in the Yucatán with lodgings that were so primitive that once I returned to Mexico City I checked into an upscale hotel for two days, languishing in a Jacuzzi and ordering room service."

Merrick pressed a kiss to her forehead. *"Pobrecita, eso es porque tu er es una chica rica maleriada."*

"That's where you're wrong. My parents never spoiled me, but I'll never take running water and indoor plumbing for granted ever again."

He wanted to tell Alex that she *was* spoiled. He'd lost count of the number of times when he was denied a bath and food because he wouldn't do something his foster parents had ordered him to do. The physical and emotional abuse he'd encountered as a child gave him the strength he needed to survive the rigorous training to become a marine who remained in a constant state of readiness for all types of combat situations.

"I didn't know what you wanted to eat, so I decided to wait until you got here to go to the supermarket."

Pulling back, Alex smiled at Merrick. "Let's go, because I'm starved."

"Didn't you eat on the plane?"

"No. I had a couple of cups of coffee, but that's all."

Reaching for her hand, Merrick held it firmly as he bent and picked up her single piece of luggage. "I'll fix something for you before we leave."

Alex pulled back. "I can pick up something at a fast-food restaurant."

"Not today, beautiful. We'll save the calories and fat-laden preservatives and additives for another day."

She gave him a sidelong glance. "Don't tell me you're monitoring your figure," she teased.

"What I'm monitoring is my heart and arteries." Merrick knew he was going to have to take a physical even for a desk position, and he didn't want anything to compromise his passing.

Alex walked up the porch steps and followed Merrick into the house where she'd spent a wonderful four days. Nothing had changed as she felt an invisible warmth envelop her with a sense of homecoming.

Merrick closed the door to keep the cool mountain air out of the house, and when she turned to face him she saw it. Her eyes widened. "What's that?"

Merrick saw the direction of her stunned gaze. A high-powered rifle was propped up against a wall next to the front door. "It's a rifle."

"I know it's a rifle, Merrick. But why is it there?"

"It's for bears."

"What about bears?" she asked.

"It's spring and the bears are out with their new cubs looking for food."

"Are you going to shoot them?"

"No, Ali. It's more to scare them."

"What if you don't scare them?"

Merrick captured Alex's anxious gaze with his. "Then there'll be one less bear around these parts."

Alex wrapped her arms around her body in a protective gesture. She knew there was something dangerous about Merrick, and seeing the rifle had just confirmed her suspicions. "Let's hope you won't have to kill one."

His expression softened as he smiled. "I've lived here for two years and I've never had to shoot another living creature. And that includes the deer who feed on the brushes behind the house. Some of them are so used to humans that they don't even run when they see you."

"Promise me you won't shoot Bambi or Smokey."

Turning his head, Merrick successfully hid a smile. There was no doubt his girlfriend had a soft spot for animals. "I can't promise that, Ali, especially if a four-hundred-pound bear is standing on my porch looking for food. I can always shoot to wound, but a wounded bear is more dangerous than one who isn't. Stay out of this, darling, and please don't ask me to do something that would put our lives at risk."

The familiar mask had descended again and Alex felt the closeness between her and Merrick dissipate like a drop of water on a heated surface. It was one thing to be separated from Merrick by more than a thousand miles, and another completely when they stood less than a foot apart, yet there was a chasm because of a disagreement.

"Okay," she conceded reluctantly. "I'll stay out of it."

It wasn't until Merrick let out an audible sigh that he realized he'd been holding his breath. He didn't want to fight with Alex. All he wanted to do was love her. "I'll take your bag upstairs, then I'll feed you."

Alex nodded as she shrugged out of her wool swing coat and placed it on a chair near the door. She was standing in the middle of Merrick's living room because she'd missed him. She hadn't come to West Virginia to fight with him over the area's wildlife population but to spend every night, hour and minute with the man with whom she'd fallen in love, until she had to return to Mexico.

Crossing the living room, she made her way to the half bath off the kitchen to wash her hands. She met Merrick as he entered the kitchen. Sitting on a stool at the cooking island, Alex rested her elbows on the countertop and watched Merrick as he prepared an impromptu lunch.

Chapter 13

Merrick had been pushing a shopping cart up and down the wide supermarket aisles, stopping whenever Alex stopped to read the label on every product she placed in the cart.

He groaned for the third time within a matter of minutes. "Do you always spend this much time reading labels?" he asked.

"Yes," she answered, not bothering to look at him. "I have to know what I'm eating, Merrick."

Shaking his head, he let out another groan. "Baby, please."

Alex glanced up, meeting his tortured gaze. "Why don't you wait for me in the truck?"

Does this mean you do everything your wife wants? Merrick recalled his query to Michael, and his friend's reply, *I know enough when to advance and when to retreat.*

He and Alex weren't husband and wife, but living together for a week, sharing meals and a bed was no different from what Michael had with Jolene. Merrick was aware that a successful relationship was based on compromise, and he also knew he had to find a middle ground with Alex or what they had, what he hoped to have with her would end in a supermarket because it was his practice to get in and out within half an hour. He didn't read labels, interrogate the in-store butcher about cuts of meat, or the produce manager as to the delivery date of fruits and vegetables.

Abandoned at birth, a loner by nature and by choice, Merrick realized having a relationship with a woman, one whom he loved, was a new experience for him. What he had to do was to learn when to advance and when to retreat.

Forcing a smile, he winked at Alex. "That's all right. I'll wait."

Alex placed the can in the half-filled cart. "I think I have everything." She'd planned menus that included Caribbean-inspired dishes she'd learned from her mother.

"Are you sure?"

She smiled at Merrick. "Of course I'm sure. Haven't we spent enough time here?"

"Too much," Merrick mumbled under his breath. "Yes, dear," he said loud enough for her to hear.

An elderly woman wheeling her cart in their direction patted Merrick's arm. "What a nice young man you are. I've been married for more than forty years, and I've never been able to get my Danny to come grocery shopping with me." Her brown eyes sparkled like copper pennies as she reached over and patted Alex's hand. "He's a keeper, honey."

Alex returned her smile. "I know."

Waiting until the woman was out of earshot, Merrick wound his arm around Alex's waist inside her coat. "Are you going to keep me, *querida?*"

She affected an attractive moue. "I'll think about it."

Lowering his head, he brushed a light kiss over her parted lips. "Perhaps that'll help you make up your mind."

Staring up at Merrick through her lashes, Alex's gold-brown eyes moved slowly over his face, cataloguing each of his well-defined features. "I think I'm going to need a little more convincing."

Desire darkened his eyes and tightened the skin over his high cheekbones. It'd been more than a month since he'd been with Alex, and the time away from her just served to increase his need for her. He, Merrick Grayslake, who'd lived his life believing he didn't need anyone, needed Alexandra Cole. Unwittingly, she'd become a part of him, the part that made him whole.

"I believe I have the answer." Leaning closer, he whispered, "Let's go home."

Alex lay in bed, listening to the sound of sleet pelting the windows. It was as if spring had forgotten the Alleghany Mountain region. Midday temperatures rose to the mid-forties but dropped below freezing with the setting sun. A popping sound of burning wood joined the rhythmic tapping. Merrick had started a fire in the fireplace before going into the bathroom to shower. He'd asked her to join him but she'd turned him down. It was their last night together and as the seconds ticked off she felt as if she were losing tiny pieces of herself each time they made love.

The tears welling up in her eyes overflowed, dotting the pillow under her head. How, she thought, was she going to make it through the next ten weeks without the man she loved? She'd made a mistake, a grievous error in returning to the States—in coming to see Merrick rather than her family—because it made leaving him that much more difficult. The side of the mattress dipped and she felt the warmth of the man who'd managed to occupy her every waking moment. Shifting on her side, she went into his strong, protective embrace.

"This is our last night together," she whispered tearfully.

"Don't say that, Ali," Merrick countered softly. "It is not our last night together. Our last night won't come for a very long time."

She pounded his shoulder with her fist. "You know what I'm talking about."

He caught her wrist. "No, I don't know what you're talking about. Your school term will be over in a few months, then we can be together—every day, every night."

"We can't do this again."

"Do what, *querida?*"

"We can't see each other until I finish my courses." A fresh wave of tears ensued.

Tightening his hold on her body, Merrick eased Alex to lie atop his body, her legs sandwiched between his, the fingers of his right hand making soothing motions on her back.

He closed his eyes. "Is it your intent to rip my heart out?"

She buried her face between his neck and shoulder. "What are you talking about?"

"This is not about you, Ali. You're not in this by yourself. I've shared and said things to you I've never told another person. It was as if I had to wait thirty-five years to feel what should be a natural human emotion—love. The love a baby feels for its mother or father, the love between a man and a woman and the love one feels for those with whom one shares a family bond.

"You've taught me to laugh, that it's all right to tease, be teased, and for that I will love you forever. Being with you has taught me that where I've come from is not as important as where I'm going. And wherever I go I want you with me."

Alex's right hand trailed down Merrick's shoulder; it

moved still lower along his rib cage, her fingers feathering over the curve of his buttocks and muscled thigh. All of her senses were intensified as she inhaled the clean masculine scent of his body, her fingertips grazing the crisp mat of chest hair and the firm flesh covering muscle and sinew. Merrick Grayslake reminded her of the statues of tall, powerful Mexican gods.

Reaching between their bodies, she cradled his flaccid sex; it swelled against her palm, increasing in girth until her fingers did not meet. The heat, hardness and the strong throbbing against her palm ignited a fire that swept through Alex like a lighted fuse. Her body vibrated liquid fire, the tremors between her thighs and groin buffeted by gusts of desire that rendered her close to fainting.

"Love me," she chanted over and over until it became a litany.

Merrick had told Alexandra that he loved her, but it never seemed to be enough. He had to show her. Reaching for the condom on the table on his side of the bed, he slipped it on. Slowly, methodically, he became a cartographer, charting every inch of her body as he began at the top of her head and moved slowly down as if sampling a sweet, frothy confection. He ignored the soft moans coming from Alex's throat, the rise and fall of her firm round breasts over her narrow rib cage, the contracting muscles in her flat, firm belly and the trembling of her legs as she writhed on the sheets.

Merrick was relentless as he alternated laving the folds at the apex of her thighs with plunging his tongue into the most secret recess of her body. It was as if he wanted to devour her whole, put her inside himself wherein she would be with him even when separated by thousands of miles.

When his own passion rose to fiery proportions, he eased himself inside her, making them one. He felt her heat as it rippled under his hands, inhaled the rising scent of their lovemaking that had become an erotic aphrodisiac. His desire for Alex, his love for her, surpassed every longing, craving and aspiration he'd ever known.

Alex cried for the second time within minutes, this time as waves of ecstasy washed over her. She closed her eyes, gasping in the sweet agony tearing her asunder. It eased slightly before she was hurled higher, climaxing, her orgasms overlapping one another until she lay, struggling to catch her breath.

Merrick felt the strong contractions squeezing his blood-engorged flesh, the sensations sending him over the edge. Cupping her hips, he quickened his thrusts until the dam broke and he spilled his passion into the sheath when it was Alex's body he craved.

The pleasure she'd offered him was pure and explosive, satisfying and sweet. A deep feeling of peace entered him as he savored the remnants of the lingering sensation that rendered him as weak as a newborn.

"Te amo," he whispered in her ear.

Alex smiled, enjoying the weight of his body pressing hers down to the firm mattress. *"Yo, también, mi amor."*

They loved each other, but what were they going to do about it? She would complete her studies and return to the States as an architectural historian. She planned to secure a position with a historic preservation, trust or museum, then what?

Would she or Merrick be content to see each other whenever she was free or would she want more? And she refused to think of marriage and children as the more.

He'd admitted he didn't want to marry or father children, but she did—though not now. Not when she wanted a career. Alex willed her mind blank. She couldn't afford to think of a future with Merrick Grayslake when marriage and children weren't her priority.

Without warning, he reversed their positions. They lay

together until their breathing deepened and they fell asleep, his body still joined with hers.

The sky had brightened with the dawn of a new day, it appearing a hoary gray, when Merrick and Alex resumed their dance of desire, leaving both hungrier for each other than at their first coupling.

Both knew it was a mistake, but love wasn't touted to be rational or judicious. And when Merrick saw Alex off at the airport before she boarded a private jet scheduled to land in Mexico City, he knew when he saw her again the meadow surrounding his house would be filled with wildflowers.

He would honor Alex's request and wait for her return.

There was one thing life had taught him and that was patience. It had served him well when he'd become a marine sniper, and it had saved his life as a covert operative.

Merrick knew there was something special the moment he laid eyes on the petite woman, unaware that she would be the one to change him and his destiny.

Chapter 14

Alex tightened her grip on the cell phone, the pressure leaving an imprint on her palm as she stared out the oval window of the ColeDiz jet as it circled the Fort Lauderdale–Hollywood International Airport in preparation for a landing. It was after two in the morning.

Her father had called her forty-eight hours before to inform her that the family was gathering in West Palm Beach to celebrate Timothy Cole-Thomas's retirement as CEO of ColeDiz International, Ltd. She'd vacillated whether to call Merrick to let him know she would be in the States for the weekend but changed her mind; there wasn't enough time and seeing him would reopen the wound that had healed from their last encounter.

She'd returned to the *universidad* assailed with feelings that left her in an agonizing maelstrom of acute loss. She'd spent a restless two days trying to figure out why she'd fallen in love with a stranger, why Merrick Grayslake and not some of the other men she'd dated. And her love for him wasn't some silly schoolgirl crush or virginal infatuation. She would turn thirty in November, which meant she was a grown woman, an independent woman in control of her life and destiny.

Merrick admitted that he'd told her things about himself he'd never told anyone, yet when she replayed their conversations she realized he actually had told her very little about himself. She knew he'd been orphaned at birth, had been in the Marine Corps and had been recruited by the Central Intelligence Agency. What he hadn't disclosed was how he supported himself, nor had he explained the many scars marring his body.

Alex was mature enough to admit that she'd been drawn to the enigmatic man because he radiated a danger that turned her on. He was akin to a graphic comic superhero prowling the nighttime streets and alleys looking to rescue the weak and right the wrongs perpetrated by those who opposed justice. She'd dubbed him Sir Grayslake, and he'd become her knight in shining armor.

She would spend two nights in Florida before returning to Mexico. Then she would begin counting down the weeks until she was reunited with the man she loved.

Alex was surprised to see her brother Gabriel waiting for her once she cleared Customs. What shocked her was his uncanny resemblance to their father. Gabriel had become a professional musician like David Cole, and like the elder Cole, Gabriel had solidified his place in history as a Grammy Award winner. Gabriel had surpassed his father when he earned an Oscar for a movie sound track.

Smiling, she quickened her step. Gabriel met her and swung her up off her feet. "What's with the mustache?" she asked, kissing his cheek. Pulling back, she stared into a pair of large gold-brown eyes, the only feature they'd inherited from Serena Morris-Cole. His long, thin nose, high cheekbones, olive coloring and wolfish dimpled smile were David Cole's. He'd pierced both ears, and tiny gold hoops were suspended from each.

"I thought I'd try it out for a while."

"Are you trying to look older?" Alex teased as he put her down. Gabriel, the eldest of David and Serena's four children, had recently celebrated his thirty-fourth birthday.

Smiling his wolfish, lopsided grin, Gabriel shook his head, his long, wavy, prematurely gray–streaked hair secured in a ponytail at the base of his neck, swaying with the motion. "No, Alex. The gray hair is enough."

Most of the men in her family who were direct descendants of her grandfather, Samuel Cole, had inherited his gene for graying prematurely, and her brother was no different.

Looping an arm around his waist, she hugged him. "Why don't you dye it?"

Gabriel ruffled her short hair, then reached for her hand. "I'll admit to being a little arrogant, but vain is not in my vocabulary."

Alex fell in step with her brother as he led her out of the airport to where he'd parked his car. "You're arrogant *and* vain, Gabriel Morris Cole."

At six-three, Gabriel slowed his stride to accommodate his sister's shorter legs. "Dad was sorry about the short notice, but it couldn't be helped."

"I thought Timothy was going to stay at least through the summer."

"Apparently, he changed his mind. Timothy says that Diego is more than prepared to take over as CEO."

She gave Gabriel a sidelong glance. "What do you think?"

Gabriel lifted a shoulder. "I wouldn't know one way or the

other. I promised myself a long time ago that I'd never get involved in the family business. Aunt Nancy and Josephine's children eat, sleep and breathe the stuff. I'm a musician, so that lets me off the hook."

"So was Dad, but he was still CEO of ColeDiz for nine years before he met and married Mom."

"That's true, but he couldn't wait to transfer the responsibility to Timothy."

"Dad gave up ColeDiz and then set up Serenity Records," Alex argued softly. "Musician or not, he was still a businessman."

David Cole had set up his own record company to showcase new and upcoming talent in all music genres. Although his company was small when compared to the larger ones, he'd earned two Grammys for Producer of the Year and his recording artists had earned and garnered more than a dozen nominations.

"Dad knows I don't want to become involved with Serenity. That's why he turned it over to Ana and Jason."

Gabriel led Alex over to a Porsche GT2. Pressing a button on a remote device, he unlocked the low-slung, silver sports car. Opening the passenger-side door, he waited until Alex was seated before he closed it and came around to sit beside her.

"When did you get this?" she asked. "It smells brand-new."

Starting the engine, Gabriel shifted into gear and pulled out of the parking space. "I've had it for about a month. It is my birthday present to myself."

"It's about time you came out of your pocket and got a decent ride," Alex mumbled. Gabriel had become the brunt of family jokes because when he wasn't touring with his band he drove a clunker that had seen better days. "What else are you holding out on me?"

Gabriel smiled. "I'm buying a house."

Shifting on her seat, Alex stared at him and asked, "Where?"

"Cotuit. It's on Cape Cod."

"What or who is in Cape Cod?"

Gabriel had to remember that he hadn't seen his sister since the beginning of the year. "I've been accepted as an artist-in-residence at a high school in a Boston suburb."

"Wouldn't it be better if you rented a place?"

"No, because I've found the perfect little house."

"How little, Gabe?"

"It's a restored two-story farmhouse set on six acres of beautifully landscaped waterfront property. I plan to renovate it by raising the ceilings in the second-floor bedrooms and expand both floors by at least a thousand square feet on either side."

"It sounds as if your little house is going to become a big house."

"I'm used to having a lot of space."

Alex nodded. They'd grown up in a house with nearly ten thousand square feet of living space, and they each had their own bedroom suites.

"How did Mom and Dad react when you told them you were moving to Massachusetts?"

Gabriel's teeth showed whitely under his trim mustache. "They had the nerve to open a bottle of champagne and toast each other."

"That's cold, Gabe."

"You think? After Dad downed two glasses he said, 'It's about time. The next piece of good news should be that you're getting married.'"

Alex shook her head. "What's up with our folks trying to marry us off?"

Gabriel maneuvered off a four-lane road and onto the interstate in the direction of Boca Raton. "They want grandchildren, Alex."

"Well, they're not going to get one out of me for a long time," she said.

"Same here," he concurred.

Eyelids drooping, Alex relaxed against the back of her seat. "Wake me when we get home." Although she'd lived in Virginia for two years, she still thought of Boca Raton as home.

Alex woke up late the next morning to knocking on her bedroom door. Bright Florida sunshine poured through the many windows. "Come in," she called out.

The door opened and Ana walked in wearing a sundress over her bathing suit. "Rise and shine, sleepyhead! We're leaving for West Palm in half an hour."

Pulling a sheet over her head, Alex moaned, "Please tone it down, Ana."

"What time did you get in?"

She lowered the sheet and pushed herself into a sitting position as Ana flopped down on the side of the bed. "The plane landed around two-thirty, and we didn't get here until four." Combing her fingers through her short hair, she smiled at her younger sister. "Who's here?"

"Everyone came except Chris. Emily said he's involved in a federal racketeering case that just went to the jury." Their first cousin's husband, Christopher Delgado, a former governor of New Mexico, was now a judge.

Pushing back the sheet, Alex swung her legs over the side of the bed, undoing the tiny pearl buttons on the front of her cotton nightgown as she headed for an adjoining bathroom.

"Did Mom make coffee?" she asked.

"I think Dad made it this morning, because it was strong enough to grow hair on my chest."

"I need it strong. Can you please bring me a cup?"

Ana moved off the bed to do her bidding while Alex

stepped out of her nightgown, leaving it on a low bench in the corner of the expansive bathroom. She was tired—no, the fact was she was exhausted. The late flight and not enough sleep had her out of sorts. Opening the door to the shower stall, she stepped in, turned on the faucets and adjusted the water temperature. The cool water was the antidote. It revived her and by the time Ana returned with a steaming mug of coffee Alex was wide awake.

Five generations of Coles had gathered on the lawn at the family West Palm Beach compound to salute Timothy Cole-Thomas's undaunted dedication to running a business empire that included coffee plantations in Mexico, Jamaica, Puerto Rico, and several banana plantations in Belize. At sixty, Timothy had successfully shepherded ColeDiz International, Ltd., through recessions and economic instability to realize a profit every year in his thirty-year term.

Alex sat next to Dana Nichols-Cole, whose three-month-old daughter had fallen asleep in her arms. "May I hold her?" Dana put the infant in Alex's outstretched arms.

Dana and Tyler were seeking to legalize the adoption of the baby they'd named Astra. Tyler Cole had delivered the infant, but couldn't save her fifteen-year-old mother who'd been abandoned by her own mother at the age of seven. Unfortunately, the pregnant teenager had spent most of her short-lived life in foster and group homes.

Gabriel leaned over Alex's shoulder. "Hey, Mama," he teased, winking and flashing his trademark dimpled smile.

"I'm going to hurt you, Gabriel Cole."

He leaned closer. "I'll let you hurt me after you get pregnant."

Dana stared at her husband's cousin. "Are you pregnant?"

Alex swatted at her brother. "Get the hell outta here, Gabriel!" she hissed through clenched teeth.

"Who's pregnant now?" Tyler Cole asked as he sat down beside his wife. Tyler had become the family resident ob-gyn.

Alex rolled her eyes at Tyler. "Don't look at me."

Gabriel rested an arm on Tyler's broad shoulder. The first cousins looked enough alike to pass for brothers. "Unlike your sisters, mine have struck out in the romance department because they can't seem to tell the difference between a winner and a loser."

Alex opened her mouth to announce that she'd fallen in love with a winner but caught herself in time. What she had with Merrick would remain her secret—for now.

"Speak for yourself, Gabriel. Why is it I don't see a woman hanging on your arm?"

"That's because I'm not one to advertise my business."

Alex's retort was thwarted when Diego stood and tapped the handle of a knife against a water goblet. All gazes were focused on the tall, powerfully built man in a white *guayabera* and jeans. "May I please have everyone's attention?"

"I want to e-e-e-at n-o-o-w!" wailed a young child before being hushed by his mother.

Diego lowered his chin and bit back a smile. "I believe that's my cue to make this quick." His head came up, black eyes smoldering with a lazy seductiveness that fired the imaginations of the few women who'd come to know him intimately.

"As most of you know, my father is a man of few words, preferring instead to let his actions speak for him. If it worked for him over the past three decades, then why should I try to fix what isn't broken?" He raised his goblet in a mock salute. "To my uncles, Martin and David, and my father, Timothy Cole-Thomas, I salute you and pray for your blessings as the next CEO of ColeDiz International, Ltd." He turned and extended the glass to his fretful nephew. "Now we can eat."

All of the young children stood up and cheered while their

parents and grandparents shook their heads. Collectively, the descendants of Samuel and Marguerite-Josefina Cole were boisterous, and at times bodacious, but they were also protective of and fiercely loyal to anyone who claimed Cole blood. And there was an unspoken rule that if you threaten one, the threat extends to all.

Gabriel patted Alex's back. "Don't get up. I'll bring you something to eat."

She rolled her eyes at him, still smarting about his remark that she'd picked up losers. "Don't try to placate me, big brother."

A smile slipped through her impassive expression as her brother walked toward the table where servers were filling plates with mounds of hot and cold dishes. It was on a rare occasion that one saw an adult Cole woman standing in line waiting to be served. The tradition, which had begun when Martin Cole became CEO, was that the women rule and their men serve. The result was all females were protected, pampered and adored.

Dana held out her arms for her daughter. "Let me take her into the house and put her to bed."

At the exact moment she relinquished the sleeping infant, a chorus of screams sliced through the undercurrent of voices raised in conversation and laughter. Four preteen boys and one girl had jumped into the Olympic-size pool—fully dressed. It was another tradition that had survived several generations.

Alex laughed when she heard the colorful language of their parents chastising them for their unruly behavior. She'd lost count of the number of times she'd jumped into her grandparents' pool, or into her own, much to the dismay of her parents, who couldn't understand why their children would want to sit around in wet street clothes when they could've worn a swimsuit. What the adults failed to understand was that it was an open act of rebellion in order to flaunt their independent spirit.

Her smile faded when she recalled a few occurrences when as an adolescent she'd challenged her mother's authority. Alex had learned to get over on David Cole, but Serena was another matter. It'd taken only two confrontations with her mother to come to the conclusion that she'd better get her act together or spend her teenage years in lockdown.

A faraway expression filled her eyes when she tried imagining what kind of mother she would become if or when she opted for motherhood. Would she be indulgent and tolerant like her grandmother Marguerite-Josefina, or straightforward and practical like her own mother?

There was never a question of not understanding what Serena said or meant. However, Alex had lost count of the number of times she'd gone to her father to enlist his support to soften her mother's stance. That all changed when David Cole called a rare family meeting, explaining that he would not tolerate his children's attempt to undermine their mother's authority, and that put an end to Alex's clandestine meetings with her father.

Prerecorded music blared from speakers as the noise level escalated. Alex lifted her eyebrows when she saw an attractive young woman with stylishly-cut, shoulder-length hair talking to Diego. Even from this distance, he appeared to be equally enthralled as he moved closer to listen to what she was saying.

"Now, that looks serious," whispered a familiar voice.

Alex turned to find Ana taking a chair next to her. "Who is she?"

"She's a weather girl with one of the television networks. If she believes she's going to become Mrs. Diego Cole-Thomas, then she's in for a world of hurt."

Alex nodded. "He told me that he's not ready to settle down."

Ana emitted a delicate snort. "Now, if the woman was named ColeDiz, then she'd at least have a fighting chance."

The sisters discussed their marriage-shy cousin until their brothers returned carrying plates of food. Jason served his twin while Gabriel placed Alex's on the table in front of her.

Ana gave Jason a forlorn look. "Can you please bring me something to drink?"

"Me, too," Alex said, chiming in.

"Damn, Ana," Jason snarled. "You should've told me when I was up there."

Gabriel wrapped an arm around Jason's neck, pulling him close. "Don't let them stress you out, little brother. I'll get the drinks while you fix me a plate."

Alex squinted at her younger sister as Ana dipped a piece of calamari into a small cup of piquant sauce. "Sometimes you ride Jason a little too hard."

The seafood dangled from the tines of Ana's fork as she hesitated putting it into her mouth. "Jason's a good sport."

"He's a good sport because you're his twin sister. But you overdo it."

Ana affected a pout. "You have Gabriel and I have Jason."

"But I don't take advantage of him, Ana."

Taking a bite of the calamari, Ana chewed it thoughtfully. "All right, Alex. I'll ease up on him."

As fraternal twins, she and Jason were inseparable, existing in a private world where one was able to finish the other's sentences. Older by eight minutes, Jason had always protected his twin although her stronger personality overshadowed his more laid-back, quiet one.

Alex spent the rest of the afternoon eating, drinking, dancing, swimming and interacting with her many relatives. The sun had set, the caterers were gone and those who'd planned to spend the remainder of the weekend in West Palm Beach claimed bedrooms in the twenty-four-room mansion.

Michael and a very pregnant Jolene decided to stay with his parents at their Palm Beach condominium. With his wife in her eighth month of confinement, Michael had opted to drive to Florida in lieu of flying.

Alex returned to Boca Raton with her parents while her siblings stayed behind to hang out with their many cousins. There was talk of them going to a popular West Palm Beach dance club.

She was scheduled to fly back to Mexico Sunday morning along with Emily Kirkland, her three children and her cousin's sister and brother-in-law, Sara and Salem Lassiter, and their children. The Kirklands and Lassisters would deplane in Las Cruces, New Mexico, before the jet continued on to Mexico City.

She checked her cell phone and realized she'd missed Merrick's call. Pressing a button, Alex listened for a break in the connection. She smiled when hearing his signature "Hey, baby."

"Hey, yourself," she whispered. "What are you doing up so late?" The glowing numbers on the clock on the bedside table read 1:10 a.m.

"I couldn't sleep."

Vertical lines appeared between Alex's eyes. "I've never known you to have insomnia."

A deep sensual chuckle came through the earpiece. "That's because whenever we're together I don't have a sleep problem. You're like morphine."

"What do you know about morphine?" she teased.

There was a moment of silence, and Merrick said, "Forget I mentioned it. Even though it's a little after midnight where you are I'll let you go. I'd planned to call earlier, but thought perhaps you'd gone out with your friends."

"I'm not in Mexico City, Merrick."

"Where are you?"

"I'm in Florida. I came early this morning and I'm leaving later on today. The family got together to celebrate my cousin Diego taking over as CEO of ColeDiz. I wanted to call you and ask if you wanted to meet me here, but there wasn't enough time."

There came another pause from Merrick. "Have you told anyone—your family, about us?"

"No. And I don't like keeping secrets from them."

"You want them to know about us?"

"Yes, I do, Merrick."

"I'd like you to wait before you tell them."

A cold chill snaked its way down her spine, and she went completely still. There was something in his voice that set off warning bells in her head. "Why do you want me to wait?"

"I can't tell you now."

"What are you hiding from me?"

"Nothing, Ali. It's something I'd rather not discuss on the telephone. I'll tell you everything when we see each other again."

"That's not going to be until the beginning of June," she said in protest.

"That's when I'll tell you."

She squeezed the tiny instrument in frustration. "You offer me some cryptic mumbo jumbo and expect me to wait two months for an explanation."

"What I'd like for you to do is trust me, Ali."

"You want me to trust you when you're hiding things from me. I really don't know who you are, what you do, how—"

"Stop it, Alexandra!" Merrick hadn't shouted the command, but the stinging effect was the same. "I'm going to end this call," he said in a dangerously quiet tone. "We won't discuss this again until I see you. Have a safe flight back, and I'll call you tomorrow night."

"Goodbye, Merrick."

"No, Ali. Good night."

The willfulness she'd struggled all of her adult life to control surfaced, making her unwilling to compromise. "Goodbye, Merrick," she repeated, then abruptly disconnected the call.

She threw the phone and it landed on an armchair. Alex flopped down to the bed and closed her eyes. She asked herself for the first time since coming face-to-face with Merrick Grayslake, was she in over her head?

Chapter 15

Moira knocked on the open door to Alex's room and walked in. Clothes were stacked in neat piles atop the double dresser and bedside table. Alexandra Morris was preparing to leave Mexico City. Classes had ended the day before and final marks were posted in the lobby of the converted convent earlier that morning.

Alex turned and smiled at her friend. "Well, this is it. We're done."

Moira flopped down on a straight-back armchair. "*You* are done."

Alex halted folding a pair of jeans. "What are you talking about?"

"I'm staying on."

She stared at Moira, baffled. The week before, Moira had suddenly burst into tears, and when Alex questioned her, she said she'd suddenly had an attack of homesickness.

Closing the distance between them, Alex sat on the arm of

the chair and looped an arm around Moira's neck. "What's up, girlfriend?"

Moira's dark blue eyes filled with tears but didn't fall. "I'm pregnant."

Alex's mouth formed a perfect O before she pursed her lips. She didn't know whether to be happy or sad for her friend, but decided on the former. "Congratulations."

Eyelids fluttering, Moira rested her forehead on Alex's arm and cried happy tears. "Thank you."

"When's the big day?"

"Early December."

Sitting up straighter, Alex swept her gaze over Moira's slender body. "You're already three months pregnant?"

Moira nodded. "I'd suspected for some time that I was carrying Hernando's baby, but you could say I was in denial."

"Hernando," Alex repeated, her voice rising slightly. "Are you talking about our Professor Hernando Rivera?"

Moira nodded as she blushed to the roots of her pale hair. "Yes."

Alex wrinkled her delicate nose. "I don't believe it. Here I thought you were fooling around with Umberto but instead it was our brilliant, esteemed *Professor* Rivera."

Moira bit down on her lower lip. "I hadn't planned on having an affair with him—"

"Don't you dare apologize to me," Alex said, interrupting her. "You're a grown woman, Moira."

Her head came up, her expression soft and angelic. "He's wonderful, Alex, as a lover, teacher and husband."

"You're married?"

"Yes," Moira said, smiling.

"When did you get married?"

"Yesterday. Because I'm not Catholic, we decided on a civil wedding."

"Do you love him, Moira?"

"Yes, I do."

"Then, that's all that matters."

A warm glow flowed through Moira and she felt freer than she had in hours. She'd called her father to tell him that she wasn't coming home because she'd fallen in love and married a Mexican man. Her father hadn't waited for her to explain that the man was one of the world's most respected art historians when he'd hung up on her.

"I wanted to wait until after the baby is born to marry Hernando, but he refused because of his position at the *universidad*."

"He's right, Moira, even though it's not frowned upon for a woman to have a child without the benefit of marriage nowadays."

Moira hugged Alex. "I knew you would be happy for me."

Alex returned the hug. "Why wouldn't I be happy for you? I wish you all the happiness you deserve—and more."

"I hope we'll stay in touch with each other, Alex."

"Of course we will."

"Will you come by tomorrow night and have dinner with us? I told Hernando that I didn't want you to leave Mexico without saying goodbye."

"Of course I'll come." That meant she would have to delay going back to Virginia.

Moira popped up like a jack-in-the-box.

Leaning over, she pressed a kiss to Alex's cheek. "I'll see you tomorrow."

Alex was still sitting on the arm of the chair when Moira left, closing the door quietly behind her. Alex's friend had accused Hernando Rivera of having the hots for her when it was Moira Morgan he was actually in love with.

Rising from the chair, she had resumed the boring task of

packing, when her cell phone rang. Reaching for the instrument, she flipped open the cover without looking at the display.

"Do you have a flight schedule for me, Joelyn?"

"Ali?"

"Merrick?"

"I can assure you that I'm not Joelyn."

"And I wouldn't want you to be her." Sitting down on the edge of the bed, Alex stared at the worn terra-cotta floor. After their rather heated exchange what now seemed aeons ago, she and Merrick had resumed their nightly telephone calls.

"Did you pass everything?" he asked.

Her smile was dazzling. "I managed to get top honors."

"Congratulations."

"Thank you."

"I'd like to give you a gift."

"For what, Merrick?"

"It's not every day that someone earns a graduate degree."

"Thousands get graduate degrees every year."

"How many people get to become architectural historians?"

"Well, you're right," she conceded.

"I know I'm right. And because I'm bigger and stronger than you it would be in your best interest to accept what I'm offering."

"What's with the intimidation?" she teased.

"What's with the interrogation?" he countered.

"Okay, Merrick. What is it?"

"I've arranged for a private jet to fly you to Rome Friday morning. Try to get some sleep because I have something special planned for the evening. Later on today a courier will deliver a packet containing your e-ticket and flight information. I've also arranged for ground transportation to get you and your luggage to the airport. When you arrive I'll be waiting for you once you clear Customs." There was a pause before he said, "Hold on, Ali. *Porterò l'un col rubino.*"

"Merrick?"

"Yes, baby?"

"Where are you?"

"I'm in Rome. How's your Italian?"

She couldn't believe he was calling her from Italy. "It's definitely not as good as yours."

"I'm going to have to hang up because the store clerk is glaring at me. I'll see you Friday night."

Before Alex could accept, reject or protest, he ended the call. Falling back on the bed, she kicked her legs the way she'd done as a child.

She never would've predicted that her life would change so dramatically since New Year's Eve. Her life had changed, she had changed and when she saw Merrick Grayslake again she would thank him for helping her to become a woman in the truest sense of the word.

Within minutes of exiting Customs, Alex spied a man holding a placard with the name Cole printed in large black letters. She approached him. "I'm Alexandra Cole."

"Dare il benvenuto a Roma, signorina. Prenderò il suo bagaglio."

He spoke Italian too quickly for her to understand more than *welcome* and *baggage*. She smiled. *"Grazie."*

The man picked up her bags and motioned for her to follow him. It was 9:00 p.m. in Rome and the airport was teeming with departing and arriving travelers.

Alex had taken Merrick's advice and slept during the transatlantic flight. An hour before they were scheduled to touch down at the Leonardo da Vinci Airport, she'd showered in one of the onboard bathrooms and changed into the ubiquitous little black dress and strappy sandals. The instructions in the packet indicated a 10:00 p.m. dinner reservation.

She saw Merrick leaning against a column. He straightened when their gazes met. They hadn't seen each other in three months, and he'd changed. His hair was longer and the sun had darkened his face to a deep copper-brown. If it hadn't been for his distinctive eye color Alex wouldn't have recognized him.

Merrick did not move forward because he couldn't at that moment. Rooted to the spot, he watched the muscles in Alex's bare shapely legs and thighs flex and relax as she made her way toward him. The skimpy black dress with a scooped neckline and capped sleeves outlined the delicious curves of her sexy, petite body. Her hair that looked as if she'd styled it with her fingers framed her round face in sensual disarray.

It was when he saw her face that a quiet storm stirred in his groin. Smoky eye shadow, a coat of mascara on feathery black lashes and the vermilion color on her lush, full lips made him want to strip her naked and make love to her. But he hadn't invited her to Italy to make love to her, but to show her much he was in love with her.

Go to her, a silent voice urged Merrick. He took one step, then another, closing the distance. He let out his breath when he felt the crush of her breasts against his chest.

Cradling her face between his hands, he lowered his head and brushed his mouth over hers. *"Dare il benvenuto a Roma."*

"Grazie, mio amore."

Merrick released her when he hadn't wanted to. "Are you hungry?"

Alex stared at the man whom she loved beyond reason. "Yes." She hadn't eaten anything since early that morning. She was hungry, but not for food. She'd missed Merrick, missed everything about him.

Putting his arm around her tiny waist, he pressed a kiss to

her hair. "Let's get out of here. I made a reservation for dinner at a restaurant not far from our hotel."

The drive from the airport took longer than expected, and when Merrick and Alex arrived at the hotel on the Via Veneto there was only enough time to store her luggage in the room before they had to leave.

Tucked away in an alley off a side street, the restaurant resembled a grotto with brick-and-mortar walls, a vaulted ceiling and water flowing from a fountain into a pool.

The flickering light from the candle on the table shimmered off Alex's flawless brown face. Merrick stared at her. Three months. It'd been that long since he'd last seen Alex and it appeared as if she'd changed. The change wasn't her looks, but her demeanor. She'd matured during their separation; a woman had replaced the open, spontaneous girl.

Alex took a sip of wine, then touched the corners of her mouth with a napkin. The restaurant's ambience, her dining partner and the food were incredible. She'd ordered chicken in a light wine and butter sauce while Merrick had chosen linguine with a broiled seafood medley.

"What made you choose Italy over some other country, Merrick?" Her query shattered the comfortable silence.

He put down his wineglass. "I remember you saying you enjoyed visiting here, and when you finished your studies you'd planned to come back not as a student but as a tourist."

Her eyebrows flickered as she met his steady gaze. "Do you remember everything I say?"

"Yes," he admitted. "But only if it's worth remembering."

Alex studied the man sharing the small round table with her. He'd become a chameleon. Dressed in a sand-colored linen suit with a sky-blue shirt and navy blue tie, he appeared sophisticated and urbane. And with his hair texture, eye color and sharply defined features he could be a citizen from any country in the world.

"How long can you hang out here with me?" Merrick asked.

She stared at the food on her plate. "No more than two weeks." She looked up, meeting his gaze. "I have an interview with the National Trust for Historic Preservation at the end of the month."

"Where's the interview?"

"Boston."

Merrick nodded. "I'll have you back in plenty of time." Shifting his chair, he moved closer to Alex. "You've accused me of hiding things from you, and I promised I would tell you what you need to know about me when we saw each other again."

Alex took another sip of wine, staring at Merrick over the rim of her glass. "We don't have to talk about it now."

Reaching for her hand, he gave her fingers a gentle squeeze. "Yes, Ali. We can't move forward unless we clear the air about things that bother you."

Alex didn't want to talk. All she wanted was to enjoy the moment because for the first time in her life she'd gotten everything she'd ever wanted: she'd completed her graduate program and looked forward to securing a position as an architectural historian and she planned to spend the next two weeks touring Italy with the man she loved.

"If whatever you plan to tell me is going to upset me, then I don't want to hear it, Merrick. Not tonight."

"When do you want me to tell you?"

"Tell me on the flight back to the States."

He shook his head. "No."

Her delicate jaw dropped. "No," she repeated.

"N—O," Merrick said, spelling the word. "You will sit and hear me out, because I'm not going to wait two weeks to tell you what you demanded to know three months ago."

Alex froze as she stared at Merrick. His voice was absolutely emotionless. A fist of fear squeezed her chest as she met the steely-eyed gaze of a stranger, a stranger who'd replaced the man she thought she knew and loved. Her breath seemed to solidify in her throat and all she could do was nod.

Merrick leaned closer, his mouth within inches of Alex's ear. "I'm going back to the CIA."

Alex closed her eyes and slumped against his shoulder. "Why?" she whispered. She couldn't imagine not seeing Merrick for months, waiting for him to return from a clandestine mission.

"Because I need normalcy in my life."

"Can't you do something else?"

"No."

She opened her eyes and shook her head. "Is it because you need money?"

"Money is *not* the issue, Ali. I joined the Marine Corps within a week of graduating from high school because the recruiter promised a signing bonus and educational benefits. I joined and took advantage of everything they had to offer. I gave them ten years before the CIA came looking for 'a few good men.'

"I was hired and trained as a covert operative. I'd always believed I would die somewhere far from home, but it was at home where I almost lost my life when someone shot me, then left me on a street corner in D.C. to die."

Her eyes widened. "What happened?"

"Three men accosted me, demanding I give them whatever I had on me. If it had been just two of them I knew I could've taken them, so I cooperated and handed over whatever money I had. However, the one holding the gun panicked and shot me in the stomach. If it hadn't been for Michael Kirkland being where he was that night I wouldn't be sitting here talking to you. He'd taken a shortcut through southeast D.C.

on his way home and found me in a pool of blood. Not waiting for an ambulance, he put me in his car and took off for the nearest hospital where I spent six hours in surgery.

"The bullet had nicked my spleen, mangled my left kidney and when I woke up in recovery I was told that I'd lost my kidney and half my body's blood supply." Merrick ignored the look of horror in the gold eyes staring at him.

"How long were you hospitalized?"

"A month."

"What happened after that?" Alex asked, her voice barely above a whisper.

"I went home and was placed on medical leave for five months. When I returned to work it was to permanent desk duty. Three days later I walked into the director's office and handed in my resignation."

Alex heard the sound of her runaway heart in her ears. "What did you do after that?"

Merrick paused, then said, "I gave up my Silver Spring apartment and bought the house in Bolivar. I didn't have a wife or children to support, so whatever I'd earned I'd invested. I'd always followed the market, so when tech companies were issuing IPOs I bought in, tripling and sometime quadrupling my investments." What he didn't tell Alex was that once he made his first million, he'd stopped buying and selling stocks. His investments were now in long-term, tax-free municipal bonds.

"If you go back…when you go back," Alex began, "will it be to a desk position?"

Merrick traced the outline of her ear with his forefinger. "Yes. I suppose I had to get over the stigma of becoming a desk jockey when I'd been a field agent. It took time and my being with you to realize that I still can protect our country but in a different capacity."

Her arching eyebrows lifted. "That's true, but why me, Merrick, and not some other woman?"

He gave her a long, penetrating look. "Because you're not *some* other woman, Ali. I fell in love with you because you're intelligent, determined, spunky and breathtakingly beautiful."

Merrick traced the outline of her cheekbone with a fingertip. "And what would it look like if my girlfriend got up every morning to go to work and left me home to lie around on my behind like a scrub? I couldn't do that and still feel like a man, *querida*."

Alex closed her eyes and rested her head on Merrick's shoulder. He'd referred to her as his girlfriend, but at that moment she wanted to be more than a girlfriend. She wasn't certain whether her stance had changed toward marriage because she'd found herself more in love with Merrick Grayslake, or if it was seeing Moira and Hernando Rivera together as husband and wife, but she no longer wanted to be a girlfriend but a married woman.

"Merrick?"

"Yes, darling?"

"I'm ready to go back to the room."

Beckoning to their waiter, Merrick settled the bill, then escorted Alex out of the restaurant, walking the three blocks that would take them back to the hotel.

As soon as they exited the elevator, Alex felt the intensifying effects of jet lag. She didn't remember Merrick undressing her, putting her to bed or joining her in the king-size bed. She dozed off and on for the next two days, and when her circadian rhythms stabilized she looked forward to reuniting with Merrick *and* Rome.

Chapter 16

Alex woke to find Merrick sitting at the table in their hotel suite, in a pair of pajama pants, sipping coffee and reading a newspaper. The strands of his coarse hair stood on end as if he'd run his fingers through it.

A smile parted her lips. It was the first time she'd seen him wearing pajamas. In fact, she didn't know that he'd even owned a pair because he'd always come to bed naked.

She lay motionless, studying the man with whom she'd fallen in love, the man whom she prayed she would one day call husband. The reasons she resisted marriage were always the same: she hadn't met the right man, and because her parents were exerting pressure for one of their adult children to marry and make them grandparents—her father in particular. David Cole resented his four older siblings' good-natured teasing that he would never become a grandfather when all of their married children had made grandparents and great-grandparents.

And she'd asked herself over and over, was Merrick Grayslake the right man? And each time the answer was a resounding *yes!*

Alex had disclosed to Merrick that eventually she wanted to marry and have children sometime in the future. His response was that he had no desire to marry or father children, which had proven an amicable arrangement for both—at that time. But with time she'd changed and her feelings toward him had changed.

She'd agreed to meet him in Italy, knowing that she would never become Mrs. Merrick Grayslake. What Alex had to resolve before she returned to the States to begin a new career was whether she would continue in a relationship that represented perpetuity without matrimony.

Without warning, Merrick turned and stared at her. "Good morning, Sleeping Beauty."

She smiled at him. "Good morning, Sir Grayslake. How long have I been out of it?"

Merrick folded the newspaper. "A couple of days. You were good as long as we were moving, but every time you sat down you fell asleep."

Pushing into a sitting position, Alex stretched her bare arms above her head. She hadn't remembered putting on the pale yellow nightgown, so it was obvious Merrick had dressed her for bed.

"It usually takes me a couple of days to adjust to the time difference whenever I cross the international date line. What did I miss?"

He angled his head, unable to believe Alex hadn't remembered anything since she'd arrived. Was she that affected by jet lag or was she that exhausted?

"What do you remember?"

Sighing, she closed her eyes. "I remember we threw coins in the Fontana di Trevi."

The tradition was to throw a coin into the fountain if one wished to return to Rome. The Trevi was Rome's most famous fountain. Neptune, the fountain's central figure, flanked by smaller figures representing a calm and stormy sea, had become the focal point of the classic romance film *Three Coins in the Fountain*.

Merrick smiled. "Do you remember what you said when you tossed your coin?"

Alex sat up straighter. "No."

What she did remember was that she'd drunk too much wine at dinner that night. They'd eaten at a sidewalk café around Piazza Navona and met an American couple visiting Rome for the first time. They spoke no Italian and their waiter, who spoke very little English, was unable to communicate with them until Merrick intervened. They wound up sharing a table for four and the native Chicagoans ordered several bottles of wine to accompany dinner.

"Did I do or say something embarrassing?"

Pushing back the chair, Merrick stood up and walked over to the bed. He crawled in beside Alex, rested his back on the headboard and pulled her gently to his bare chest.

There was a full minute of silence before he spoke. "You said you wanted to come back to Rome for your honeymoon."

Letting out her breath in an audible sigh, Alex met his penetrating gaze. She hadn't embarrassed herself. "I've always said if I married I'd want a Roman honeymoon."

"You want to get married?"

A slight frown furrowed her smooth forehead. "I told you before that I want to get married and have a child."

"Some other man's child?"

Pulling out of his loose embrace, Alex's frown deepened. "What are you talking about?"

"You're not going to marry another man."

Alex was totally baffled at Merrick's behavior. He was talking in riddles. "What I'm not going to do is marry you."

"Why not?"

"Because you're not the marrying kind."

Merrick shrugged his shoulders. "I changed my mind."

Going to her knees, Alex leaned closer. "Just like that," she drawled, snapping her fingers, "you've changed your mind. I'm sorry, but I don't buy it, Merrick. Wasn't it you who said there's no reason why we can't enjoy each other without marriage and children becoming part of the equation? I told you what I want for my future and you've told me what you want, and we're not in agreement."

"That's where you're wrong, Ali. I do want what you want. I want you to become the mother of our children."

Wave after wave of shock assaulted her senses as a buzzing in her head increased to a roaring that made it impossible for her to think, hear, feel. Rage replaced her shock as she launched herself at Merrick.

"Don't play with my head!"

Ali was quick, but Merrick was quicker when he held her wrists, shaking her gently. "I'm not trying to play with your head, darling. I love you too much to do that."

"But I'm confused."

"What about?"

"About you, Merrick, about us. We start out as friends, then become lovers. I respect what we have because we're able to talk about everything—what we like, don't like. What we want and don't want. And we decided to have a relationship that would *not* end in marriage.

"I've floundered for years, and now when I'm back on track

you try to derail me with mixed messages. You say you love me and you want to spend the rest of your life with me although marriage will not become a part of our future. I love you, Merrick. I love you more than I've ever loved any man, yet—"

"Then marry me, Alexandra Cole," Merrick said, cutting her off.

"No!"

He tightened his hold on her wrists. "Why not?"

Her eyes filled with tears. "Because you don't believe in marriage, Merrick Grayslake!"

A wry smile parted his lips. "That was before I met you."

Alex struggled to free her hands. "Let me go."

"Why? So you can hit me?"

Her eyes narrowed. "I'm going to do more than hit you," she threatened.

Merrick released her, then extended his arms out to his sides. "Take your best shot, Ali," he beckoned. "Come on, baby. Hit me if it will make you feel better." The seconds ticked off as they stared at each other in what had become an impasse. His expression softened as he reached out and cupped her chin in his hand. "You don't want to hurt me any more than I can hurt you." Warm, fat tears dotted his palm. "If you'd changed your mind about marriage I would've accepted it without question because you'd claim it's a woman's prerogative. Well, what's good for the goose is also good for the gander. Don't dudes have equal rights? Are we not allowed to change our minds?"

Alex smiled through her tears. "Yes."

Resting his forehead against hers, Merrick kissed her nose. "Yes, what?"

"Yes, you're allowed to change your mind."

"Good. I'm glad we've settled that." He kissed her again. "I love you, and I want you to marry me. It doesn't have to be now. It can be next year, the following year, whenever you want."

Alex wanted to accept his proposal, but something Merrick said nagged at her. Something he'd said about not wanting to lose her to another man had triggered warning bells. Did jealousy play a part in his changing his stance toward marriage? Or was it because once she began working and traveling she wouldn't be *that* available to him?

"I'll let you know," she said softly. Even though she wanted to commit, she couldn't. Not yet.

Cradling her face between his palms, Merrick pressed his mouth to her throat. Increasing the pressure, his mouth moved lower as her stomach muscles contracted.

Alex barely had time to react when she found herself in Merrick's arms as he slipped off the bed and carried her into the bedroom. Time stood still, the earth stopped spinning on its axis as they stood under the warm water from an overhead shower and demonstrated wordlessly their love for each other.

With her legs wrapped around Merrick's waist, her back pressed against the tiled wall, she breathed the last of her passion against his throat. This coming together was different from the other times. Merrick hadn't used contraception.

Alex didn't panic because it was the *safe* phase of her menstrual cycle. "This cannot happen again," she gasped, trying to catch her breath.

Merrick supported her body until her feet touched the floor of the shower stall. "You mean making love in the shower?"

"No, Merrick. Making love without using a condom."

"I pulled out in time."

Resting her cheek on his chest, she looped her arms under his shoulders. "And if you get me pregnant, then I'm going to name the baby Pull Out."

Merrick threw back his head and roared with laughter. He didn't know what he was going to do with Alexandra Cole except love her until his last breath.

* * *

Alex arrived in Venezia, or Venice, reuniting with the city built on water and made up of canals; she felt like a glutton consuming copious amounts of food yet never feeling satiated. If she loved Rome, then it could be said she had a passion for Venice that was akin to an unrequited love.

She'd never tired of the crowds, the countless pigeons in Piazza San Marco, the overrated and overpriced gondola rides, the museums, galleries, the dark *callesellas* or alleys, or high-priced souvenirs.

Merrick had secured lodging on an upper floor of a furnished *palazzetto* along the Grand Canal. Alex opened a bedroom window and inhaled a lungful of air.

"It smells like Venice."

"How is Venice supposed to smell?" asked the voice behind her.

Alex turned and smiled at Merrick. If possible, she'd fallen more in love with him. He hadn't mentioned marriage again, and for that she was grateful. She knew he wanted her as his wife, and when the time came for her to marry she knew it would be to Merrick.

"Like the sea."

Merrick stared at the petite woman with the curvy body with whom he'd begun his days *and* ended his nights. He never tired of making love with her. He also had acquired a newfound appreciation for art. Unlike when he and Alex had toured the D.C. museums, they'd embarked on a walking tour of Rome, and whenever he asked about a particular statue or building Alex would explain its origin and identify the artist.

And because he was more fluent in Italian than she, he assumed the responsibility of ordering meals, negotiating with shopkeepers and asking directions. She taught him how to navigate crossing the streets with traffic coming in both directions as Vespa-riding Romans played a frightening game of tag with pedestrians brave enough to step off the sidewalks. Alex also turned him on to gelato, and he set out on a campaign to sample every variety of the custard-based Italian ice cream.

They'd spent five days in Rome before traveling northward to Florence. They'd varied their nighttime routine of walking to sitting on their hotel's rooftop as the lights of the city sparkled below. Florence was a shopper's haven for jewelry and leather goods. Larger than usual crowds cut short their stay in Tuscany, and Merrick decided to end their two-week European sojourn in Venice.

Reaching for his hand, Alex threaded her fingers through Merrick's. "Beautiful, decadent Venice is like a woman no man can resist."

Wrapping his free arm around her waist, he pulled her close. "Then your parents should've named you Venezia rather than Alexandra."

She lifted her chin to see gray eyes boring into her. As of late she'd begun analyzing everything Merrick said to her to uncover a hidden meaning. It was as if she had to erect a wall of defense to shield herself against him.

Standing on tiptoe, she kissed his cheek. "We should try and relax until siesta is over. I can assure you that we'll get very little sleep tonight, because Venice doesn't really start jumping until after sunset."

As in France and Spain, Italian shopkeepers, banks and other places of business closed for several hours in the afternoon for siesta.

Merrick disengaged his hand and began the task of unbuttoning her blouse. His touch was deliberate as he pushed it off her shoulders and it floated to the floor. Reaching around her back, he unhooked her bra, and it, too, joined her blouse. Alex went completely still as he unzipped her slacks, pushing them and her panties down her legs until they pooled around her feet.

She stepped out of them at the same time she repeated his action when she unbuttoned his shirt; a minute later, both stood nude in the middle of the bedroom in an apartment dating back to the 13th century.

Hand in hand, they made their way to the antique bed, floating down to the crisp, ironed sheets. She wanted Merrick, craved him because she was ovulating.

Her body felt heavy, like ripened fruit waiting to be picked. Her breasts were tender and she couldn't control the spasmodic trembling between her legs.

"Hurry," she pleaded as he slipped on a condom.

Merrick knew this joining would not become the unhurried, leisurely lovemaking he was used to sharing with Alex. Her quick, shallow breathing, the lines of tension on her face and the bite of her fingernails on his biceps urged him to follow her command.

There was no foreplay as he entered her in one, sure swift thrust. Her urgency was transferred to him and he rode her like a man possessed by invisible spirits whose intent was to swallow him whole.

Her hot flesh pulsed around his sex, squeezing tighter and tighter. Every muscle, nerve and tendon in his body screamed for release. The sound of his runaway heart was that of a galloping horse as he struggled not to release his passion—not yet. It was too quick.

Alex's raw sensuousness lifted him beyond himself, her fire spreading to him, and he lost it; he lost himself in a fiery downpour of uncontrolled passion in which he experienced *la petite mort* for the first time in his life.

Flames of fire heated the blood in Alex's veins as she surrendered all she was and had to the man who'd taken her to unknown heights of passion. Their shared moment of ecstasy ended, Alex too emotion-filled to speak.

They lay together, entwined, the burning memory of their first day in Venice imprinted in their memory forever.

"Walk faster, Merrick." Alex, a vision in white, pulled Merrick along with her as she turned down an alley.

He smiled. She was like a child in FAO Schwarz at Christmastime. The white sundress with an empire waist and tiny pleated skirt that ended at her knees made her appear younger, virginal. He hadn't been the one to claim her innocence, but he could've been when he thought about the first time he'd made love to her. It was obvious she had only experienced conventional lovemaking because whenever he introduced another technique she'd become shy or embarrassed by it. Not one to push, Merrick waited for her to take the initiative before adding it to their sexual repertoire.

They left the alley and crossed a small bridge. The sight unfolding before him was humbling. The setting sun had turned the sky blood red, the outline of magnificent structures across the lagoon standing out in stark relief.

"It's incredible." There was no mistaking the awe in his voice. He pointed. "What's that?"

Alex followed the direction of his finger. "Chiesa della Salute."

"How do you remember the names of every church, cathedral, or *duomo?*"

"Memorization. Unlike you, I don't have a photographic memory."

Merrick stared at her delicate profile. "Who told you I have a photographic memory?"

She turned and stared directly at him. "No one. You proved that the day we were in the National Museum of African Art.

You'd recalled works of art I'd forgotten we saw. You're not just smart, Merrick. You're brilliant. Now I see why the CIA wanted you. And now I know why you're going back.

"You told me you need normalcy in your life, but I believe it's because you feel as if you're losing it, losing your edge. You miss the thrill of being offered a new assignment, and with the heightened threat of terrorism you believe you have to do something to protect your country."

Merrick took her face in his hands, his eyes making love to her. "You're right, Ali. But you left out one piece of the puzzle."

"What's that?"

"You didn't mention yourself."

"How do I figure into the picture?"

"You've helped me to know what love is."

A shy smile flitted across her face. "Love is not taught, Merrick. Either you feel it or you don't."

He angled his head. "It could be I hadn't met the right woman."

Her smile widened. "I'll accept that because I've dated my share of losers."

"Were they losers, or you just weren't compatible?"

"Probably both." Standing on tiptoe, she brushed a kiss over his mouth.

Curving an arm around her waist, he dipped his head and kissed her soft, parted lips. "Are you ready to eat?"

"Does a cat think it's the meow?"

Shaking his head, Merrick smothered a laugh. One thing he was certain of, and that was life with Alexandra Cole would never be boring.

Chapter 17

Alex returned to the States, tanned, relaxed and more in love. It took two days for her to air out, dust and stock the pantry and refrigerator in her Arlington condo.

She called Michael to get an update on Jolene but got the Kirklands' voice mail. Three hours later Michael called to inform her he'd become a father. Jolene had given birth to a perfectly formed, healthy girl. They'd named her Teresa April Kirkland in honor of her paternal grandmother and one of Jolene's clients. Mother and daughter were well, and Alex told Michael she'd come by the hospital the following day to see Jolene and meet her newest cousin.

Alex walked into the small private hospital set on twenty acres of prime property in affluent Georgetown. The medical staff housed in a former Georgian mansion provided one-on-

one care for patients wealthy enough to pay five-figure-per-day fees for maximum privacy.

Jolene Kirkland's room wasn't a room but a suite with a balcony overlooking a formal English garden. She sat up in bed, pillows cradling her shoulders for support, watching a flat-screen television.

A cradle was positioned on the right side of the bed.

Alex rapped lightly on the door. "Hello, Mommy."

Jolene, reaching for the remote device, turned off the television. "Please come in, Alex."

Carrying a cellophane wicker basket filled with aromatherapy items, Alex walked in and placed the basket on a damask-covered table. Jolene looked incredibly beautiful for a woman who'd just endured thirteen hours of difficult labor.

"There's something in that basket for mother and baby." She approached the bed and hugged Jolene. "Congratulations."

Jolene smiled. "Thank you."

Alex walked around the bed, peering into the cradle. Wrapped in a pale pink blanket was an infant with tufts of jet-black hair. "She looks like Emily."

"That's what I told Michael."

"What color are her eyes?" Alex wanted to know if Teresa had inherited her father's green eyes.

"I don't know. Little Miss Willful has yet to open them."

Alex sat on a cushioned chair next to the cradle. "Is she a good baby?"

"No," Jolene said without hesitating. "The only time she isn't crying is when she's eating and sleeping."

"Perhaps she has gas."

"Perhaps she wants to be held," Jolene countered.

"But she's only a day old. And who's been holding her?"

Jolene rolled her eyes. "Take a guess, Alex."

"No!" Alex moaned. "Please don't tell me that Michael has begun spoiling her already."

"You didn't hear it from me."

"I can't…" Alex's response was preempted by a knock on the door. Turning, she saw Michael's broad shoulders filling out the doorway.

He gave Alex a bright smile. "Hey, cuz." He walked into the room and kissed her cheek before he rounded the bed to kiss his wife.

"Congratulations, Michael. Your daughter is beautiful."

With clear green eyes dancing in excitement, Michael shook his head in amazement. "I still can't believe she's here."

"She looks like Emily."

"That's what I told Jolene."

"If she's as outspoken as your sister, then you're in for it," Alex predicted.

"You're a lot more candid than Emily," Michael said in defense of his sister.

"Is this a private family gathering?" asked a deep voice that sent a shiver of excitement throughout Alex. She turned to find Merrick standing in the doorway in a tan suit, with a white shirt and chocolate silk tie.

Suddenly she found breathing difficult as her gaze met his. Would Michael know just seeing them together that his friend was sleeping with his cousin? Was this the time when she'd reveal her relationship with Merrick?

"Come on in, Gray." The two men shook hands, at the same time exchanging a rough embrace. "Have you met my cousin, Alexandra Cole?"

Merrick extended his hand, belaying her fear that he would reveal the extent of their involvement. "Yes, I have. We met New Year's Eve."

Alex shook his hand, smiling. "We shared a dance New

Year's Eve." She now was able to relax. Merrick hadn't let on that they'd just spent two weeks together in Italy. He'd given her a tangible graduation gift on the flight back to the States: an Etruscan-inspired gold necklace with a magnificent ruby briolette.

Merrick inclined his head. "You're right." Reaching into his jacket, he took out an envelope and gave it to Jolene. "Congratulations. It's just a little something for your daughter."

Jolene reached out and patted his hand. "You didn't have to give her anything." The moment Teresa drew breath she'd become heir to a share of the ColeDiz billion-dollar empire.

"That may be true, but I've been told that little girls *and* big girls can never have too many clothes."

Jolene opened the envelope and stared at its contents before handing the envelope to Alex. Merrick had given Teresa Kirkland a gift certificate to the finest children's boutique in the Capitol District.

Jolene smiled at the man who despite being her husband's friend frightened her. She'd found him too quiet and very mysterious. "Thank you, Merrick. Teresa's certain to be one of D.C.'s best-dressed babies."

Merrick moved over to stare down at the sleeping infant, his expression softening. "Nice work, Kirk."

Alex and Jolene exchanged looks that spoke volumes. "He did have some help," Alex drawled.

"Speak, sister," Jolene chimed in.

Wincing, Merrick put up his hands. "Did I say the wrong thing?"

"Hell, yeah!" the two women chorused.

"I suppose that's my cue to escape while I can," Merrick teased.

"Where are you off to?" Michael asked him.

"Langley."

Alex knew the CIA was headquartered in Langley, Virginia. And like marriage, Merrick's return to the CIA was not a topic she welcomed—at least not at this time. She knew she was either selfish or in denial, but the only thing she wanted to focus on was securing a position with the National Trust. After that she would deal with her future with Merrick.

Merrick left as quietly as he'd come and she spent another thirty minutes with the Kirklands before driving back to Arlington. She'd purchased the brand-new Acura Integra a month before closing on her condo, and in two years she still hadn't put more than three thousand miles on the vehicle. Instead of flying to Boston for her interview, she drove, stopping and touring the states in the Trust's northeast region.

CIA Headquarters...Langley, Virginia

Merrick sat in an interview room, answering the same question posed at least three different ways. What he detested most was the information necessary for security clearance. It was as if the interviewer wanted to know why he'd been born.

"Have you traveled out of the country in the past three years?"

"Yes, I have," he answered truthfully.

"When?"

"Three weeks ago."

"Did you travel alone?"

"Yes."

"Were you alone during your return to the United States?"

"No."

"Who did you travel with, and what is your relationship to said person or persons?"

"I returned to the United States with a woman. Her name is Alexandra Cole."

"Did you and Ms. Cole reside together during your travels?"

"Yes."

"Is Ms. Cole a citizen of the United States? If not, then what country?"

"She is a citizen of the United States."

"Where does she reside?"

"Arlington, Virginia."

"Has Ms. Cole always been a resident of the Commonwealth of Virginia?"

"No. Ms. Cole was born and raised in Boca Raton, Florida."

The interrogation went on for hours, every answer recorded for dissemination and follow-up. Merrick was mentally and physically drained when he got into his car in the visitors' parking lot and drove away. His association with Alex had drawn her into an investigation that was not of her choosing. Her family name or wealth meant nothing to a governmental agency intent on dissecting her life.

He'd gotten security clearance once and there was no doubt he would again. But he wondered if the Justice Department would uncover something about Alexandra he didn't want or need to know. And as if he'd executed the maneuver countless times, Merrick took the road leading to Arlington. Activating the hands-free device, he pressed the number to Alex's cell phone.

"Hello, stranger," she crooned.

"Hello, Miss Cole," he countered, playing along with her. "What do I have to do to convince you to come out and play?"

"What are you playing?"

"Strip poker."

She chuckled. "Does stripping translate to the removal of articles of clothing?"

"Shame on you. Get your mind out of the gutter, naughty girl."

"Would you like me if I were a good girl?"

"I'd like you if you were toothless, bald and covered with carbuncles."

"What in the world are carbuncles?"

"Warts."

"Dis-gus-ting." She drew the word out into three syllables. "When should I expect you?"

Merrick took a quick glance at the dashboard clock. "Sometime after five."

He disconnected the call, then began the process that would disassociate of what had transpired in the tiny room back in Langley. He'd relived his entire life during the session, and unfortunately there were events he'd relegated to the deepest recesses of his mind, hoping never to resurrect them. However, they'd resurfaced and would take days if not months to purge again.

Carl Ashleigh listened to Merrick Grayslake's taped responses, comparing them to his previous security clearance report. Not much had changed in two years. The only exception was his involvement with a woman—a woman who just happened to be heiress to a family-owned conglomerate.

It wasn't what Carl's superiors wanted, but it couldn't be helped. They needed Grayslake to flush out a big fish; but if his lady got caught up in the trap it would become Grayslake's responsibility to protect her.

Picking up the phone, he dialed an extension. "He looks good," he said into the mouthpiece. "But there may be one hitch. He's involved with a woman, and I'm not certain whether we'll be able to keep her out of the picture until we spring the trapdoor. Don't worry. I'll keep you posted on everything."

Carl hung up, staring at several framed photographs on the opposite wall. The director was counting on him to put Operation Backslap into motion before the end of the year. He had eight months to bring down the country's most powerful lobbyist, Chandler Duffy. With Duffy out of the way, the popular incumbent president was certain to lose his party's nomination for reelection.

Chapter 18

It took four days for Alex to drive to Boston for her interview, but she accomplished the return drive to Virginia in ten hours. On the trip northward she'd stopped and toured the historic districts in Pennsylvania, New Jersey and Connecticut, staying overnight in the respective states' capitals. She'd planned on calling Merrick her first night on the road, but when she checked in to her hotel the only thing she'd wanted was a warm shower and firm bed. When she checked her cell-phone voice message, there was a call from him. His terse reprimand about her not checking in with him raised her hackles, and she waited another day before calling him back.

She had her first serious disagreement with Merrick when she told him that she hadn't needed to check in with anyone since she'd celebrated her twenty-first birthday, and now at twenty-nine, soon-to-be thirty, she wasn't going to begin.

Alex couldn't remember his brusque retort because she'd abruptly ended the call.

The volatile interchange forced her to rereevaluate her relationship with Merrick Grayslake, that perhaps she hadn't married or had a serious relationship because she unconsciously valued her independence; that she was unable to commit to sharing her life and future with a man.

Her interview had gone well, and with her degree and outstanding grades she was offered a position with the National Trust for Historic Preservation. She'd formulated a game plan and had accomplished everything she'd set out to do.

Alex loved Merrick, enough to marry him and become the mother of his children, but she refused to be subjugated by him or *any* man. She'd been reared to think for herself, nurtured and taught to take care of herself, and being a Cole meant she would always be able to take care of herself.

It was late afternoon when Alex crossed the state line from Maryland into the District of Columbia. An accident backed up traffic for miles along the road leading to the Key Bridge, so she headed south to the Fourteenth Street Bridge to cross the Potomac River. It was a longer route to Arlington, but at least she wouldn't have to sit in traffic.

Half an hour later, she pressed a device, raising the door to one of the four garages in the rear of her building, parked, then alighted from the car where she'd spent too many hours. Not bothering to remove her luggage from the trunk, Alex unlocked the front door, mounted the staircase and opened the door to her apartment, encountering a blast of hot air that forced her to take a backward step.

Placing her keys and handbag on the foyer table, she pressed a button, activating the central cooling unit, while chiding herself for not leaving it running during her absence.

Going into the bathroom adjoining her bedroom, she

stripped off her clothes and placed them in a wicker hamper. Just as she prepared to step into the shower, the telephone rang. She returned to the bedroom to answer the call. A smile parted her lips. It was her sister.

"Hi, Ana."

"Where have you been?"

"Let's begin again, little sister," she chastised softly. Ana was as bad as Merrick. What was with them clocking her? "Hello, Ana."

"Sorry about that. Hi, Alex."

Alex smiled. "What's up?"

"I'm in Georgetown. I've been staying with Michael, Jolene and the baby for the past two days. Alex, she is the most adorable little girl."

Alex hadn't seen Teresa since the day she'd come to the hospital because she wanted to give Jolene time to recover before she had to entertain visitors. The fact that Michael, as a teacher, did not work summers would make Jolene's transition from wife to mother easier than it would if she had full responsibility of caring for Teresa.

"She is beautiful. Why are you staying with them when you could've stayed here?" Before she'd left for Europe Alex had given her sister and brothers the key to her condominium so they could use her extra bedroom whenever they were in the D.C. area.

"I called you, but when I didn't get an answer I decided to hang out with Michael."

"I was in Boston on a job interview. Why didn't you call my cell?"

"I just got a new cell phone, and I hadn't programmed in your number. Do you want company?"

"Of course. Come on over."

"I'll see you in a bit."

Alex hung up and headed for the bathroom.

* * *

Ana lay at the foot of Alex's California king bed, her head resting on a mound of pillows. The flickering light from candles on tables provided the only illumination in the air-cooled space.

"I can't believe you're going to get a real job," Ana teased her sister.

Alex shifted until she found a more comfortable position against the headboard. "I *had* a real job, Ana Cole, when I worked for that art gallery."

Ana sucked her teeth. "That was play-play and you know it. Now, working for the National Trust is real."

Alex smiled. "I think the most exciting aspect of the position will be the traveling and meeting with groups whose focus is on preserving our history for future generations."

Turning over on her side, Ana tried making out her sister's face in the subdued light. "I don't understand how you get so excited about broken-down old buildings."

"That's because you can't see the beauty in them. What you see as broken down and worthless I see as the fading beauty of magnificent wraparound porches, moldings, lintels, columns and newel posts. Only in America do we tear down to make way for the new, which isn't necessarily better or prettier than what stood before. That's why I love going to Europe, because they value their architecture and history."

"Don't forget that the United States is an infant when you compare it to the rest of the world, Alex."

"But that's no reason not to respect past artisans. Many of the antebellum mansions were designed and built by African slaves."

Ana closed her eyes and listened to Alex recount the names of the mansions that rose to glory and splendor under the human toil of their ancestors. She was so caught up in the history that she jumped as if jolted by a bolt of electricity when the telephone on the bedside table rang.

Reaching for the instrument, Alex picked it up. "Hello."

"Hello, cuz," said a deep voice with a distinctive Southwest intonation.

"What's up, Michael?"

"My folks just called to say they're coming up for the Fourth. Jolene's parents are also coming in to see Teresa, so I decided to throw a little something. If you and Ana aren't doing anything, then come on by any time after noon."

"Hold on, Michael." Alex covered the mouthpiece with her hand. "When are you going back to Boca?"

Ana sat up and stared at Alex. She'd come to the D.C. area to meet with a young female vocalist who'd sent Serenity Records a demo, but once she met with the fifteen-year-old she realized she wasn't the one who'd recorded the songs. Livid because she'd been duped, Ana hadn't bothered to stay and uncover who'd actually recorded the demo and decided to extend her stay to visit her sister and cousin.

"There's no rush for me to go back. Why?"

"Michael wants us to come over for the Fourth. Uncle Josh and Aunt Vanessa are coming up to see the baby. He said Jolene's folks are also coming in from Chicago."

Ana flashed her dimpled smile. "Count me in."

Alex removed her hand. "We're in. Do you want us to bring anything?"

"No. I've got everything covered."

"How about dessert?"

"I'll order pies and cobblers from Rudy B's."

"Hot damn!" Alex had discovered Rudy B's by accident when she drove through northwest D.C. The original Rudy B's, a one-room log cabin, was built behind the small house that belonged to Reuben Brown in 1908. It was expanded after World War I, then again in the sixties, and had undergone extensive renovations in 1998 for its ninetieth anniversary. The family-owned restaurant had earned the reputation of serving the best soul food in the Capitol District. The first time she ate a slice of sweet-potato pie she was hooked!

"I guess that means we'll just show."

Michael laughed. "You do that."

Alex hung up, smiling. "Save your appetite because Michael's ordering dessert from Rudy B's."

"Who or what is Rudy B's?" asked Ana.

"It's the best soul food joint in the world."

Ana lifted her eyebrows. "Did you say the world?"

"You heard me."

Swinging her legs over the side of the bed, Ana pushed her feet into a pair of sandals. "Get up. We're going on a food run."

Alex took a quick glance at the clock next to the telephone. It was 8:48 p.m. "Are you sure you want to eat this late?"

Combing her fingers through her short hair, Ana gave Alex a knowing look. "Don't play yourself, Alexandra. You know it's never too late to eat. Especially when the food's good."

Grinning, Alex swung her legs over the bed and pushed her feet into a pair of worn leather flip-flops. "Let's roll."

Merrick had spent the night vacillating over whether to accept Michael's invitation to come to Georgetown for a cookout or stay in Bolivar because he knew Alex would be there; she'd hung up on him, and his pride, false pride, wouldn't permit him to call her back.

He missed her, missed their nightly chats even when they were hundreds of miles apart. He missed her so much that his heart ached. There had been a time when he'd accused her of ripping his heart out, and she had, leaving him to bleed emotionally.

Perhaps, he mused, he wasn't cut out to be a good boyfriend because he didn't know how to be a boyfriend. There were women, women he'd slept with, but they weren't someone with whom he would plan a future.

Love, the emotion that had eluded him, had come into his life like a slow-moving mist, the silent paws of a stalking cat and death when it came stealing to reclaim the breath given at birth. It was so unexpected that he wasn't given the opportunity to reject it.

Slumping lower in the porch chair, he stared at a doe and her fawn feeding on blackberries. Something must have startled them because they took off running in the direction of the woods.

Merrick closed his eyes, sighing heavily. Love. Men and women sang about it, poets wrote sonnets about it, people took their own lives and killed others for it.

He'd fallen in love with a slip of a woman who made him look for the next sunrise, a woman he had proposed marriage to and wanted to have his children with, a woman who had pulled him from a morass of self-pity and irrelevance where one day turned insignificantly into the next. He opened his eyes, pushed off the chair and went into the house. Grasping the hem of his T-shirt, he pulled it over his head.

He had to stop the bleeding, and the only way he could do that was to confront Alex.

Merrick drove from Bolivar to Washington, D.C., utilizing back roads and pushing the speedometer above ninety. Crossing the Virginia state line, he slowed to the speed limit. He'd made the trip in half the time.

He made one stop on Connecticut Avenue at Dupont Circle. Returning to his truck with his purchase, he drove the short distance to Q Street NW. Fortunately, Merrick found parking outside Michael's house. The cars lining the driveway bore Virginia and Florida license plates.

Hoisting a box to his shoulder, he walked around to the rear of the house. A large awning and colorful beach umbrellas shielded the Kirklands' guests from the blazing summer sun as they sat at tables eating, drinking and laughing.

Merrick saw her, and went completely still. Alex had her back to him so he was given the opportunity to observe her unnoticed. A baseball cap covered her hair and a pair of sunglasses shielded her eyes. His gaze caressed the smooth brown skin on her back and shoulders under a halter top.

"Hey, man. What do you have there?"

Merrick lowered the box and put it in Michael's outstretched arms. "It's just a little something to quench your thirst."

Michael's eyes, hidden behind the lenses of a pair of sunglasses, crinkled when he smiled. "What is it?"

"Your favorite sake."

"All right," Michael drawled. He'd acquired a fondness for the Japanese brew when he'd been stationed in Japan. "Why don't you circulate while I take this in the house. I'll make the introductions later."

Merrick wanted to tell Michael that he didn't need an introduction, at least not one to Alexandra Cole. He knew not only her name, but every inch of her compact body. He knew how to make her moan and sob in ecstasy. He knew what made her laugh and cry. And he'd heard her admit to loving him as much as he loved her.

Alex felt Ana's fingers tighten on her wrist. "He's here," she whispered close to her ear.

She frowned at her sister. "What are you talking about?"

"The guy from our New Year's Eve party. You know, the one who was staring at you and I told you he was hot."

Alex forced herself not to move, react. She knew Ana was talking about Merrick. She'd wanted to ask Michael if he had invited him, but hadn't wanted to appear that interested. What her cousin didn't know was that not only did she know Merrick, but she was also in love with him.

"Don't get crazy," she whispered, sotto voce.

"He's looking this way, Alex. I take that back. He's coming this way."

She removed her glasses and schooled her expression to one of indifference when she saw Merrick making his way toward her. He wore a dark blue shirt with large green leaves over a pair of jeans that were molded to his lean hips and thighs. When he was less than three feet away, she stood up and extended her hand.

"It's nice seeing you again, Merrick."

Merrick ignored her hand for several seconds, and his expression was that of complete unconcern. He saw a flash of fear in her eyes; she didn't want her family to know how well they knew each other; she was still hiding their affair. Reluctantly he took her hand, certain he heard her exhalation of breath. He decided not to out her.

"Same here, Alex."

She mouthed a thank-you. "Do you know everyone here?" she asked louder than necessary.

He released her hand. "I'm afraid I don't."

Looping her arm casually through his, she steered him toward her sister. "Alex, this is Merrick Grayslake. Merrick, my sister, Ana."

Ana flashed her dimpled smile. "Hi, Merrick."

He inclined his head. "My pleasure, Ana."

Before Ana could utter another word, Alex escorted him over to her aunt and uncle. "Aunt Vanessa, Uncle Josh, I don't know if you remember Michael's friend from the—"

"Oh, I didn't know that you were making the introductions," Michael interrupted.

Alex released Merrick's arm. "He's your guest, so I'll let you do the honors."

That said, she walked away, feeling the heat from Merrick's gaze burning into her back. She made her way into the house and a bathroom off the gourmet kitchen. Sitting on a chair, she closed her eyes. She had to get Merrick alone; they had to talk, but not in front of a crowd of people.

Alex lingered in the bathroom long enough to splash cold water on her face, before patting it dry with a paper towel. She knew she couldn't hang out in the bathroom, so pulling back her shoulders she opened the door, stopping short when she saw Merrick in the kitchen with Jolene. He'd cradled Teresa to his chest, smiling and making cooing sounds. The sight of him holding a baby stopped her breath. He'd talked about having a child—their child.

Jolene's dark eyes sparkled like polished onyx. "It appears as if my daughter is partial to men. The minute a woman, other than myself, picks her up she cries."

Merrick's head came up and he smiled at Alex. "Does she cry with you?"

"I haven't held her."

"Come hold her," Jolene urged.

Alex took half a dozen steps and held out her arms for the two-week-old infant. She smiled when feeling the slight weight. "Hey, baby girl," she crooned and Teresa opened her eyes. Brilliant green eyes met a pair in gold. The two cousins regarded each other for a full minute before Teresa yawned, closed her eyes, then fell asleep.

"I guess there goes your theory about her preferring men," Alex said proudly, handing the infant to her mother.

Jolene cradled the baby to the shoulder draped with a cloth diaper. "There must be something about you that Teresa likes, because she won't let my mother or Vanessa hold her. I've told her it's not nice to shun her grandmothers because they're always more indulgent than grandpas."

"You're right about that."

Jolene shifted her baby to a more comfortable position. "Alex, would you mind seeing that Merrick gets something to eat?" She smiled at Merrick. "Now, *if* you were family, then it would be the reverse."

Crossing his arms over his chest, Merrick angled his head. "What do you mean?"

"If you were married to Alex, then it would be you bringing her a plate, not the reverse."

There came a beat of silence as Merrick regarded Alex. "I wouldn't have a problem serving Alexandra."

His response seemed to surprise Jolene, who'd lifted her arching eyebrows. She never would've expected Merrick Grayslake to be accommodating, especially to a woman.

"How interesting," she said in a quiet tone as she gently rocked her baby.

Alex winked at Merrick. "Let's go, Mr. Grayslake. Enjoy this while you can."

Merrick took long strides as he followed Alex. "When are you going to let me serve you, *querida?*"

"We'll talk about it."

"When, Ali?"

She stopped, turned and glanced up at him. "I'll come to you after my sister goes back to Florida."

Merrick held her gaze for a full minute. He wanted to ask her when, but held his tongue. He would wait as long as it took, not because he wanted to but because Alex was worth it.

Chapter 19

Alex navigated Deadman's Curve, her heart in her mouth. It had taken three weeks to fulfill her promise to come to Merrick. Their relationship had changed. The nightly telephone calls had stopped, replaced by one or two a week. The urgency to see each other had waned, replaced by a waiting as to when they would be reunited.

She also found it odd that her feelings for Merrick had intensified. It was as if the separation allowed her to take a step back to confirm what she did share with him was love and not lust.

Alex would've come to West Virginia sooner if Ana hadn't extended her stay in Virginia another two weeks; the morning of her sister's departure she received a letter of hire from the National Trust and that they wanted her to return to Boston for an orientation session; this time she flew to Massachusetts instead of driving.

Within miles of her crossing the West Virginia border the

weather changed. An oppressive humidity and green-gray haze made normal breathing nearly impossible. She chanced glancing away from the curving, winding roadway for a second to adjust her car's air-conditioning.

Alex hummed a tuneless ditty to take her mind off the road ahead of her, while chiding herself for driving to Bolivar and cursing Merrick for living in the wilderness. She decelerated when she saw the bumper of a pickup several car lengths in front of her. It was apparent she wasn't the only driver going under twenty miles per hour.

Deadman's Curve leveled off as she maneuvered into a valley nearly obliterated by the thick haze. She continued along the paved road, peering through the windshield for the turnoff to Merrick's house. She missed it the first time and had to reverse directions.

Then she saw it! Merrick's house was ablaze with light, a beacon in a darkened sky that looked more like night than day. It was only ten in the morning. She maneuvered around to the garage where he housed his classic cars, parking behind his truck.

Merrick heard the sound of a car's engine, followed by the solid slam of a door. He was on his feet and on the porch in a matter of seconds. A smile curved the corners of his mouth when he spied the petite figure in a tank top, jeans and running shoes.

He'd waited patiently for Alex to come. Whenever they talked he'd wanted to ask her when, but couldn't bring himself to tell her how much he missed and wanted to see her. The three weeks had given him the space he needed to assess his feelings for the only woman to whom he'd given his heart. He loved Alexandra Cole, loved her enough to give up his life for her.

Merrick realized in introspect that he'd made a gross error in judgment when he'd attempted to monitor her whereabouts. How had he forgotten that she was an independent woman who'd traveled and lived abroad, a woman who didn't need him or any man for her day-to-day existence? Alex was educated, independently wealthy and had focused her energies on beginning her career, and for that he was forced to respect her.

He came down off the porch to meet her. The first thing he noticed was that she was thinner, her face and body. Her hair was styled differently. Her ubiquitous tousled, mussed look had been replaced by a chic cut that framed her tiny face.

Extending his arms, he closed the distance between them. It wasn't until he felt the soft crush of her breasts against his chest, inhaled the familiar scent of her perfume and felt the softness of her mouth when he kissed her that he knew she wasn't a figment of his imagination.

His mouth caressed hers as if it were fragile porcelain. Her lips parted and he deepened the kiss; there was a dreamy intimacy that hadn't been in any of their kisses; his lips parted in a soul-searching journey to taste every inch of her mouth.

Alex wound her arms under Merrick's shoulders, holding him fast. Her knees shook, her heart pounded a runaway rhythm as she struggled to catch her breath. His mouth revived her troubled spirit like rain soaking the parched earth. She'd missed him—oh how she'd missed everything about him!

"Take me inside," she whispered as pleasure radiated from the core of her body outward. Heat rippled under her skin, increasing with each second until she felt as if her entire body was on fire.

Her thoughts spun out of control, her emotions whirled, skidded and raced headlong into a whorl of sensual delight from which she never wanted to escape.

She loved Merrick, loved him more than she could've imagined loving a man. She wanted and needed him to remind her why she'd been born female.

"I love you so much," Merrick whispered against her lips. Tears filled her eyes with his passionate confession.

"Take me to bed and I'll show you how much I love you," Alex promised.

Merrick needed no further urging. He climbed the steps and walked into the house, closing the door with his foot. The entire house was ablaze with light to offset the eerie darkness that had settled on the region. It wasn't noon, yet the sky was black as pitch.

Cradling Alex's slight weight, he took the stairs, two at a time, and walked into his bedroom. Gently, he eased her down onto the bed, his body covering hers. He wanted to go slow, but his body refused to reason with his brain.

A roll of thunder shook the earth, followed by a crack of lightning that rent the air. The approaching storm was no match for the one racing through the bedroom. Buttons were ripped from their fastenings as pieces of discarded clothing littered the large bed.

Merrick reached over and swept everything off the mattress with the flick of his hand. Wrapping an arm around Alex's waist, he tucked her beneath him, parted her legs with a knee and entered her body in one sure upward thrust.

They gasped in unison with the joining of flesh akin to smoldering metals. There was no time for exploration, as Alex's urgency matched Merrick's long-denied needs.

She couldn't control the moans slipping from her parted lips, her hips writhing in a dance of desire, her breath coming in long, surrendering gasps. She rose to meet Merrick's powerful thrusts in a moment of unrestrained passion that exploded, then freed them in a firestorm of uncontrollable ecstasy. They lay together, waves of lingering passion flowing between them and making them one.

Alex woke hours later, alone in bed, ravenous. Sitting up, she swung her legs over the side of the bed and stood up. She hadn't taken a step when she felt the evidence of her passion session with Merrick trickle down her inner thigh. Her heart lurched. They'd made love without using protection. They'd gambled before, rolled the dice and had come up winners; however, this time the odds were against them.

Alex walked out of the bedroom and into the bathroom. She didn't want to think about the possibility that there was a new life growing inside her—not now, not when she'd just started her career.

The thunderstorm continued unabated as torrents of rain lashed the roof and windows. Alex stepped off the last stair and followed the mouthwatering smell.

She stood under the entrance to the kitchen watching Merrick as he placed a cover on a wok. If she'd changed in the short time they'd been apart, so had he. He'd cut his hair again, the dark reddish-brown strands hugging his scalp. There was no doubt he'd spent a lot of time outdoors as evidenced by the rich mahogany brown of his face and arms. Without warning, he looked up and smiled, his silver-gray eyes shimmering like newly minted quarters in his dark face.

"Did you sleep well?" he asked.

"How long was I asleep?" The first time she'd come to Merrick's house she couldn't find a clock. It was only when she set the clock on his microwave with the time on her watch that she was able to discern the hour.

"About six hours. You must have been exhausted."

Walking into the kitchen, she stood on tiptoe and kissed his cheek. She smiled. "Exhausted and hungry. What did you cook?"

Wrapping his arms around her waist, he pulled her to his length. "London broil, garlic roasted potatoes and stir-fried green beans."

Alex rested her head against his shoulder. "I think I'll keep you."

He pressed a kiss on her damp hair. "You better, because we're stuck with each other."

She closed her eyes for several seconds. "Speaking of being stuck with each other, we took a risk this morning when we made love without using protection."

Merrick let out an audible sigh. While Alex slept he'd agonized over what they'd done. It wasn't his intent to make love to her without a condom, but at that moment it was as if he'd taken leave of whatever common sense he had.

"I'm sorry, Ali, I didn't—"

She stopped his apology when she placed her fingertips over his mouth. "Don't apologize, Merrick. I should've stopped you."

Grasping her wrist, he pulled her hand down. There was a lethal calmness in his eyes that made it impossible for her look away. "Why didn't you, Ali?"

Lowering her gaze, she stared at the stark-white T-shirt stretched across his solid chest. "I don't know."

"Whatever happens I don't ever want you to forget that I'm in this with you."

She nodded, closing her eyes. "I suppose you'll remind me if I ever forget, won't you?"

"Hell, yeah," he said, smiling. "Let me feed you before you faint on me."

He dropped his arms and steered her to the table in the corner of the large kitchen that had been set with place settings for two. He pulled out a chair and seated her. Leaning over, he pressed a kiss to the column of her neck.

A knowing smile softened Alex's face as Merrick placed a bowl of avocado salad on the table. Merrick would fit in perfectly with the men in her family. He could cook, and he was secure enough with his masculinity to serve his woman.

Alex took a glance at her watch for the umpteenth time. The meeting of the northeast Trust's Waterfront Historic Action League in New Bedford, Massachusetts, was running late. As liaison for the National Trust, she had come to support the WHALE project, whose focus was the rehabilitation of a fire-damaged commercial building in the historic whaling community, but the queasiness persisted. And she didn't have to see a doctor to know the source of the nausea.

She was pregnant!

What she'd hoped for in the future had become a reality— now. She would marry Merrick and make David and Serena grandparents.

Mercifully, the meeting ended and Alex gathered her notes. She would decipher them during the flight back to Virginia; she would then type them and forward copies to her supervisor.

Alex liked her position as a liaison because she was like a doctor on call. She didn't have to go into an office, except for monthly meetings, and she worked independently on the projects to which she'd been assigned. Not knowing where she would be sent was the only drawback. It could be Delaware one week, then two weeks later Rhode Island or New York. She refused to think about being stranded in an airport in Vermont or Maine during a snowstorm.

Not waiting to confer with the members of the board, she rushed out of the building to the lot where she'd parked her rental car. By the time she maneuvered into a strip mall, the nausea had stopped. A quarter of an hour later, she was back in her car, driving in the direction of her hotel.

Alex lay across the bed in the darkened room, staring up at the ceiling. She'd pulled the drapes, shutting out the strong autumn sunlight. The home pregnancy test had confirmed her suspicions. She was pregnant with Merrick Grayslake's baby, and by her estimate she would deliver a son or daughter early May of the following year. They'd made love countless times after *that* time, but had always used protection.

Rolling over on her side, she reached for her cell phone on the bedside table. Merrick answered after the third ring.

"Hey, baby."

She smiled at his sensual greeting. Whenever he called her baby it came out in a deep, sexy growl. "Hey, you," she countered.

"How are you?"

"Pregnant." The sound of heavy breathing echoed in her ear. "Did you hear what I said, Merrick?"

"Yes, I did. When are you coming home?"

"I'll be home in a couple of days, but I'm not going to stay," she said.

"Where the hell are you going? And to do what?"

Alex heard the rage *and* panic in his voice. She decided to ignore his query as to her whereabouts. This was not the time to fight with him. "I'm going to see my mother. I'm going to need her help in planning our wedding."

There was a beat of silence. "Ali?" His voice was softer, calmer.

"Yes, Merrick?"

"Do you want me with you when you tell your parents?"

"No, *mi amor.* I have to handle this by myself. As soon as

the arrangements are finalized I'll let you know when you should come to Florida."

"Ali...baby, I...I don't know what to say."

She smiled. "How about congratulations?"

"Congratulations to you...and to me!"

"You're silly, Merrick Grayslake."

"No, I'm not. I'm going to become a daddy."

"After I check out tomorrow I'm going down to the Cape to see my brother Gabriel. I'll spend the night with him, then fly out of Logan Saturday morning. I'll call you as soon as I touch down."

"Please don't make me worry about you, Ali."

"I won't. I love you, Merrick."

There was a pause. "I love you, too."

Alex ended the call. Picking up the receiver for the hotel phone, she ordered room service. Afterward she thought about calling Gabriel to let him know she was coming, but decided to surprise him. And no doubt he would be very surprised when she told him he was going to be an uncle.

Chapter 20

Alex maneuvered her midsize rental car into the driveway leading to her brother's house, coming to a stop in front of the two-car garage. It was nine forty-five at night, and she prayed Gabriel was home, and if he was, that he hadn't gone to bed. She got out of the car. She was in luck. Gabriel bounded off the porch, arms outstretched.

"Hey! What are you doing here?"

Alex kissed her brother's cheek. "I had to see you and give you my good news."

Cradling her face between his palms, Gabriel smiled at the same time he shook his head. "You could've used the telephone, Alex."

"I was already in Boston for a meeting."

His hands came down, and he held her at arm's length. "Look at you, Miss Corporate. You look wonderful."

An attractive blush suffused her face under a deep summer

tan. She'd traded her jeans and T-shirts for a black wool crepe suit, ivory silk blouse, black leather pumps and a strand of perfectly matched pearls with matching studs in her pierced lobes.

"Thank you."

Gabriel reached for her hand. "Come inside and we'll talk."

Alex followed him up to a wraparound porch and into a spacious entryway. A formal living room held two facing gleaming black Steinway concert pianos.

"So much for your little place," she murmured. "This house is enormous." Bleached pine floors, French doors and pale walls projected an atmosphere of openness.

"It'll do," Gabriel said with a hint of pride. He led the way to the family room. He indicated a love seat. Alex sat, Gabriel taking the cushion next to her. "Do you want anything to eat or drink?"

"No, thank you. I ate dinner at the hotel before I left." She glanced around the meticulously furnished room. "I really like what Aunt Parris has done here." Martin Cole's wife, Parris, was a highly trained interior decorator. "Your house looks like a home. All you need is a wife and a few kids to make it look completely lived in."

Deliberately ignoring her reference to a wife and children, Gabriel peered closely at his sister. "Tell me your good news."

A mysterious smile curved Alex's lush mouth. "I'm getting married."

A muscle tensed in Gabriel's jaw. "Who is he?" The three words were squeezed out between clenched teeth.

Alex stood up and walked over to the French doors overlooking the rear of the house. Strategically placed floodlights illuminated the backyard. She so wanted her brother to be happy for her.

"Please, Gabe."

He stood up and walked over to her. "Please what?"

Her hands closed into tight fists, her nails biting into the tender flesh of her palms. "Don't say it like that."

"How else can I say it, Alex? You come to me in the middle of the night with the news that you're engaged. I'm shocked, stunned and surprised."

Turning around, she stared up at Gabriel. Her heart sank when she saw his expression. "I thought you would be happy for me."

"I am, Alex. But…but it's so unexpected. You never said you were seeing anyone." He hesitated when she smiled. "Do I know him?"

She nodded. "Yes."

His eyes narrowed. "A name, Alexandra."

"Merrick Grayslake."

Gabriel went completely still. "Michael's friend?"

Alex lifted her chin and placed her hands on her hips. "Do you know another Merrick Grayslake?" she spat out.

Gabriel threw up his hands at the same time mumbling a savage expletive. "How the hell did you hook up with him?" he shouted in Spanish.

"Don't you dare yell at me!" she warned in the same language.

Running a hand over his face, Gabriel counted slowly to ten. He'd run interference more times than he could remember to scare away men who'd considered his sisters fair game; he'd heard a few refer to Alex and Ana as *"fresh meat."*

He knew Merrick Grayslake was his first cousin Michael Kirkland's friend. He'd met him at Michael's wedding, and had found the man mysterious and somewhat sinister looking.

Why was it, he thought, that his sister was drawn to men who were the complete opposite of her? If they weren't walking on the wild side, then they were on the edge. He didn't know much about Merrick except that he lived somewhere in West Virginia and had at one time worked for the CIA.

Grasping her hand, Gabriel led Alex back to the love seat, sitting and pulling her down next to him. "Talk to me, Alex."

"Where do you want me to start?"

"From the beginning."

"I met Merrick at Michael's wedding. We shared a few dances, and he asked me for my number. I gave him my cell phone because I was between the States and Mexico. I must confess that I felt uncomfortable around him for a while, and then one day it disappeared and I saw him in a whole new light." She didn't reveal the whole new light was when they went from being friends to lovers. "At first I was impressed with his intelligence, but once I got past that I saw him as a lonely man."

Gabriel shot her an incredulous look. "You're marrying him because you feel sorry for him?"

"Of course not. I'm marrying Merrick because I love him. I also want to tell you that I'm…"

"You're what?" he asked when she did not complete her statement.

"I'm pregnant."

Gabriel's expression of shock and annoyance gave way to a brilliant smile. "Hot damn! I'm going to be an uncle."

Alex put her arms around his neck. "Thank you for being happy for me."

He kissed her forehead. "How can I not be happy for you? When's the wedding?"

Pulling back, her eyes sparkling like multifaceted citrines, Alex blinked back tears of joy. "Soon."

"Does Grayslake know he's going to be a father?"

Alex nodded. "Yes. I told him last night."

"How far along are you?"

"Probably about six weeks."

"Have you seen a doctor?"

"Not yet. I have an appointment for Tuesday morning. You're the first one to know—other than Merrick of course."

"Why didn't you tell anyone you were dating him?"

"I didn't want to say anything until I was certain he was the *one*. Our relationship changed after he called, asking me to join him in Italy after I'd graduated. Of course I'd been there before as an art student, but I saw it differently because I realized then that I had fallen in love with Merrick."

Gabriel's smile was tender. His sister was in love. "You're really happy, aren't you?"

She nodded. "So much so that I'm frightened."

"Have you guys set a date?"

"No. But I don't want to wait too long. Looking like someone who swallowed a melon isn't too cool for a bride. I know you're teaching, but when are you off?"

"We're off Columbus Day, Veterans Day, Thanksgiving and of course winter recess."

Alex shook her head. It was the second week in September. "That's too far off. It looks as if you're going to have to fly down to Florida for a weekend. I want you to sing at my wedding."

"Let me know and I'll be there." He angled his head. "What about your position with the Trust?"

"If there's an opening in the southern region, then I'll request a transfer."

"And if there isn't?"

"Then I'll sit home knitting booties and piecing quilts until the baby comes."

"What do you want?" he asked. "Boy? Girl?"

"I don't care as long as it's healthy."

Gabriel ruffled her coiffed hair. "Will I be able to find you in the hills of West *Virginnie?*"

"We're going to use the house in West Virginia for weekends and vacations. We plan to live at my place until we find something bigger in a D.C. suburb."

"Do you have to live near D.C.?"

"Merrick is going back to the CIA as an intelligence training specialist, so living in or around D.C. would be a lot more practical."

"That sounds like a good plan. You, Michael and Jolene can raise your kids together."

"What's nice is that our children will get to see one another more than we saw Michael and Emily."

"You're right," Gabriel agreed. Michael and Emily Kirkland had grown up in Santa Fe, New Mexico, and they usually saw them at family gatherings once or twice a year. Emily still lived in New Mexico with her husband and three children, but her brother had moved to the D.C. area after having been assigned to the Pentagon as a captain in the U.S. Army. Michael met his future wife, Jolene, in Georgetown.

"When do you plan to tell Mom and Dad?"

"I'm going to try and see them before next weekend."

Gabriel glanced at the watch strapped to his wrist. "I hope you know you're spending the night here."

She nodded. "I don't think I could make it back to Boston without falling asleep behind the wheel."

"Did you bring luggage?"

"I have a bag in the trunk of the car."

"Go upstairs and get ready for bed. I'll bring your bag in. You can take the bedroom at the top of the stairs on the left."

Alex stared lovingly at her older brother. "Thank you, Gabe."

"For what?"

"For being you."

He cradled her to his chest, kissing her cheek. "Love you, sis."

"Love you back, bro."

She handed Gabriel the keys to the rental, then made her way up the staircase. A wave of fatigue swept over her. If it wasn't the nausea, it was fatigue.

Alex stayed on her feet long enough to wash her face, brush her teeth and take a quick shower. When she returned to the bedroom she found her bag by the closet door. She took out a nightgown, slipped it over her body, and as soon as her head touched the pillow she fell asleep.

Chapter 21

A bright rising sun and the tangy smell of salt water greeted Alex when she woke up in the strange bed. Then, she remembered. She was at her brother's house on Cotuit. Gabriel had begun vacationing off-season on the Cape, but she'd never expected him to settle down in New England.

Pushing back the sheet, she moved off the bed and made her way to an adjoining bathroom. The gnawing feeling in her belly had intensified. She had two options: eat or faint.

Gabriel was in the kitchen when she walked in. His long damp hair hung down his T-shirt-covered back like satin ribbons. The aroma of freshly brewed coffee wafted into her nostrils. "Now that smells wonderful."

Gabriel turned and smiled at Alex. "Good morning. How are you feeling?"

"Hungry."

He pointed to the table in the breakfast nook. "Sit down

and I'll make you some *café con leche*." They'd grown up drinking warm milk with a small amount of brewed coffee.

Alex sat down. "Please don't make it too sweet."

Gabriel flashed a lopsided grin in an unshaven face. "Is it because you're sweet enough? Does Merrick think you're *sw-e-e-e-t?*" he drawled, unable to resist teasing her.

"Why don't you ask him?" she retorted.

A sobering expression came over Gabriel's face. "I will when I see him again."

"He doesn't frighten that easily, Gabe, so forget about trying to intimidate him the way you've done with a few of the other men I've gone out with."

Gabriel's eyebrows lifted. "Oh, so you know about that?"

"Know, Gabe. Some of them told me what you said to them."

He shrugged a shoulder. "I was just trying to protect my sister. Some of those clowns you called dates defied description." He poured milk into a saucepan and heated it. "I was usually pretty good in sending them packing—all except for Duane Jackson. It took a face-to-face to get Mr. Hip-Hop Master to stop seeing you." Alex's jaw dropped as she stared at him as if she'd never seen him before. "Close your mouth, Alex. Yeah, I met with Duane."

"But you had no right to interfere in my affairs," she spat out once she recovered her voice.

Gabriel winked at her, smiling. "If I hadn't interfered, then you wouldn't be sitting here telling me that you're planning to marry Merrick Grayslake."

A wave of heat stung her cheeks. "You're right about that."

He cupped an ear with his hand. "Can I get a thank-you, Alexandra Cole?"

"Like, thank you, Gabriel," she drawled in her best Valley-Girl imitation.

Alex thanked her brother again when he set a large mug

with the steaming milk and coffee in front of her. She took a sip, moaning softly. It was perfect. The warm liquid slid down the back of her throat, heating her chest and belly. Gabriel filled his mug with coffee, joining her at the table.

Her hand halted in midair as she attempted to take another sip of coffee. A young, very pretty woman stood under the arched entrance to the kitchen dressed in a gray sweatshirt, matching pants and running shoes. Her hair, secured in a single braid, fell over one shoulder.

A mysterious smile softened Alex's mouth. "Shame on you, brother," she said softly in Spanish. "You didn't tell me you had a girlfriend."

Gabriel jumped up, his chair crashing to the floor in a loud clatter.

"I'm not his girlfriend. We are colleagues." Walking into the kitchen, the woman extended her hand. "I'm Summer Montgomery."

Rising to her feet, Alex leaned over the table and shook Summer's hand. "Alexandra Cole. Your *colleague's* sister."

Gabriel, righting his chair, pulled it out for Summer. "Would you like a cup of coffee?"

"No, thank you. I usually don't eat or drink anything before jogging."

"What would you like for breakfast?"

"Fruit, a slice of toast and decaf coffee."

Alex smiled at Gabriel. "If you're taking orders, then I'll have grits, eggs, bacon or sausage and biscuits."

He leveled a frown at her. "If you keep eating like that, I'm going to start to call you porky."

"Bite me, Gabriel Morris Cole!"

"Sorry, sis, but I'll leave that task to Merrick."

Alex stuck out her tongue at her brother. "You're gross."

Summer pushed back her chair and stood up. "I'd like to complete my jog before the sun gets too hot. I'll be back later."

Alex watched Gabriel watching Summer's retreating figure, a knowing smile curving her lips. "She's beautiful." With her long hair, dark eyes and nut-brown coloring, Summer Montgomery looked exotic.

"That she is," he said matter-of-factly.

"You like her, don't you?"

Gabriel didn't meet his sister's gaze. "Yes."

"Does working with her pose a problem for you?"

"For me, no."

"What about her, Gabe?"

"She's reluctant."

"Does that matter to you?" Alex asked, continuing her questioning.

Shifting slightly, Gabriel stared at Alex. "No. I can't change how I feel about someone just like that." He snapped his fingers. "We've agreed to take it slow and see what becomes of it."

"That's the same thing Merrick said to me. And now I have to plan a wedding."

Gabriel held up a hand. "Back it up, Alex. No one said anything about getting married."

"Don't you want to get married? Start your own family?"

"I don't consciously think about it."

"You didn't answer my question, *Gabriel*."

"And I don't intend to answer it, *Alexandra*."

"You don't have to," she said smugly. "And because you're being evasive tells me that you do."

"Just because your fairy godmother sprinkled you with fairy dust, it doesn't mean it will happen to me."

"It's going to happen, Gabe," Alex predicted. The expression on Gabriel's face when Summer walked into the kitchen was one she'd never seen before, and Alex had seen her brother with enough women to know this one was different.

A frown appeared between Gabriel's eyes. "Next you're going to tell me that you can read palms."

Alex clapped a hand over her mouth at the same time she pushed back her chair. She made it to the half bath near the pantry just in time to purge the contents of her stomach. Morning sickness had attacked with a vengeance.

Alex waited for the sleek jet to touch down on the private airstrip before turning on her cell phone. She pressed a button. "I'm on the ground," she said when hearing Merrick's greeting.

"I'm waiting by baggage claims."

She'd called him earlier that morning from Logan Airport to let him know she'd chartered a private jet to return to D.C. She'd been one of ten passengers on the flight that made for an interesting and entertaining experience.

She deplaned and made her way down the gangway, through a long corridor that led to a waiting area for commercial departures. Navigating her way through the crowds, she found herself in baggage claims.

"Looking for someone?" whispered a familiar voice close to her ear.

Turning around, she tilted her head and smiled at Merrick. She handed him her carry-on. "Yes, I am. And I believe I just found him."

Wrapping his free arm around her waist, Merrick dipped his head and kissed her. "Welcome home."

Alex wound her arm around his waist inside his jacket. "Please get me out of here before I pass out."

Merrick led her toward the automatic doors. "Are you feeling all right?"

"It's the crowds."

"Do you want to wait here, or come with me to the lot to pick up my truck?"

"I'll come with you." She'd never felt bothered by crowds, so Alex assumed it was an idiosyncrasy attributed to her being pregnant.

Alex lost track of time. She knew she was back in her Arlington condo, but other than that she caught glimpses of the world going on around her whenever she stayed awake long enough to eat and go to the bathroom. She woke several times during the night to find Merrick in bed with her. They talked, but she couldn't remember what they'd talked about.

"What day is it?" she mumbled, her face pressed to the pillow.

"Sunday."

"What time is it?"

"Eight twenty-two."

"At night?"

"No, baby. It's morning."

Rolling over on her back, she smiled at Merrick leaning over her. She combed her fingers through the crisp hair on his chest. "What happened?"

"Nothing earth-shattering or catastrophic since you went into Sleeping Beauty mode."

She gave him a shy smile. "I'm sorry I wasn't very good company."

Straddling her body, Merrick supported his weight on his forearms. "We're not together to become each other's entertainment. You were exhausted, so you slept."

"I think it's the baby that has me so sleepy."

Merrick moved off her, and sitting back on his heels, he splayed a hand under her hips and relieved her of her nightgown. "Let's see what we have here."

Embarrassment washed over Alex, bringing a burning heat

that began in her face and spread lower. She attempted to cover herself with her hands. "No, Merrick."

He brushed her hands away with the ease of swatting a gnat. "It's too late to act innocent, *querida*. I've seen, touched and tasted everything you have."

Alex closed her eyes, shutting out his intense stare. "Please leave me some pride, Merrick."

His hands moved up between her thighs. "You're hardly going to be thinking about pride when you go into labor and your knees are spread east to west."

She opened her eyes and slapped at his hand. "Stop!"

He cradled her mound. "It's too late for that, beautiful."

Alex closed her eyes again, enjoying a touch that was as soft and gentle as a butterfly's gossamer wings. His fingers trailed over her belly, breasts, throat and around the outline of her ears. He'd become a sculptor, committing every dip and curve to memory.

"What are you doing to me, Merrick?"

"Making love to the mother of my child."

"Are you happy about the baby?"

He smiled. "Very, very happy."

"I'm not marrying you because I don't want to be a baby mama."

Merrick's smile faded. "Then why are you marrying me?"

Alex rested her hand alongside his stubbly jaw. "I love you."

Merrick wanted to tell Alex that he would marry her even if she didn't love him; there was no way he was going to father a child and not become a part of his child's life.

"Do you want a son or a daughter?" Alex asked after a comfortable silence.

Nuzzling her neck, Merrick pressed a kiss under Alex's ear. "It doesn't matter."

It didn't matter to Merrick whereas she secretly wanted a

girl. A little girl she would dress in frilly clothes, share tea parties, shopping sprees and intimate secrets with. She wanted for her daughter what she'd shared with her mother.

"Do you feel like going out for breakfast?"

Excitement fired the gold in her eyes. Merrick had mentioned food, which had become her number-one priority. "You don't have to ask me twice."

Merrick slipped off the bed and swung her up in his arms. "We'll save time if we share a shower."

Alex looped her arms around his neck. "Do you think we can take time to do something else?"

"What are you talking about?" he asked, not breaking stride.

"You know."

Merrick stopped several feet from the bathroom. "I know what?" Pressing her mouth to his ear, Alex whispered what she wanted him to do to her. Easing back, gray eyes flattening with an unreadable emotion, Merrick shook his head. "None of that until you see the doctor. I don't want anything to happen to you or our baby."

"Couples make love right up until the time a woman is ready to give birth."

"What if you're not one of those women, Ali?"

"And if I am, are you going to wait around for nine months and take care of yourself?"

His eyes widened until she saw glints of blue in his silver gaze. "And why not?" he asked glibly. "It won't be the first time."

Alex affected a saucy smile. "If it comes to that, then I'll do it for you."

Merrick stared at the woman in his arms, shock freezing his features. With whom had he fallen in love *and* committed his future to? He knew life with Alexandra Cole would never be boring, but he hadn't realized it would also be fun.

* * *

Alex shocked her parents when they walked into their kitchen early Friday morning to find their eldest daughter sitting at the table eating a bowl of oatmeal.

David's dimpled smile deepened the network of tiny lines around his obsidian eyes. "I told you we should change the locks," he said to his wife.

Alex waved her spoon. "If you change the locks, then you're going to have to change the alarm's security code."

Serena smiled at her daughter. "Never mind your father. He's as fussy as an old settin' hen, but he knows he loves it when his children come back home."

David leaned over and dropped a kiss on Alex's damp hair. "Speak for yourself, Mrs. Cole. Hi, baby," he crooned in the same breath.

Alex patted his arm. "Hi, Daddy." She smiled at her mother, who'd come over to hug her. "Hi, Mom."

Serena sat down beside her daughter. "What time did you get in?"

She and David had gotten used to their four children coming and going at odd times and hours. They would be there, then hours later jetting off to another state or country. Gabriel had become the most stable of the quartet. He loved teaching and living in Massachusetts. Even though Alex had purchased property in Virginia, she continued to travel—first for her education and now with her career.

Serena had come to realize that Ana and Jason were the least independent of her four children. And because they were twins, albeit fraternal, it would be difficult for them to sever the connection that began in the womb.

Alex swallowed a mouthful of cereal. "I got in after one."

As David filled a carafe with water to brew coffee, he

narrowed his gaze. There was something different about Alex, but he couldn't pinpoint what it was.

"If you came to hang out with Jason and Ana, then you're out of luck. They'll be in Los Angeles until next week."

Alex stared at her father, then her mother. "I didn't come to see them. I came to talk to you."

David felt his heart lurch; he mumbled a silent prayer for strength. "What about, cookie?"

Alex smiled. It'd been years since her father called her that. "Please sit down, Daddy."

Resting his left hand over his chest, long, slender fingers outstretched, David shook his head. "If what you're going to tell me is going to hurt my heart, then I'd rather not hear it."

"Sit down, David," Serena urged quietly.

Waiting until her father sat beside her mother, his right arm draped over the back of Serena's chair, Alex said, "I'm getting married."

"When?"

"To whom?"

Serena and David had spoken in unison.

Alex smiled at Serena. "When? As soon as you can get the family together." She angled her head, grinning broadly at her father. "His name is Merrick Grayslake."

David's expression did not change. He'd complained about his children not getting married, but now that Alexandra had expressed an interest in changing her marital status, he didn't feel the joy he thought he would've felt.

"Why the rush, cookie?"

"I'm pregnant."

Serena gasped, her eyes widening with each passing second while David jumped and pumped his fists in the air.

"Yes! Yes!" he shouted, cutting a dance step around the kitchen. He came back to the table and pulled Alex from her chair. He swung her around and around until both she and Serena screamed for him to stop.

"David! You could hurt the baby," Serena chastised angrily.

He set Alex gently on her feet as he managed to look contrite. "I'm sorry, cookie. It's just that the news that I'm going to be a grandfather is the best that I've had in a very long time."

"I thought winning a Grammy as Producer of the Year was the best."

"Oh, hell no," he said in protest. "The day your mama told me that I was going to become a father tops the list. Knowing that I'll be a grandfather comes in at number two."

Serena got up, filled a glass with orange juice and placed it in front of Alex. "How far along are you?"

"I just made seven weeks."

"Did you see a doctor?" Serena asked, continuing her questioning.

"Yes. He says everything looks normal."

"How and where did you meet this Grayslake dude?"

Alex rolled her eyes at her father. "He's not a dude, Daddy."

"If he's not a dude, then what is he? A she?"

"Mommy, can you talk to your husband?"

Serena leveled David a knowing look. "Please, darling. This is serious."

"So am I, Serena. Don't I have a right to know something about my future son-in-law?"

Alex took a deep breath, then let it out slowly. "Daddy, you and I will talk later, because Mom and I need to plan a wedding."

David ran a hand over his close-cropped silver hair. "Okay, cookie. When are you going back to Virginia?"

"Sunday night."

He nodded. He was outnumbered two to one, so he knew when to retreat. "Just remember to save time for your old man."

"I will, Daddy."

David filled a mug with coffee and walked out of the kitchen; an indescribable feeling filled his chest; there was going to be a wedding on the property of his Boca Raton estate for the first time; somehow he'd thought his sons would give him grandfather status, but it appeared as if his globe-trotting, art-loving daughter had beat them to it.

It no longer mattered because now his brothers would have to stop teasing him about his marriage-phobic children.

Chapter 22

Merrick's arrival in Boca Raton coincided with two inches of rain that delayed flights into and out of Florida. He and others waited more than six hours before boarding a jet scheduled to land at the Fort Lauderdale–Hollywood International Airport. He'd called Alex to inform her that he would be late, followed by a call to the hotel where he'd made a reservation to inform them of his late arrival.

Alex had insisted he stay at her parents' house, but he rejected her offer, preferring instead to reserve a suite at a nearby hotel chain. Merrick reassured her that there would be other occasions, after they were married, when he would willingly accept his in-laws' hospitality. After all, he was a stranger, a man who would marry their daughter and change her name from Cole to Grayslake, a man who had no known relatives with whom to share the joy of his upcoming nuptials.

He saw Alex before she spied him. She stood in the baggage claims area holding a sign with his name. "I'm Mr. Grayslake," he whispered, startling her. "How are you, beautiful?"

Alex lowered the placard and looped her arms under his shoulders. "I'm good. Welcome to the Sunshine State."

Merrick gave her a skeptical look before he brushed a light kiss over her mouth. "Surely you jest," he teased.

Her eyes took in his powerful presence. "Dad said it's the first hard rain in weeks."

Switching his carry-on bag to the opposite hand, he reached for her fingers. "Did you check the almanac for Saturday's weather?"

Alex gave him a sidelong glance as she led him out of the terminal. "Do you really follow what's in the almanac?"

Merrick nodded. "It's more accurate than not."

"Well, it's not going to rain on our wedding."

He lifted an eyebrow. "Why? Because you say so?"

"Yes," she said confidently.

Waiting until they were seated in a late-model Lexus sedan, Alex gave Merrick an overview of their wedding scheduled for Saturday afternoon at four, and that family members had been gathering in Florida all week since David and Serena Cole had announced their upcoming nuptials.

"Where is everyone staying?" Merrick asked as Alex maneuvered in and out of traffic like an Indy car driver.

"Most will stay in Palm and West Palm Beach. Michael and Jolene will stay with his parents at their condo. The property where we met will accommodate at least fifty. It'll be a tight fit, but it will be like a gigantic sleepover. My aunts Nancy and Josephine have enough room to put up another thirty or forty between them."

"What's on the agenda for tomorrow other than getting a license?"

"That's it. I picked up my dress yesterday and shoes earlier today."

"What about rings, Ali?"

Her mouth formed a perfect O. "I forgot about them."

"Do you want an engagement ring?"

She shook her head. "No." Alex wanted to tell Merrick that if they'd had a formal engagement period, then yes.

"Can you take a few days off for a honeymoon?"

Alex slowed and then came to a complete stop at a red light. "We can't do Venice in a few days."

"But we can do Key West."

She bit down on her lower lip to keep from screaming. "I'd love to spend my honeymoon in the Keys."

Reaching over, Merrick rested his hand on her knee. "I'll call a few places to see if we can't rent a bungalow. The summer season is over, so we should be able to find something."

"What can I do to make you change your mind about staying in a hotel?"

He squeezed her knee. "There's nothing you can do, baby. I'll meet your folks tomorrow."

"Are you worried that I'll slip into your bedroom and jump your bones?"

Throwing back his head, Merrick laughed. "There's not going to be any more bone-jumping until after we're married. Getting you pregnant before I married you was not what I'd planned."

"Are you sorry that I'm pregnant?"

Merrick heard the hitch in her voice and his heart turned over. "No, baby, I'm not sorry. But if it was the only thing that convinced you to marry in *this* century, I would've made it my business to get you pregnant the first time we slept together."

"That's diabolical and underhanded."

"All's fair in love and war, *querida*."

* * *

Merrick felt as if he were reliving New Year's Eve. There were Coles everywhere. They drifted in and out of David and Serena's house, leaving wrapped gifts and envelopes; they hugged and kissed Alex, overwhelming her until she burst into tears. He took charge of his fiancée when he led her into the house, put her to bed, staying with her until she fell asleep.

There came a soft knock on the door. Merrick left the chair next to Alex's bed, crossed the room and opened the door. Serena motioned to him. "How is she?"

Merrick smiled at the petite woman with graying reddish-brown curls. He met her gold-brown eyes, eyes she'd passed along to her four children. "She's sleeping."

Serena exhaled. "I didn't want to say anything about the baby, because that's something you and Alex should make public. I should've known she was getting overwhelmed when she stopped talking." Lowering his head, Merrick smothered a grin. "Oh, I guess you know that she talks a lot."

"One of us has to be the talkative one."

Serena rested a hand on his arm. "That's what I told David. He kept saying 'he's kind of quiet,' but I had to remind my husband that every Cole carries the loquacious gene." Standing on tiptoe, she kissed her soon-to-be son-in-law on the cheek. "Thank you for taking care of her."

Merrick met Serena's unflinching stare. "I'll always take care of her."

Turning on her heel, Serena retraced her steps. She'd told David that he had nothing to worry about. There was something about Merrick Grayslake that reminded her of David's brother, Joshua Kirkland. Both men were quiet and radiated a danger that could take the nerve of the bravest man.

She was proud of her daughter. There was no doubt she'd chosen well.

* * *

Merrick sat around the heated pool with Alex's twenty- and thirty-something relatives as catering staff unloaded their vans, setting candles out on each table. Within twenty minutes dozens of candles flickered like stars while a long table groaned under platters of food set up buffet style.

It was to be his last night as a single man, and Michael teased him about being *whipped.* He'd come to like Alex's family. They were friendly, outgoing, unpretentious and brutally honest. In a few short days they'd become his family: father, mother, brothers, sisters, cousins, aunts and uncles.

Merrick sat up straighter, going completely still when he saw Gabriel Cole with a woman from his past. He remembered her even if she didn't remember him. He stood up with the other men at their approach. Gabriel made the introductions, and when they stood in front of him Merrick noticed the stiffness in her slender body.

Gabriel smiled at Merrick. "Last, but certainly not least, is the prospective bridegroom, my soon-to-be brother-in-law, Merrick Grayslake. Merrick, this is my friend and colleague, Summer Montgomery."

Merrick wanted to tell Gabriel that he knew who she was. Casually dressed in a pair of tailored taupe slacks and an ivory-hued silk shirt, and her hair pulled off her face in a loose knot, she looked nothing like the woman he'd trained. DEA special agent Summer Montgomery had completed her training at the FBI facilities in Quantico, Virginia, and had applied to take an additional course in intelligence training. Merrick, on loan from the CIA to the FBI and the DEA, had facilitated the four-week training.

Summer inclined her head. "Merrick. Best wishes on your upcoming nuptials."

Smiling, he leaned over and kissed her cheek. "Thank you,

Renegade." He'd whispered her code name. He saw a flicker of gratitude in her eyes before she shuttered her gaze. It was apparent Gabriel Cole was totally unaware that his girlfriend was an undercover drug agent.

Not waiting for the others, Merrick went over to the serving station. Reaching for a plate, he had the servers fill it with vegetables, sliced chicken and cubed fresh fruit. He approached the table where Alex sat with Ana, Summer and Clayborne Spencer's fiancée and fellow medical student, Kim Cheung.

He placed the plate in front of Alex. Resting both hands on her shoulders, he massaged the muscles in her neck and upper back. "What do you want to drink?"

Smiling up at him over her shoulder, Alex crooned, "A fruit juice, darling."

Merrick walked away to do Alex's bidding and Ana covered her hand with her fingers. "Michael's right," she whispered. "He is *whipped!* And speaking of whipped, I owe you one, dear sister."

Alex swallowed a mouthful of avocado. Some women craved pickles and ice cream, she craved avocados. "For what?"

"For pretending you didn't know Merrick when you two were knockin' boots."

"How long have you known Merrick, Alex?" Kim asked.

"I met him New Year's Eve just like the rest of you." Alex smiled at Gabriel's girlfriend. "Everyone except Summer."

"I saw him, but I wasn't introduced to Merrick until he came to Michael's house on the Fourth," Ana said. "By that time he and Alex were knee-deep in the hot sauce."

"My sister's pissed because Miss Sherlock Holmes couldn't find out my business."

Ana wiggled her fingers. "That's because your man is tall, dark and mysterious."

Kim flipped several strands of straight black hair over her shoulder. "He's gorgeous."

"It's his eyes," Ana crooned, batting her lashes. "They're like lasers. Do they change color when he makes love to you?"

"Why don't you ask him?" Alex said, glaring at her sister.

"Ana," Kim whispered, "you shouldn't ask your sister that."

"Why not?" she asked.

"Because it's disrespectful."

"You tell her, Kim," Alex chimed in.

Summer Montgomery rested her forehead on her arms and laughed until tears rolled down her cheeks. Gabriel's sisters were like a stand-up act.

Merrick returned, carrying a glass of juice, followed by Clayborne, Gabriel and Jason, who set down plates in front of Kim, Summer and Ana.

Having assuaged her temporary pangs of hunger, Alex drank her juice, then dabbed her mouth. "Summer, you can share my room tonight because Kim will be in Ana's. Let me know if you'll need a massage, manicure, pedicure, or if you want your hair styled. Mom has contracted with a group of beauty consultants to hook us up tomorrow."

Summer flashed a wide grin. "Count me in for the massage and hair."

The women sat eating and chatting for several hours until Alex stood up. "I don't know about the rest of you, but I must get some sleep."

Pushing herself into a standing position, Summer said, "I think I'm going to join you." She smiled at Ana and Kim. "I'll see you tomorrow. Good night."

"Wait for us," Kim called out as she and Ana followed Alex and Summer.

Chapter 23

It was minutes from midnight when seven men sitting around a table lifted glasses filled with brandy and toasted Merrick Grayslake.

Jason, the mirror image of Gabriel, sans long hair and pierced ears, offered the first toast. "To Merrick, my soon-to-be brother-in-law. May your days be sunny and your nights warmer than my esteemed older brother's." First Gabriel had been teased about driving a hoopty, and now it was because he'd moved from warm sunny Florida to frigid New England.

"Hear! Hear!" came a chorus of deep male voices.

Merrick raised his glass, put it to his mouth and downed it in one swallow.

"Hot damn!" federal district court judge Christopher Delgado crowed. Slender and elegant with salt-and-pepper wavy hair, he leaned over and slapped Merrick on the back.

"You're going to fit nicely in this family because you drink like an *hombre!*"

"Are you signifying something, brother?" Michael asked his brother-in-law.

"Some male relatives…who I will not out tonight…have a problem holding their Kool-Aid."

Jason cupped his ear. "Do I hear throw down?"

Christopher smiled. "I don't know about throw down, but the last time I stepped in as bartender I heard complaints about the Kool-Aid being a wee bit too strong."

Gabriel shook his head. "Don't play yourself, Chris. You know right well that stuff you mixed up wasn't legal."

"It's as legal as I am," Chris retorted, dodging a barrage of rolled-up cocktail napkins thrown at him. "Jason, check your dad's liquor cabinet and bring out the good stuff."

Jason popped up from his chair. "I know he has the Three Kings."

"The Three Kings?" asked Algerian-born fashion designer Silah Kadir. Silah was married to Martin Cole's youngest daughter. "Are you talking about the Magi?"

Merrick laughed along with the other men. "Jason is talking about Johnny Walker, Jim Beam and Jack Daniel."

"Why do you call them Three Kings?" Silah asked in French-accented English.

Clayborne rested an arm over his uncle's shoulder. "Because if you drink enough of them you'll think you're seeing not only the kings, but also their camels."

"Go get them," Gabriel urged his younger brother. "We're here to toast Merrick, and it should be a night to remember."

Dr. Tyler Cole looped one leg over the other. Tyler, Martin's only son, was the heir apparent to the family dynasty. "Don't look for me to resuscitate any fool who gets so drunk that he'll mistake the pool for a bed."

"Grandpa told me that you were in your cups at Michael's reception." Tyler, glaring at his nephew, smothered a curse. "Did Dana give you mouth-to-mouth?"

Tyler waved a hand. "Get this young pup outta here. This is grown-folk business."

"Wait up, Jason," Clayborne called out. "I'll help you."

Leaning back in his chair, Michael extended his glass to Merrick. "Friend. Soon-to-be cousin. Welcome to the family." He, too, downed the brandy in one shot.

Someone refilled Merrick's glass and he tossed it back, the heat of the smooth liquor spreading throughout his chest. He'd never been much of a drinker, but tonight he would make an exception.

Jason and Clayborne returned with a plastic crate filled with bottles of scotch, gin, vodka, tequila and bourbon. The liquid flowed, the tongues got looser, the men toasting Merrick for having the good sense to marry into the family; eventually the conversations turned to when the men first made love to their wives and girlfriends.

Merrick got drunk, drunker than he'd ever been in his life; he was as talkative as the others with one exception: he didn't disclose the circumstances surrounding his birth, the covert missions for the CIA and the most intimate details of his relationship with Alex.

Sometime around three Gabriel climbed onto one of the chaises set up around the pool and fell asleep.

It was Serena Cole who found Christopher, Tyler and Silah asleep on the deck of the pool. Michael, Jason, Merrick and Clayborne managed to make it into the house, falling asleep where they lay.

None had made it to their designated bedrooms.

Merrick tied the light gray silk tie in a Windsor knot, then turned down the spread collar on the white shirt. When he'd

finally regained consciousness earlier that morning it was to
a pounding headache, but after several aspirins washed down
with black coffee he felt more human than he had in hours.

The male bonding/mock bachelor party was unlike any in
which he'd participated. Grown men had become boys, fueled
by an alcoholic haze wherein they'd confessed their shortcom-
ings. To the world they were rich, powerful, successful men;
however, they displayed their very human side when they spoke
of the difficulties of parenting and their willingness to compromise in order to save their marriages. Merrick would've
thought them conventional, but the various tattoos and ear
piercings that crossed generations shattered that perception.

Sitting on the leather bench at the foot of the bed in the
suite that had belonged to Gabriel, Merrick closed his eyes
and did what he hadn't done in a very long time—he prayed.
He was still in the same position, eyes closed, when Jason
knocked on the door and walked in.

Tall, broad-shouldered, he cut a handsome figure in formal
attire. His silk tie matched Merrick's. "Thinking about
backing out, Brother Merrick?"

Merrick's head came up at the same time he stood up.
Reaching for the jacket to his tuxedo on the foot of the bed,
he slipped his arms into the sleeves.

"No."

Jason flashed a dimpled smile. "It's time we get going, but
Dad wants to see you downstairs in his study before you
marry my sister."

Merrick followed Jason down a curving staircase of a house
constructed in three sections. The elder Coles occupied one
section that included a guest wing, the four bedroom suites took
up another section and the third section contained a state-of-
the-art recording studio and Serenity Records' corporate office.

Merrick walked into the large cool room with floor-to-ceiling shelves packed with books and musical scores. A large glass-top rosewood desk and matching table complemented leather chairs in a rich maroon.

David Cole was not alone. His brothers, Martin and Joshua Kirkland—the latter the result of an illicit liaison between Samuel Cole and Teresa Maldonado Kirkland—sons Jason and Gabriel, and Matthew Sterling, family friend and father-in-law to Emily Kirkland Delgado, made the large room appear small. The men, all in formal dress, staring at Merrick radiated power and danger, and if he hadn't been who he was he would've been intimidated. However, he'd experienced too much, stared death in the face too often to be intimidated—by anything or *anyone*.

David, who sat on the edge of the desk, rose to his feet. Recessed light glinted off his silver hair. "Merrick, I've asked you to come here because there is something I must say to you. I've asked my brothers, sons and a lifelong friend to be here because I want them to be aware of what's in my heart at this moment.

"In fifteen minutes I will place my daughter's hand in yours. And when that happens I will relinquish all claim and responsibility for Alexandra. My wife and my children are my most precious gifts, and I'm generously offering you the gift of my eldest daughter.

"I will say this only once, Merrick Grayslake. Love her, and protect her with your life. But if you fail to do this, then look for me to come after you."

The nostrils of Merrick's aquiline nose flared as he let out the breath he'd been holding. His future father-in-law had just threatened him. He blinked once. "Warning heeded, David." His eyes widened. "You've had your say, so let me have mine. At four o'clock Alexandra will become *my* wife and therefore it will become *my* responsibility to protect her.

"I love her and the child she carries in her womb. And because I love her, I've broken a vow I made almost three years ago when I said I'd never go back to the CIA. Well, I'm going back because I'll have a wife and child to support." He paused for effect. "So, that should put your mind at ease as to whether I have a job." Everyone turned and stared at David, who managed to look sheepish.

"No, you didn't, David," Gabriel said softly.

"Damn, brother, that's cold," Joshua Kirkland whispered, shaking his head in disbelief.

Merrick lowered his head, hiding his own grin when Martin Cole and Matthew Sterling dissolved into a paroxysm of laughter that left them with tears in their eyes.

His head came up and he stared at David. "I don't have as much money as Alexandra, but I can assure you that I can support her and the children we plan to have." He nodded to the other men. "I don't know about you guys, but I have a wedding to go to in three minutes." Turning on his heels, he walked out of the study, leaving his bride's family members staring at his retreating back.

Martin Cole's silver hair was a startling contrast to his deeply tanned olive-brown skin. Shaking his head, he glared at his younger brother. "David, you never cease to amaze me. Why the hell did you have to ask the man if he had a job?"

Crossing his arms over his chest, Joshua continued to stare at his half brother, green eyes sparkling in amusement. "If you'd wanted to know about Merrick you could've asked Michael."

"Dad would never do that," Jason said. "Whenever it concerns Alex or Ana he goes straight for the jugular. He wasn't even diplomatic about it. He could've said, 'By the way, my man, are you a scrub?'"

Matthew Sterling stared at Jason. "Scrub?"

"Pimp, gigolo, deadbeat—"

"I get the picture, Jason," Matt interrupted.

Martin patted David's back. "I know all of this is new for you, but you'll get through it." All of Martin's children were married and had made him a grandfather of five.

Joshua took David's arm. "Come on, brother. After the first time it gets easier."

David narrowed his eyes at his brothers. They'd teased him for years about his children not wanting to marry and have children. But all of the teasing would come to an end in a few minutes.

Shaking off his brother's hands, he walked out of the study to give his daughter away in marriage to a man he now respected enough to think of him as a son.

Chapter 24

Alex was certain her father could feel her trembling as she clung to his arm. She'd decided on simplicity: no brides-maids, groomsmen, ring bearer or flower girl. Her father would escort her over a red carpet to where Merrick waited with a judge to make her his wife.

She closed her eyes when Gabriel sang her favorite song, the top-chart blockbuster classic hit "I Will Always Love You." Gabriel's fingers skimmed the keyboard as his melodious voice came through the powerful speakers and something within her burst.

Alex wasn't certain it was the fullness of the love she felt for Merrick, the hormonal changes playing havoc with her moods or the knowledge that within minutes her life would change dramatically. The times when she thought only of herself and what made her happy were over. Every decision she made would be predicated on its effect on her husband and child.

The tears flowed down her face, landing on the bouquet of white lacecap hydrangeas with dozens of faux-pearl sprays, bead flowers, seashell flowers and seashells on wires tied with yards of ribbons in different widths and edging. The song ended with many seated on the organza-draped cushioned chairs blotting the corners of their eyes.

The assembled rose as one when Gabriel played the familiar chords to the wedding march.

"Let's go, cookie," David murmured to his still-weeping daughter.

Alex wanted to move, but her legs refused to follow the dictates of her brain. "I can't, Daddy," she sobbed.

Murmurs escalated when David Cole wrapped his arms around his daughter's bare shoulders. "If you don't want to marry him, then say so, cookie."

Alex shook her head. She wanted to marry Merrick. He'd been the only man she'd ever wanted to marry. "I want him, Daddy."

David kissed her hair, careful not to dislodge the tiny rosebuds pinned into her black curly hair. All he'd ever wanted from the moment he became a father was to protect his children and see to their happiness. But as Merrick had stated so arrogantly, Alex was no longer his responsibility. It was now up to Merrick Grayslake to protect his daughter and unborn grandchild.

Merrick watched the interchange between his bride and her father, his heart racing uncontrollably. Had she changed her mind? Did she wait until the very moment that they were to exchange vows to change her mind?

He'd heard of Dear John letters, brides and grooms being left at the altar and runaway brides. Was he, he agonized, about to become another statistic?

A sense of strength came to Merrick, one stronger than any he'd experienced in the past. He'd languished in foster and group homes, endured verbal and physical abuse and still managed to survive. He did not give his heart to a woman only to lose her in front of hundreds of people.

"I'll be back," he said to the elderly black-robed judge watching the unfolding scene with an expression of distress on his lined face.

Gasps filled the warm autumn afternoon when Merrick marched down the red carpet like a marine during a dress parade. He rested a hand on her back and she went completely still.

"*Querida.*"

Alex felt the comforting touch on her bare flesh, inhaled the familiar cologne. She couldn't move, couldn't go to Merrick so he'd come for her. Turning, she smiled up at him through her lashes. The moisture had turned her eyes into pools of gold.

Her lips parted in a trembling smile. "*Mi, amor.*"

David reached for Alex's hand and placed it in Merrick's outstretched one. "Take her."

Reaching into the pocket of his dress trousers for a handkerchief, Merrick gently blotted the tears on his bride's face. Lowering his head, he kissed her forehead. "Are you ready to do this?"

She wrinkled her pert nose. "Yes."

Alex looped her hand over the sleeve of Merrick's jacket as he retraced his steps, bringing them to stand in front of the elderly judge who'd officiated at many a Cole civil wedding. He winked at Alex, then began the ceremony he could recite in his sleep.

Merrick's voice was strong and clear as he took his vows. His gaze never strayed from Alex's face as she recited hers.

He loved her, had openly confessed to loving her, had shown her in the most intimate way possible that he loved her, but he doubted whether she knew the depth of the love he felt for her.

When it came time for the exchange of rings he reached into his breast pocket and slipped a diamond eternity band onto her slender finger. Alex handed her bouquet to her father as she took the platinum band off her thumb and slipped it onto Merrick's left hand.

Sighs of relief, cheering and whistles followed the judge's pronouncement that Merrick and Alexandra Grayslake were now man and wife. Looping his arms around her waist, Merrick picked up his wife and kissed her soundly on the mouth.

"Congratulations, Mrs. Grayslake."

Her dimples deepened when she flashed a joyous smile. "And congratulations to you, too, Mr. Grayslake." Tightening her hold around his neck, she kissed him again. "I can't believe we're married."

"Believe it, baby," he whispered, "because I'm going to remind you of it every day and every night."

He set her on her feet, one arm going around her waist as he shook hands with David. "Scared you for a moment, didn't it?" he asked his father-in-law.

"Hell, yeah," David admitted. He patted Merrick's shoulder. "You did good, son."

Serena came over and kissed her daughter, then her new son-in-law. "Congratulations."

Merrick wound his free arm around Serena's trim waist. "Thank you, Mrs. Cole, for your daughter and putting everything together so quickly."

Frowning, Serena shook her head slowly. "You call my husband David and me Mrs. Cole?"

Merrick's eyebrows lifted. "What do you want me to call you?"

"Mom will do nicely, thank you."

Merrick was momentarily speechless in his surprise. His foster mothers had wanted him to call them Mom or Mother, but he'd never been able to bring himself to do it. Not when they saw him as a check from the state, not when they punished him for what they'd considered the slightest infraction.

Today his life changed when he became husband, son and brother-in-law. It had taken him nearly thirty-six years to find a family he could claim as his own.

"From now on it will be Mom, Mom." He nodded to David. "I'm going to take Ali to the table where she can get off her feet."

"Are you all right?" Serena asked her daughter.

"I'm good, Mom. I'm going to skip the receiving-line routine."

"Why, cookie?" David couldn't believe Alex wanted to break the tradition.

"I don't know what it is, but since I've become pregnant I can't stand crowds of people. I freak out if they get too close to me."

"Don't tell me you're not going to save your father a dance."

"Of course I am. Do you think I'm going to cheat you out of that honor?"

"I hope not," David mumbled. He took Serena's arm. "Come, sweetheart, let's circulate."

Merrick steered her over to where a table had been set up for the bride, the groom and her parents, parents that he now thought of as his own.

Prerecorded music blared from speakers set up on the property and the partying began in earnest. Those who came over to greet Alex found her ravishing in an off-the-shoulder platinum gown with a sunburst-pleated silk-chiffon bodice topping a silk-satin skirt. The garment was perfect for her petite figure. Three inches of jeweled Manolo Blahnik wedding sling backs put the top of her head at six-foot-three-inch Merrick's shoulder.

She'd decided on a buffet rather than a more formal sit-down dinner. The caterer had delivered dozens of tables, each with seating for six. Vases of pale-colored roses lined the courtyard and patio.

David had hired a disc jockey to spin tunes, and a portable dance floor had been set up between the pool and tennis court. Serena had the pool covered, much to the disappointment of the younger children.

Merrick pressed his shoulder to Alex's bare arm. "You have the same food on your plate, so why is it you're eating mine?"

"Whoever fixed my plate added salt."

"I would've gotten you another plate, Ali."

She rested her head on his shoulder. "That's all right."

Angling his head, he kissed her hair. "Are you all right?" She'd seemed out of sorts after dancing with him, her father and then her brothers.

"I'm feeling a little tired."

Merrick knew her little tired was more than that. There were times when she was so lethargic that she fell asleep while eating. "We're leaving."

Her head came up, and suddenly she was wide awake. "We can't leave now."

"And why not?"

"It's too soon."

"Soon for what, Ali? You're lethargic and out of sorts. Have you forgotten that you're two months pregnant?"

"How can I forget?" she countered. "Between the nausea and fatigue I feel like a punching bag."

"That's why we're leaving." Rising, he eased her up from her chair. "We'll change, then head over to the hotel." They'd made plans to spend their wedding night in a hotel before driving down to the Keys the following morning.

"You're a bully, Merrick Grayslake," she hissed through clenched teeth.

"Yeah, yeah," he drawled. "A bully who loves you and that little baby inside you."

Leaning against his side to keep her footing, Alex permitted Merrick to lead her back to the house where she'd grown up. She thought about his comment that he loved the baby inside her. How could he love something he'd never met or seen?

There were other questions she wanted to ask her enigmatic husband, but Alex decided to wait, wait until after they returned from their honeymoon.

PART THREE

Silent Witness

Chapter 25

CIA Headquarters...Langley, Virginia

Leaning back in his chair, Merrick pinched the bridge of his nose with his thumb and forefinger. His eyes were burning from nonstop reading. The terrorist act of September 11 had changed the course of action for securing America's borders and its citizens.

He'd spent the past week reading about new and updated security protocol that had been put in place within days of the horrific destruction of the World Trade Center.

Merrick forced his concentration away from what he'd mentally recorded to that of his wife. He and Alex had celebrated their third month of marriage the night before. Even though she professed she wanted a quiet dinner at home, he overrode her protests and took her out to one of her favorite D.C. eating establishments.

Alex was now in her second trimester and without warning her nausea had vanished along with her lethargy. The gradual changes in her body made her pregnancy more obvious. Her face was fuller, as were her breasts, and she'd lost her waistline.

She'd contacted the National Trust, applying for a transfer to the southeast region; however, her request was denied because there were no liaison positions available. Alex existed in a blue funk for one day, tendered her resignation, then called a real estate company to set up an appointment to show her properties for their new home.

He'd been at the Company for a month, and his time was spent reading and sitting in on meetings—meetings that were of no interest or consequence to him, meetings with low-level clerks with years of seniority. He'd come back as an intelligence training specialist and so far he hadn't trained anyone.

The phone on his desk rang, and he sat up and picked up the receiver. "Grayslake."

"Mr. Ashleigh would like to see you in his office—*now.*"

Merrick hung up without verifying whether he would or wouldn't comply with the assistant director's directive. Shirt cuffs rolled up over his wrists, top button on his shirt undone and tie hanging loosely around his collar, he walked out of his closet of an office to a larger one at the end of the hall.

"Go on in," drawled a woman whose face was reminiscent of an overripe pumpkin.

Merrick met her intimidating gaze with one of his own as he brushed past her desk. He entered Carl Ashleigh's office silently, startling the man with the cold, pale blue eyes.

Carl waved a hand toward a chair facing his desk. "Sit down, Grayslake." Waiting until Merrick was seated he laced his fingers together atop a stack of papers. "I know you've been waiting for me to assign you to a training class, but I'm afraid that's not going to happen for a while."

Crossing one leg over the other, Merrick rested his elbows on the arms of the chair. "How long is awhile?"

"At least another six months."

Merrick did not visibly react to the response that he had come back to work to sit around, collect a government check and do absolutely nothing.

"Why did you bring me back now if you knew there wasn't a position for me?" What he wanted to tell Ashleigh was that he could've stayed home with his pregnant wife to await the birth of their first child.

A band of red crept up Ashleigh's neck to his face and hairline. "I have a position, but it's not what you'd requested." A hard edge had crept into his voice.

Merrick leveled a gaze at him. "What do you have?"

Ashleigh paused, hoping to make Grayslake uncomfortable. He knew about the man's pretty, young wife, and that they had a baby on the way. He knew everything there was to know about Merrick Grayslake except how to unnerve him.

"How's your marksmanship?"

Merrick didn't blink. "With what? Pistol or rifle?"

"How about a PSG-1?"

A muscle in Merrick's jaw jumped. "One shot, one kill."

Every branch in the military used snipers: the SEALs, CCT, and Army Rangers. And although they all had their respective sniper elements, there was one school that stood out from the others: the United States Marine Corps Scout Sniper School.

"We need a sniper instructor, and because you're Scout Sniper Qualified, you're the perfect candidate."

"*You* want *me* to train agents to become snipers?"

Ashleigh shook his head. "Not me, Grayslake, your *country.*"

Merrick's cold smile never reached his eyes. "Because you put it that way how can I refuse?"

It'd always been the triumvirate: country, Corps and

mission. The trinity would always be there, but along the way he'd added family.

"Do you still have your rifle?"

"Yes." He'd stored his rifle in a special case, and hidden it beneath the floorboards in a closet in West Virginia.

"I recommend you dust it off and start practicing."

"When do exercises begin?"

"The first Monday in January." Ashleigh knew he had to keep Merrick busy until he received word that Operation Backslap was ready to be executed.

Merrick nodded. He had about two weeks to bring himself up-to-date on the rigorous ten-week-long course broken down into three phases—land navigation and marksmanship, stalking techniques, field skills and fire rehearsals—and the last that encompassed everything from communications to surveillance performance.

"How many will be in the class?"

"Five."

Uncrossing his legs, he placed both feet on the floor. "I'll be ready."

That said, he pushed off the chair and walked out of Ashleigh's office. Sniper training wasn't what he wanted to do, but it was better than sitting around doing nothing.

Merrick placed Alex on her side on the thick, thirsty towel covering the bed, then took his time drying her body. It'd become a nightly ritual for them to share a shower. She let out a moan when he kneaded the muscles in her legs.

"Am I hurting you?"

She smiled, not opening her eyes. "Are you kidding? It feels wonderful."

"What on earth did you do today?" The muscles in her calves were tight as fists.

"I did a lot of walking up and down staircases. One house had an attic and a basement, so that was four flights."

"Do you really want a house that big?"

"The question should be, do *we* need a big house, Merrick."

"Do we, baby?"

She smiled. "Yes."

"There's going to be only three of us." Sonogram pictures showed one baby—a girl.

"Three for now. What about in a couple of years? I don't want to decorate a house, then leave it when we outgrow it."

His hands moved up her thighs. "How many babies do you plan on having?"

She moaned again. "As many as you plan on making."

Lowering his head, he pressed a kiss to the nape of her neck. "Realistically, we could have one every year until you're about forty."

"That's madness! There's no way I'm going to have ten kids."

"Why not? We could name them Pull Out, Quick on the Draw, Rhythm. That is, if we decide to use the rhythm method, Oops, my bad."

Alex couldn't help herself as she burst out laughing. It wasn't often that her very serious husband displayed his wicked sense of humor.

Merrick removed the towel and lay down next to Alex, his chest against her back. He placed an arm over her waist, his hand cradling her rounded belly.

"Don't make any appointments for house tours this weekend."

"Why not? I thought you'd want to go with me."

"I can't because we have to go to Bolivar."

Alex stiffened. "For what?"

"I have to pick up something."

"Can you identify what the something is?"

"It's a sniper rifle."

Alex threw off his arm and sat up, but he eased her back down to the mattress. "What the hell do you need with a sniper rifle, Merrick? You told me that you sit at a desk. Do you plan to go into the office and shoot up the place? Or perhaps you're thinking of becoming another D.C. Sniper."

"You don't know what you're talking about."

"Enlighten me, Merrick. Please tell me why you need a weapon that can make someone's head explode with one bullet."

"There will be some things I can tell you, and others that I can't because they're classified."

"Is this sniper business classified?"

"No. I've been assigned to facilitate sniper training."

"Why you, Merrick?" Her voice was softer, calmer.

"I was a sniper in the Corps, and the Marine Corps has the best sniper program in the world."

"You're just going to do training?"

"Yes, Ali."

She covered the hand over her swollen belly, whispering a prayer of thanks. Alex didn't know what she would do if Merrick put himself in danger. "I'm sorry I went off on you."

He kissed her damp hair. "I can think of a way for you to apologize for jumping to conclusions."

"How?"

He kissed her again. "Sit on me."

"You really like it when I ride you?"

His smile was dazzling. "I love it." Merrick loved when Alex became the aggressor in bed.

Alex sat up and straddled him as he supported his back against the headboard. Together they found a rhythm that took them to heaven and back. Leaning into Merrick, she pressed her full breasts to his chest, rested her head between his neck and shoulder and counted the strong steady beats of his heart. There was never a time when they made love that they hadn't become one with each other.

Chapter 26

The chiming of the telephone roused Merrick from a deep sleep. Reaching out in the darkened bedroom, he took the cordless instrument off its cradle before it disturbed Alex.

"Yes," he whispered into the receiver.

"You don't know who I am, but I know all about you, Merrick Grayslake." The distorted voice of a man speaking fluent Spanish came through the earpiece. It was apparent whoever had called him was using a device that scrambled or distorted the voice.

"Who are you?" Merrick asked in the same language.

"I can't tell you that. Not now."

"What do you want?"

"How would you like to avenge your mother's murder?"

Merrick depressed a button, disconnecting the caller. "Sick bastard," he whispered as he practically slammed the instrument down on the bedside table.

Fluffing up his pillow, he tried going back to sleep, but sleep was elusive. The caller knew his name, his home phone number and knew that he was fluent in Spanish. If the man hadn't mentioned his mother perhaps he wouldn't have been so disturbed.

There had been a time when he would've given anything to glean a modicum of information about Victoria Grayslake, but that time had passed. It took more than forty minutes before he finally fell asleep for the second time that night.

Merrick hadn't sat down behind his desk yet when his phone rang. He picked up after the second ring. "Grayslake."

"Don't hang up on me again or you'll be very, very sorry."

It was the same person who'd called him at home. "Are you threatening me?" Merrick asked softly. Whoever had rung him the night before knew he worked at the CIA. He was glad the call had come in at the Agency because it would be easily traced.

"No, I'm not threatening you."

"It sounded like a threat to me," Merrick countered.

"I need to talk to you."

"You're talking now," he said sarcastically.

"What I need to tell you shouldn't be recorded. I know every call you make and receive is recorded. And don't try to trace this number, because the phone will be in the garbage as soon as I hang up."

"What do you want?"

"I want a number where I can call you without the government listening in."

Merrick's curiosity was piqued. "I'll get a phone that's unlisted."

"I'll send you a phone you can use."

"When?"

"I'll have it delivered to your post office box in West Virginia. It'll be waiting for you when you get there."

"How…" Merrick's voice trailed off when he heard the break in the connection. "Who the hell are you?" he said aloud.

Was someone trying to mess with his head? Was he being set up? Not given to episodes of paranoia, he sat down and went through a mental recall of places he'd been, people he'd met and situations wherein his identity might have been compromised.

He had lots of questions and no answers. At least not one until he went to Bolivar.

Merrick turned up the heat to the highest setting as he navigated the winding West Virginia roads. "Better?" he asked Alex.

"Much better." She'd tied a cashmere shawl tightly around her neck and shoulders. "This is one year that I'm really looking forward to spending a week in Florida."

"Let's hope the cold weather doesn't go any farther south."

Winter had come early to the East Coast with below-freezing temperatures from Maine to Georgia. Only Florida had been spared.

Alex turned and stared at her husband's profile. "Are you sure you're not going to be able to take off Christmas Eve?"

"Baby, let's not start that again. I told you we'll probably shut down early, but I can't take the day. Barring airport delays, I will be in Florida before midnight."

He and Alex had celebrated Thanksgiving in Mississippi with Tyler and Dana as their hosts. It'd become an impromptu family reunion with the second generation of Coles, Kirklands, Delgados and Lassisters coming together under one roof. Gabriel's date, Summer Montgomery, was now his fiancée.

Pushing out her lower lip, Alex pouted as she'd done as a child when she couldn't get her way. "Stop it!" she screamed when Merrick reached over and tugged on her lip.

"Stop pouting. It's not going to get me to change my mind."

Her expression brightened. "I can think of something else that will get you to change your mind."

Merrick gave her a sidelong grin. "Not even that!"

She gave him a saucy smile. "We'll see."

"In another couple of months we're going to have to stop the calisthenics."

Alex lifted her eyebrows. "Why?"

"Because your belly will get in the way."

She rolled her eyes and sucked her teeth. "Don't be so parochial, *mi amor.* We can always do it doggy style."

Merrick opened his mouth and closed it just as quickly, stunned by his wife's bluntness. "You've got to stop reading those books."

"What books?" Alex asked innocently.

"The ones you hide in the basket with the towels."

"They're how-to books for pregnant women. And I don't hide them. I read them whenever I'm in the bathroom."

"I've seen the pictures and they're just plain nasty, baby. You'd have to be a contortionist to execute some of those positions."

"Where are you going?" Alex asked when Merrick took a route that led away from their home.

"I have to stop at the post office. Do you want to come in with me?"

"No, thank you. I'll wait in the truck. Can you please pick up some Christmas stamps? This weekend is as good a time as any to do Christmas cards." Alex had brought boxes of cards and several needlecraft projects with her to pass the time in Bolivar.

A quarter of a mile later, Merrick parked in a lot behind a row of stores, not bothering to turn off the engine; he got out and went into the post office. Inserting a key into his box, he took out several pieces of junk mail and a small white box addressed to him. He lingered, opening it. His mystery caller had sent four disposable cell phones, each with a thirty-minute limit.

Pushing the phones, no larger than an iPod or thicker than a credit card, into the back pocket of his jeans, he discarded the box and returned to the parking lot. The serial numbers on the back of the phones were sequential. That was a clue in attempting to trace where the phones were purchased, and by whom.

Merrick hoped the man wouldn't contact him until Monday because he wanted to enjoy two uninterrupted days with his wife.

The smell of baking apples wafted throughout the second story as Merrick opened the door to the bedroom he used for storage. He removed a footlocker and steamer trunk, then went to his knees and pressed gently on the edge of a wooden floorboard. It lifted easily. He did the same with another, then another. Concealed under the floor was a large oaken case that contained his coveted PSG-1 that had been made to fit his body's dimensions.

He opened the case, staring at the smooth stock and the various scopes. If the Corps's slogan was "the proud, the few," then he had become an expert marksman with a deeply ingrained understanding of what it meant to be a sniper.

Merrick opened the footlocker and removed several automatic handguns and ammunition; the closet floorboards had become the perfect place for concealing his arsenal of weapons. Where, he thought, would he be able to conceal the cache of arms in the Arlington condo?

Alex had embarked on a house-hunting campaign, while he'd assumed an attitude of indifference toward the undertaking. However, the day of reckoning could not be put off too much longer. They had to move, and he had to find a place in which to totally secure his weaponry.

Merrick had knelt down to replace the floorboards when

he heard movement behind him. Turning around, he saw Alex standing in the doorway to the bedroom, her gaze fixed on the holstered automatic handguns. She glanced up, her expression a mix of fear and revulsion.

Rising slowly to his feet, Merrick closed the distance between them. He reached out to touch her, but Alex took a step backward. "*Querida,* please."

Alex shook her head. "No, Merrick. Don't ask me to understand. I don't like guns, especially in my home."

"I'll make certain you'll never see them."

She gave him a long, penetrating stare. "You do that. I came up to tell you that dinner is ready."

Merrick watched her leave, unable to do or say anything that would convince his wife that the cache of weapons posed no threat to her.

Chapter 27

Three days before she was scheduled to leave for Florida, Alex found the perfect house in Old Town, the core of historic Alexandria. The unoccupied redbrick home, dating back to the nineteenth century, boasted an updated kitchen and bathrooms. Five bedrooms with adjoining baths and sitting rooms would provide ample space for living and entertaining. She'd toured the area by car and had fallen in love with the abundance of antique shops lining King Street.

"I want it," she told the real estate agent.

"Don't you want your husband to see it before you make a decision?"

Alex stared at the smartly dressed middle-aged woman as if she'd spoken a language she didn't understand. "There is no doubt my husband will like it."

"It's…it's just that I've had situations in the past where the wife wants something her husband doesn't and vice versa."

Opening her handbag, Alex took out her checkbook. "How much are you asking as a down payment?" The agent quoted a figure, and she wrote the check. "I'm due to deliver a baby in less than five months. I'd like to be settled in my new home before the end of January." She handed the startled woman the check. "Please call me when you confirm a date for closing."

Alex walked out of the house and made her way down the street to where she'd parked her car, her mind filled with how she wanted to decorate the remarkable structure. She no longer worked for the Trust, but she would have her own piece of history to preserve. Browsing for antiques germane to the period would become an ongoing project to keep her occupied until her daughter's birth and many years after.

When the obstetrician had disclosed that she was having a girl, Alex was overcome with joy. She'd begun planning all of the activities they would share: baking cookies, tea parties and browsing antique shops. Alex shuddered to think she wouldn't have a girly-girl, that her daughter would prefer firearms and restoring old cars and trucks to shopping.

Sitting in her car, she dialed the number to Merrick's cell phone. It rang twice before he answered. "I found it!"

"Found what, Ali?"

"Our house. I just put a down payment on it."

"Where is it?"

"Alexandria. It's a little pricey, but it's worth it, Merrick."

"Can we talk about this when I get home?"

A frown appeared between her eyes. "I hope we're not going to argue about money."

"Did I mention money, Alexandra?"

"You're upset, Merrick."

"Why do you say I'm upset?"

"Because you called me Alexandra. You only call me that when you're angry."

"Look, baby, I'm not angry. I don't know what the house is selling for and I don't care. If you like it, then we'll buy it."

Tears filled her eyes at the same time she bit down on her lower lip. "Thank you, darling."

He laughed softly. "You're welcome, darling. I'll see you when I get home."

"What do you want for dinner?"

"You."

Before Alex could reply or react, Merrick hung up. She sat in the car, staring through the windshield, unable to believe she could feel so incredibly happy, that her life could be so incredibly perfect.

Merrick Grayslake had come into her life when she wanted nothing to do with men. He'd become a friend, one who'd slipped under the barrier she'd created to keep all men at a distance because of her master plan. He'd waited patiently for her to complete her education, then wooed her with the skill and finesse of a libertine. And she'd taken the bait and let him reel her in.

She'd fallen in love, gotten pregnant and married. All the things she'd professed not wanting to do. But that was before she met Merrick Grayslake. His claim that he never wanted to marry or father children was shattered the moment they went from friends to lovers.

Alex closed her eyes. They would soon celebrate a new year, and she looked forward to celebrating a new life with her new husband in their new home.

Putting the key in the ignition, she started up the car and adjusted the heat. Meteorologists were predicting a white Christmas. Alex hoped the snowstorm would bypass Virginia and blow out to sea. She was so looking forward to spending the week in Florida with her extended family. She'd done all of her Christmas shopping and had shipped the gifts from her and Merrick to her uncle Martin's house in West Palm Beach.

Every year there seemed to be a new Cole baby, and it was becoming more difficult to keep up with the names that now spanned five generations.

She and Merrick had gone over names and had decided on Victoria Cole-Grayslake. The little girl would be faced with the daunting task of being a Cole, but there was no doubt she would succeed, because the Coles *and* the Grayslakes were survivors.

Merrick's phone rang just as he closed and locked his desk. He glanced at the wall clock. It was three minutes before he was scheduled to leave for the day. Most times he worked beyond his dismissal because he wanted to avoid rush-hour traffic. He and Alex usually did not sit down to dinner until seven, so he did not see the need to rush out with the other office workers.

"Grayslake." He'd decided to answer the call.

"I'm going to call you once you reach your car."

Merrick froze. It was the first contact he'd had with the mystery caller since he'd picked up the cell phones. And how, he mused, did the person know he was leaving for the day? Was something at the CIA monitoring his whereabouts?

"I assume you're going to call me on the phone with the lowest serial number?"

"You assume right. I'll call you in a few minutes."

Merrick was tempted not to leave, but then what? Would the sicko call him back on the government's line? He would leave as planned. Whoever it was that sought to push his buttons had succeeded because he was anxious to uncover just what the person wanted.

It took Merrick ten minutes to get an elevator and make it down to the parking lot. As soon as he sat behind the wheel, the disposable phone rang.

"What do you want?" His greeting was brusque, rude, but he was beyond caring about social etiquette.

"I want you to meet me."

"Where?" Merrick listened when he was told the address. "That's not a very nice neighborhood," he drawled sarcastically.

"That's why I want you to meet me there. The only vermin you'll encounter will be of the two- and four-legged variety."

He'd been instructed to go to a crime-infested section of D.C. only blocks from where he'd been assaulted and left to die years before. Unlocking the glove compartment, he took out a small automatic handgun and secured it in the small of his back.

"Come alone and come unarmed."

"I'm coming alone."

"Don't bring the firearm."

It was too dark in the parking lot for Merrick to see if someone was watching every move he made. After all, he was sitting in the parking lot at CIA headquarters with high-tech surveillance equipment everywhere.

"Goodbye."

"Wait...don't hang up."

A small smile of triumph parted Merrick's lips. "Are you saying I can bring the gun?"

"Bring it. Come to the second floor. I'll see you in an hour."

The call ended and Merrick saw a message flashing the number of remaining minutes. Their conversation had lasted exactly two minutes.

Merrick started up his truck, driving away from Langley toward southeast D.C. He hadn't gotten more than a mile when he remembered Alex's phone call about finding a house. He activated the hands-free device and dialed her number.

"Hi, baby."

Merrick smiled. "Hi, yourself. I'm calling to let you know I'll be late."

"How late?"

"I'm not certain. But I don't think it's going to take too long. Put away your pots. We'll eat out tonight, and then you can show me our new house."

"Thank you, Merrick!"

His smile widened. "You're welcome, Ali."

Merrick continued to talk to his wife until he turned down the street to the address his caller had given him. Slowing, he peered at the dilapidated and burned-out buildings lining the block. A hand-painted number in fluorescent paint shimmered in the darkness on the last house on the street. Someone really wanted him to find the building. He parked across the street.

Merrick alighted from his truck at the same time he reached around his back and gripped the handle of the holstered automatic. The gun was small enough for him to palm it easily.

He entered the building, waiting for his eyes to adjust to the light from a dim naked bulb hanging from a frayed wire. He tested the first stair. It groaned beneath his weight, but held. Counting the number of stairs, he made it to the second-floor landing. Firearm drawn, he knocked on the door.

"Come in," ordered the diffused voice.

Pushing open the door, Merrick was assailed with the smell of stale urine and other unidentifiable odors. He automatically reached for a wall switch but quickly discovered there was no electricity. There came the distinctive scrape of a match, followed by the smell of sulfur, then the weak flickering flame of a candle.

"Sit down," came the disembodied voice. Merrick complied, reaching for a wooden crate, and sat down. "This will not take long because I know you want to go home to your very pretty wife."

"Who the hell are you?"

"You don't need to know who I am. Not yet."

"And you don't need to bring my wife into this," Merrick retorted.

"She's in it because she *is* your wife."

"This is not about her, is it?"

"No. It's about your mother."

Merrick closed his eyes. "What about her?"

"I know who killed Victoria Grayslake."

Chapter 28

Merrick swayed slightly before righting himself. He tightened his grip on the gun butt. "Why are you telling me this?" His query was whispered. "Why don't you expose the murderer?"

"She wasn't my mother."

"She abandoned me, so why should I feel anything for her?"

"She abandoned you to save your life."

Merrick closed his eyes for several seconds. "In other words she sacrificed herself for me?"

"It was the ultimate sacrifice. Your mother was an undercover DEA special agent assigned to the Mexican border region. She'd infiltrated a group who'd operated openly and without impunity between the U.S. and Mexico.

"She'd been assigned to gather evidence to put several high-ranking Mexican Federales, at least eight U.S. Border Patrol agents and two Texas and Arizona ranchers in prison for the rest of their lives.

"Victoria, who'd discovered she was pregnant, requested a leave but before she was scheduled to depart Mexico she was abducted and held prisoner until it was time for her to give birth."

"Are you saying someone blew her cover?" Merrick asked perceptively.

"Yes. A senior agent gave her up."

"What happened?"

"Victoria was flown by private jet to a ranch in south Texas where she delivered a son. The baby boy was left in a church. Victoria's body was discovered weeks later in a shallow grave near the Mexican border. She'd been tortured, her tongue cut out, then shot in the back of the head."

"How do you know all this? And why are you telling me about something that happened more than thirty years ago?"

"I was her partner on one undercover mission, and I swore an oath that I would always protect her."

"It's apparent you didn't protect her. What do you expect me to do?" Merrick asked.

"I want you to expose the man who eventually became an associate director for the DEA. I want you to bring down the son of a bitch who ordered the hit on Victoria Grayslake."

"You expect me to take revenge for someone I never knew?"

"I can understand your reluctance, but Victoria gave up everything to have you. If she hadn't compromised her mission you wouldn't be here. She forfeited her life so that you could enjoy your life, your wife and await the birth of your own child."

Merrick longed to spring across the space and snatch the man by the throat. He wanted to know who was it that knew so much about him. "What do you mean she compromised her mission?"

"She cut a deal—her baby for the identities of undercover field agents."

"How do you know this?"

"It was on videotape. It sent shock waves through the DEA. Agents were pulled, assigned to desk duty or transferred to other agencies. It was the administration's most serious breach in security and the fallout was catastrophic. Victoria was tried in absentia, charged with treason and sentenced to life in prison. The man responsible for her death was promoted and is now a very influential D.C. lobbyist."

"Victoria is gone, she can't be vindicated and you want me to take this person out? Other than my being the son of Victoria Grayslake, you're going to have to give me another reason."

"He knows who you are, and he's afraid that one day you may decide to seek retribution for what he did to your mother."

"If that's true, then why hasn't he tried to take me out?"

"He did try."

Merrick froze, holding his breath until he felt his lungs exploding. The roaring in his head intensified and he felt faint. He let out a lungful of constricted breath. He knew the answer even before he asked it.

"When?"

"When you were shot and left on the corner two blocks from here. The woman who'd asked you to meet her was also in on the conspiracy."

Merrick closed his eyes, reliving the scene as if it were yesterday. Corrine Grice, who'd moved into the apartment building in Silver Spring a month after he had, was the consummate neighbor. She picked up his newspaper when he failed to stop delivery because the Company hadn't given him enough notice whenever they called for a new mission. And whenever she cooked too much she shared what she had with him.

There was never anything personal about their relationship, so a year later when Corrine told Merrick that she planned to buy property in a less-than-desirable section of D.C. because she was tired of paying rent he offered to help her with her fixer-upper.

He spent hours painting the kitchen and bathroom, and when he told Corrine he was going home she came on to him like a cat in heat. More shocked than repulsed, he told her that he didn't see her in that way and left, running headlong into three men whose intent was to rob him. What he'd thought was a botched robbery in reality had been a conspiracy for murder.

"Where is Corrine?"

"She and her three flunkies were found a little well done in a burned-out establishment around the corner. No witnesses, no blame."

Seconds ticked off into a minute before Merrick said, "Who is he?"

"Chandler Duffy."

A sardonic smile twisted Merrick's mouth. "Chandler Duffy. The unofficial president of the United States."

"The same," confirmed what Merrick now thought of as *the voice*.

"Why don't you go after him yourself?"

"I can't."

"Well, neither can I," Merrick argued softly. "If I'm going to do it legally, then you know I'm prohibited from collecting foreign intelligence concerning the domestic activities of U.S. citizens. That falls under the jurisdiction of the Bureau."

"I'll provide you with what you need to go after Duffy."

"Whatever you tell me I'll have to pass along to my superiors."

"I don't give a flying fig who pinches him. It could be CIA, FBI, DEA, ATF, Secret Service or the friggin' Boy Scouts of America."

Merrick nodded, doubting whether his informant could

see him. "I'll see what I can do." He stood up. "Now, if you'll excuse me I have to go home and get out of these clothes."

"I'll be in touch," said *the voice*.

"Oh, I'm sure you will."

Merrick gripped the gun as he made his way down the rickety staircase and out into the crisp cold air. He sucked in a lungful before letting it out. The cloying stench of human and animal waste lingered in his nostrils.

Merrick drove back to Arlington. He stood outside the door and had Alex bring him a large plastic garbage bag. Not concerned with who saw him in his birthday suit, he stripped off his clothes and shoes and left them in the bag on the floor outside the door.

It was only after he'd showered and washed his hair, twice, that he felt clean again.

Chapter 29

All eyes on the gun range were focused on Merrick Grayslake as he executed his marksmanship skills. Using his right hand, he fired at the target, all sixteen rounds hitting dead center. Expelling the spent clip, he inserted another and repeated the action with his left hand.

A spattering of applause followed the awesome exhibition as Merrick took off the protective gear covering his eyes and ears. He ignored those standing around talking quietly amongst themselves. He'd come to the gun range to let out some of his pent-up frustration.

He'd reacted like an automaton when Alex parked in front of the home where she wanted them to live. He told her he liked the style of the house, the neighborhood and the shopping area. What he couldn't tell her was what he'd gleaned earlier that afternoon. That he knew about Victoria Grayslake, who she'd worked for and how she'd died. It haunted him that she'd agreed to give up names of undercover agents to save the life of her unborn child.

Chandler Duffy. The name played over and over in his head, becoming a litany. The former DEA supervisor had set up Victoria Grayslake to be tortured and executed. Why? Merrick asked himself over and over, unable to come up with a plausible explanation.

Retribution. The word seeped into his consciousness, nagging at him like a gnawing ache. Duffy had to pay, not only because he was responsible for an agent's death; he also had the blood of four hired thugs, five if they'd killed him, on his hands and who knew how many more?

Whether it was retribution, revenge, payback or reprisal, Chandler Duffy knew who he was and Merrick Grayslake knew Chandler. It was time for him to level the playing field, settle the score.

He'd come to work earlier than usual, hoping to meet with Carl Ashleigh or William Reid, but was told that the two men were out of the building. Merrick knew he couldn't do anything to Duffy unless he cleared it with Ashleigh and/or Reid. Until then he would take his stress and frustration out on the gun range target.

Ashleigh and Reid returned to CIA headquarters later that afternoon and were told that Merrick Grayslake needed to speak to them ASAP. They shared a knowing look, then summoned him. He was forthcoming when he told them of his meeting with *the voice.*

Ashleigh spoke first. "Chandler Duffy is no small-time punk looking to make a big score. He's been peddling influence in Washington for two decades, and everyone knows he's the best at what he does."

Lacing his fingers together, Ashleigh avoided Merrick's

gaze. "He's what you'd call a power broker extraordinaire. He has backed our last two presidents."

"Do you have anything on him?" Merrick asked.

William Reid looked at Ashleigh, who nodded. "Duffy's name has come up in connection with his firm accepting cash payments from the head of an African nation who has been accused of human rights violations and rumored to offer refuge to known terrorists."

Merrick's gray gaze shifted from Reid to Ashleigh. "How do you know this and where do *we* fit into that equation?"

A rare smile found its way to Ashleigh's pale eyes. "We've uncovered an offshore account in Duffy's wife's name, and there's been talk that he brokered a deal for several senators and for our incumbent president's opponent to meet secretly with this leader."

This wasn't the news Merrick wanted to hear because personally he liked the man who was certain to receive his party's nomination to run against the weak and ineffective incumbent president.

"I'd like to request permission to head the team to investigate Duffy."

Ashleigh shook his head. "I don't know, Grayslake. It wouldn't work, because something of this nature would be too personal for you."

Leaning forward, Merrick impaled him with a lethal stare. "I'm not going to lie and say it's not personal. But I didn't have to come to tell you what went down last night. I could've gotten into my vehicle, stalked Duffy and taken him out at a thousand yards with one bullet, one kill. Far enough away to see his head explode, and far enough away not to have pieces of his DNA on me.

"The fact that I've come back to the Company is like waving a red flag in front of Duffy. Unlike the last time, I'll be ready for him and his hired thugs. But what I won't do is put my family at risk. Either you approve me going after Duffy legally or I'll take care of him my way. And you both know how that will end."

If Merrick Grayslake had been any other subordinate Ashleigh would've written him up. The director had half hoped Grayslake would take the bait, but it'd gone better than they'd planned because Duffy wasn't above killing women. And because Grayslake, dubbed the "Lone Wolf" by those involved in Operation Backslap, had taken a mate it made the mission that much more personal.

"Okay, Grayslake," Ashleigh said grudgingly. "You can be first chair on this one. Do you want to pick your team or do you want to leave that to me?"

"We can do it together."

Carl Ashleigh felt a measure of relief for the first time since he'd been ordered to indirectly involve Merrick Grayslake in the mission to neutralize Duffy.

"Good. Let's get together at the end of the first week in January." He flipped a page in his planner and circled a date. "If I can't get someone else to lead the sniper training, then we'll put it off until you close out the Duffy investigation." He closed his planner, struggling not to do the happy dance. He'd lied to Merrick. There never was going to be a sniper-training course. "If you need some time off to make arrangements to protect your wife, then take it." He stared at Merrick, then his assistant. "Gentlemen, this meeting is over."

Merrick left the conference room and returned to his office. Propping his elbows on the desk, he covered his face with his hands. How, he thought, was he going to tell Alex that she would have to stay in Florida with her parents until Duffy was either in custody—or dead? He lowered his hands and stared at a wall calendar displaying eighteen instead of the usual twelve months. He'd circled the last day in April—the day Victoria Cole-Grayslake was predicted to make her appearance.

Chapter 30

Alex's plan to change her flight reservation to leave Virginia with Merrick backfired. The snow, which had begun falling two days before Christmas, continued nonstop for three days and two nights. Snow totals from Maine to portions of West Virginia averaged more than two feet.

It would become the first Christmas that the second generation of Coles, Kirklands and Grayslakes would not celebrate Christmas and New Year's in West Palm Beach, Florida. Gabriel and Summer, Michael and Jolene and Merrick and Alexandra were unable to leave their homes.

Merrick, who lay in bed with Alex in the Kirklands' guest bedroom, rested a hand over her distended belly. They'd come to Georgetown for dinner and found themselves snowbound.

"Why don't you go to Florida when the airports are back on schedule."

Alex felt as if someone had caught her throat, not permitting her to breathe. Merrick had changed, but she'd attributed that to his work at the CIA. Most nights he came home, went directly to the bathroom where he showered, then flopped in front of the television until she called him for dinner. He always helped her clean up the kitchen, waited for her to come to bed, turned over and fell asleep.

Sitting up, she turned on the lamp on her side of the bed and shook him awake. "Merrick, are you having an affair?"

He moaned and threw an arm over his face. "What?"

"I know you heard what I said." She repeated her query.

Merrick sat up. "No. Oh, hell, no!"

Alex pulled her lower lip between her teeth. "Then, why is it we haven't made love in more than a week? Is it because I'm fat and ugly?"

"Ali, my love," he crooned, reaching for her, but she turned her back. "You are the most beautiful woman in the world."

"But I'm fat."

"Baby, you're pregnant. Pregnant women always put on weight."

Turning over to face him, Alex touched the side of his face. "You're not having an affair?"

"I would never cheat on you, Ali." Merrick combed his fingers through her curls.

"Then, what's the matter, Merrick? Why do I feel as if we're growing apart?"

Merrick wanted to tell her, unload all he'd discovered about his mother, but he couldn't. "I'm involved with something at work that has me distracted."

"Can you talk about it?" Alex asked.

"No, baby. It's classified."

She smiled. "That's all you had to say."

He kissed the end of her nose. "Any time I start acting strange, talk to me."

"You're always strange," Alex teased.

Merrick's hand searched under the hem of her nightgown, trailing up her thighs. "How's that?"

She pressed her forehead to his. "You have a way of looking at a person that makes them feel as if you have X-ray vision. Then you have a habit of sneaking up on folks wherein they look up and you're there."

"Do I frighten you, darling?"

She closed her eyes, smiling. "Not anymore."

"When did you stop being afraid?"

"The day I became Mrs. Merrick Grayslake. I knew I could never live with a man who frightened me."

"Have you given what I said some thought?"

"About you wanting me to go to Florida?"

"Yes."

"Why do you want me to go away, Merrick? And please don't tell me it's classified."

"I'm involved in something that may put you and the baby in danger."

"What is it?"

"That I can't tell you."

"You want me to go away for how long?"

"I don't know," he answered truthfully.

"No, Merrick. If you can't give me a time frame, then I'm staying here. We're buying a new house and I plan to focus all of my energies on decorating it before the baby comes."

"I don't want to fight with you, Ali."

"Then don't," she shot back.

"I will if I have to."

"Are you threatening me, Merrick Grayslake?"

"No, I'm not. I'm telling you that I'll do what I have to do to keep you safe. If that means hiring someone to watch you when I'm not here, then I will."

Alex's hands curled into fists. "I will not become a prisoner in my home."

Merrick pulled away and lay on his back. "You will become anything I want you to become until what I'm involved in is over."

Alex struggled to control her temper. "When will it be over?"

"Dammit! I don't know!"

She swung her legs over the side of the bed. Her movements were slow and awkward as she made her way over to a window. "Don't you *ever* raise your voice to me again!" she ground out between clenched teeth. "In case you failed to notice I am your wife, not your chattel. Yell at me again and you don't have to worry about hiring someone to protect me, because I'll be out of here so fast you'll forget what I look like."

Merrick moved off the bed, stalking her like a large cat. "You will not leave me. You will not take my child from me."

"Me, me, me," she mimicked. "Why is this about you? What about me?"

"It *is* about you, Ali. Everything in my life, everything I do is about you." He threw up a hand. "Do you think I really wanted to go back to the CIA?"

"Then why did you?"

"Because I needed to support my wife and family."

"I don't need you to take care of me."

He took several steps, bringing them inches apart. "What kind of man would I be if I let my wife foot the bill for everything? How long would it take for me not to feel like a man? Be a man?"

"Why are you equating your manhood with money?"

Grasping her shoulders, he pulled her to his naked body. "I have to, Alexandra, because that's who I am. Do you think your father would've given us his blessing if I didn't have a job?"

Her eyes widened until he saw into their clear gold depths. "What does my father have to do with us?"

"Your father asked me how I was going to support you."

"When?"

Merrick told her about the confrontation with her father as an expression of disbelief swept over his wife's incredibly beautiful face. Being pregnant made her lush, more feminine.

"Even though you're carrying David Cole's grandchild, he still had the stones to blindside me in front of his brothers and sons to question me about how I was going to take care of his precious baby girl."

Her lids fluttered. "I didn't know, Merrick. I'm sorry my father—"

"Don't apologize for him, Ali," he spat out, cutting her off. "What your father said came from his heart. I have to respect him for that."

Resting her palms on his pecs, Alex pressed a kiss over his heart. "I'm sorry for fighting with you, *mi amor.*"

He cradled her belly. "We don't fight, baby."

"What do we do?"

"Disagree."

"I...I..." Her eyes were wide as silver dollars. Placing her hands over Merrick's, she pressed them to her swollen abdomen. "Did you feel that?"

"Feel what?"

"The baby, Merrick. She kicked me."

He placed his hands on her belly. "I don't feel anything."

Alex gasped. "She kicked again."

"Where?"

"Here."

Merrick closed his eyes and waited. Then he felt it—a soft flutter. It happened again. A well of emotion filled his chest, making it difficult for him to draw a breath. His daughter was moving. Now she was real, very, very real.

Going to his knees, he pushed up Alex's nightgown and kissed his wife's belly. "I love my girls," he whispered, placing soft tender kisses over every inch of her swollen flesh.

Alex cradled Merrick's head as an angelic smile spread over her face. Her baby, their baby, in making her presence known, had forced a truce between her mother and father.

Merrick rose to his feet and swept Alex up in his arms. He carried her back to bed and proceeded to make love to her slowly, gently, as if he feared she would shatter into a million tiny pieces.

He gave, she received, she gave and he was there to receive. A wave of ecstasy came upon them so quickly they didn't have time to react. A fireball exploded and they fell headlong into a maelstrom of uncontrollable joy that ebbed to a deep feeling of sated peace.

Chapter 31

The following morning Merrick asked Michael to take a walk with him. He knew by the expression on Michael's face that he thought he'd taken leave of his senses; who'd want to go for a walk when some streets were still impassable because the sanitation department hadn't gotten around to removing the mountain of snow from residential neighborhoods?

Michael recognized and quickly processed the tension in his friend's request, and agreed. "What's up, Gray?" he asked once they attempted to navigate a narrow path on the sidewalk, made by booted footsteps.

"I need a favor."

Michael stared up at a startlingly blue, cloud-free sky. The warmth of the winter sun felt good on his face. "Ask away."

Merrick stomped his feet, knocking snow off his boots. "I need you to look after Alex."

Closing his eyes, Michael smothered a savage expletive. "What the hell are you involved in *now?*"

"I can't tell you. It's—"

"Classified," Michael said, cutting him off and completing his statement. He shook his head. "I thought you were going back as a trainer?"

"I did."

"But right now you're not training anything or anyone. I don't want to be the one who said I-told-you-so, but I'm going to say it anyway. I told you that they were going to recruit you for some clandestine operation. I know how *they* operate, Gray. It's one thing to be in the field and wait for your orders, and another completely when you're sitting at the top in an office making decisions as to who they can use and who is expendable. If nothing else, working at the Pentagon taught me that."

Merrick waited for Michael to finish his tirade, then said, "This is personal, Kirk." The two men stepped into a snowbank to let a woman pass.

"How personal?" Michael asked.

"It involves my mother."

"Is she alive?"

Merrick shook his head. "No. The only thing I will tell you is that she was tortured before she was executed."

"Oh, damn. I'm sorry, Gray."

"It's okay. What I find strange is that when I found out how she died I didn't feel anything. No anger, no sadness."

"That's because you never met her. Do you have a photograph of her?"

Merrick shook his head. "No." He'd tried accessing her file through an intra-agency database, but her name had been deleted.

Clasping his gloved hands behind his back, Michael gave his friend a sidelong glance. "How much danger is my cousin in?"

"Life threatening." Merrick had decided not to mince words.

"She can live with me until whatever crap you're involved in is over. I'm sure Jolene would love to have Alex around. I'll be home until the end of January. I hope you complete your mission before that. If not, then we'll have to come up with another plan."

"I want her to go to Florida and stay with her folks."

"Did you tell her that?"

"Yes."

"Did she go off on you?"

Merrick stopped and stared at Michael. "Did you hear us last night?"

Michael shook his head. "No. But I know my cousin, Gray. She's not going to Florida because she doesn't want to, but because you told her to go. Alex is sweet, funny and generous. But she's also as stubborn as a mule. You don't tell Alexandra Cole what you want her to do, you ask her. Let her think it's her idea."

Merrick frowned. "I don't have time to coax and coddle. Not with what I'm up against."

"Your wife is with child, Merrick. She is not the same Alexandra you met and fell in love with. Once she has the baby the old Alex will return. Right now you can't do anything to set her off. I'm a witness. I've lived through and survived the nine months of horror."

"Because you've survived the horror, what do you suggest I do?"

"Tell her you have to go away for a week, and that you want her to stay with me because you don't want her left alone because of the baby."

"But I'm not going away. Besides, I've never lied to Alex."

"Merrick, my friend. You *are* lying to her. Her life and that of your unborn child are at risk, yet you're telling her she has to go away. And when she asks why, you tell her it's classified. Look, man, if you have to lie, cheat or kill a son of a bitch to keep your family safe, then you do it. Tell Alex you're involved in some training program and see what she says. I'm willing to bet she'll volunteer to hang out with me and Jolene."

"Okay, I'll give it a shot. But if she balks, then it's World War Three."

Michael smiled. "If you'd told me you were fooling around with my cousin I would've given you the four-one-one on her. After all, she's a Cole woman and they are a breed unto themselves."

"Amen," Merrick said under his breath. "I'm ready to go back. Thanks for hearing me out."

Michael patted his shoulder. "No sweat. After all, we're family."

He and Michael had returned to the house at the same time Jolene and Alex walked into the kitchen. They shooed the women to the family room while they prepared a country breakfast of bacon, sausage, eggs, grits, biscuits, freshly-squeezed orange juice and brewed coffee and tea.

Michael put on several CDs, and the music flowing from hidden speakers added to the festive mood. Six-month-old Teresa, who'd begun pulling herself up in her crib, crawled around on the floor, getting underfoot. Jolene placed her in a playpen in a corner of the large kitchen and the little girl cried hysterically until Alex freed her from the mesh-covered prison.

Jolene glared at Alex. "She's spoiled enough without you adding to it. I should send her home with you."

Alex kissed Teresa's curly black hair. "Do you want to come stay with Titi Alex? I wouldn't mind taking care of you for a couple of weeks to give your mama a break."

"Why don't you hang out here with us for a couple of weeks?" Jolene suggested. "We can go shopping for baby clothes and furniture to decorate the nursery in your new house." She smiled at her husband. "Would you mind if your cousin stayed with us?"

Michael affected a stern expression. His wife had given him and Merrick the opening they needed. "Are you asking or telling me, Jo?"

"I'm asking, Michael."

He waved a slender hand. "Alex is family. You don't have to ask. Who you should be asking is Merrick. After all, he *is* her husband and he just might have something planned for the two of them."

"Merrick and I don't have any plans," Alex volunteered.

Merrick stared at Alex rather than Michael. He knew if he looked at his wife's cousin, he wouldn't be able to keep a straight face. He felt relieved that he didn't have to lie to Alex.

"Did you forget that we close on the house January ninth?"

"No," Alex said. "That's not going to take more than an hour or two. As soon as we get the keys I want Jolene to see the house."

Jolene dabbed the corners of her mouth with a napkin. "Have you decided what style of furniture you want to put in it?"

"Not really."

"Now, that's going to be fun."

Alex shifted Teresa to her other knee. "Merrick, would you mind if I stayed here with Jolene? We have a lot of shopping to do, and I would like her opinion on things like wallpaper."

"I don't mind at all," Merrick said much too quickly. He ignored Michael's incredulous stare. "You know I have no interest in wallpaper, paint colors or what fabric you want on some chair or other doodad."

"Are you sure you're not going to miss me, *mi amor?*"

"Miss you? Aren't we going to see each other at night?" Merrick affected a frown. "If you've found someone you'd rather be with, please tell me now."

Alex blushed like a schoolgirl with her first crush. "Who's going to want me looking like this?"

There was a long-suffering silence. "I want you, Ali," Merrick said, his voice filled with emotion.

Michael cleared his throat. "Damn, my brother. You don't have to show your woman you're whipped."

"Stay out of it, Michael," Jolene warned softly. "Please," she whispered when her husband opened his mouth.

Michael caught and held his wife's gaze. He knew how Merrick felt about Alex because he felt the same about Jolene. He'd fallen in love with her on sight, and each day he grew more in love with her.

Chapter 32

Merrick opened and closed his eyes in an attempt to relieve the burning. He'd been staring at the computer monitor for hours, searching one database, then another for something that would link Duffy to something—anything the government could use to issue an indictment.

He headed a team of four, including himself, who'd worked tirelessly for the past three months researching every lead given them. So far, Duffy had come up clean.

He came in early and worked late, yet his private life had remained stable. He and Alex had closed on the house in Alexandria and her priority was decorating it before giving birth.

The Kirklands' offer of their guest wing had become a necessity once the Arlington condominium was sold. Merrick was more relaxed because Alex wasn't left alone during the day. Whenever she had to see the doctor he took time off from work to take her.

Merrick was aware that Alex didn't like that he didn't go anywhere without the small but powerful handgun tucked into his waistband, but it was a topic he refused to discuss with her.

He glanced over at a female computer programmer who'd been Ashleigh's recommendation. Merrick was astounded with what she could do with one keystroke. "What screen are you looking at, Patty?"

"DEA."

"Patch me over."

Within seconds the Drug Enforcement Administration logo appeared on his monitor. The fact that Duffy had been DEA before leaving to start up his lobbying firm made them a part of the investigation.

Pen in hand, a pad of paper nearby, Merrick began scrolling down a listing of names of past and present agents, hoping to connect at least one to Duffy's present operation.

Summer Montgomery. The name jumped out at him. The undercover special agent—code name: Renegade—was engaged to his brother-in-law Gabriel. Pressing a few keys, he viewed the operation she was assigned to cover at Weir Memorial High School. He stared at the names of the students and faculty members. A slight frown furrowed his forehead. Dumas Gellis. He'd come across the name before, but where?

He scribbled the name on the pad.

"Patty?" Merrick hadn't taken his gaze off the screen.

"Yes, Merrick?"

"I need you to go to the Treasury Department site and type in Dumas Gellis."

"Dumas like in Alexandre?"

"Yes, Patty."

Soft brown eyes widening behind the lenses of her glasses, Patty smiled. "He's here. He has several offshore accounts in the Cayman Islands."

"Can you tell me how much he's deposited?"

"Give me a few minutes and I'll let you know." Biting down on her lower lip, an affectation she executed whenever she concentrated on a task, Patty bobbed her head up and down. "Got it."

"How much?"

"All totaled. In excess of three mil."

Merrick whistled. "Not bad for an assistant principal and ex-footballer." He read the name of the agent-in-charge of the Weir operation. "I believe Lucas Shelby would find Mr. Gellis's bank balance quite interesting." With a stroke of a key, Gellis's banking information was forwarded to the Drug Enforcement Administration.

Merrick knew he'd helped his future sister-in-law bring closure to her assignment, but he still hadn't gotten a single clue with which to take down Duffy.

The lobbyist was smart, but was he smarter than the team of four who were the best at what they did? Merrick knew if they were going to pinch Duffy, it would be tied to his finances.

Leaning to his left, Merrick tapped the shoulder of an accountant on loan to the CIA from the Treasury Department. A recent college graduate, Stuart Olson didn't look old enough to drive or drink.

"I need a printout of banking transactions from every international database in existence."

"Can I do that, sir?"

Smiling, Merrick nodded. "Yes, you can."

He didn't tell the accountant that the secret program, run out of the Central Intelligence Agency and overseen by the Treasury Department, initiated weeks after the September 11 attacks, permitted counterterrorism officials access to financial records from a vast international database to examine banking transactions involving thousands of Americans and others in the United States. However, the program was limited to tracing transactions of people suspected of having ties to terrorist groups.

Stuart gave a look that said he didn't believe what he'd been told. "The program is predicated in part on the president's emergency economic powers," Merrick explained.

During a briefing session, Merrick was told data from the Brussels-based banking consortium, formally known as the Society for World Interbank Financial Telecommunication, had allowed officials from the CIA and the FBI and a few other agencies to examine tens of thousands of financial transactions.

"That's going to take days if not weeks, Mr. Grayslake."

Merrick patted his shoulder again. "You have a June first deadline to come up with something on Duffy."

Stuart sat up straighter. "I'll find something on him before May Day."

Merrick redirected his gaze to his computer monitor. Patty had changed it again. He noted the time at the lower right of the screen. It was 8:05 p.m., time that he headed home.

He couldn't wait to wrap up this case so he could resume a normal life wherein he'd come home from work and have his wife greet him in their new house. A contractor had refurbished it to Alex's specifications, and she and Jolene had spent all their free time together shopping for antiques to fill up the grand structure. They'd established a routine of going to Sunday-morning mass, followed by brunch, then to the house that was to become their home once he closed the Duffy case.

Merrick knew Alex longed to spend the night in their new home, but he couldn't afford to take the risk—not even with a state-of-the-art sophisticated security system—because he never knew when he would be summoned to return to Langley.

Her advancing pregnancy slowed her gait, and she constantly held her lower back as if she were in pain. Whenever he questioned her she said it was just the baby pressing on her lower spine.

Ashleigh had given him until June first to bring down Duffy, but Merrick hoped it would be sooner. His wife was due to deliver their first baby in a month, and when he brought his daughter home he didn't want it be under a cloak of danger and secrecy.

Standing up, he rolled his head on his shoulders. "I'm done for the day."

"I'm staying," said Patty.

Stuart stared up at Merrick. "Me, too."

"What about you, Justin?" Merrick asked an information specialist whom he'd selected to join the team. Justin Jefferson bore an uncanny resemblance to a young Malcolm X.

"I guess I'll stay a little longer. Besides, I could use the overtime."

"If I see any of you in before me tomorrow, I'm going to write you up," Merrick teased. They laughed as he walked out of the room that had been set up for them.

His stomach growled loudly as he made his way to his office, reminding him that he'd skipped lunch *and* dinner. He would stop at a health-food drive-through and pick up something.

Chapter 33

Merrick had just crossed the marker indicating he'd left Virginia for the Capitol District when his cell phone rang. He reached into his shirt pocket for the phone. Without looking at the display, he answered it.

"Hello."

"Merrick, it's Michael."

His heart lurched. Michael always called him Gray. "What's the matter?"

"I'm at the hospital with Alex. She's in labor."

"But the baby's not due for another four weeks."

"It looks as if your daughter doesn't want to wait."

"I'm on my way."

He closed the phone and jammed the accelerator, taking red lights like a man possessed. He heard the siren, then the flashing lights behind him. Damn his luck! He was being pulled over. Coming to a screeching halt, he was ready for the officer when he approached his vehicle.

He handed the officer his photo identification from the Central Intelligence Agency. "I just got a call that my wife has gone into premature labor."

The officer took a glance at the ID, and then his glance lingered on Merrick's face. "Follow me."

What should've taken fifteen minutes was reduced to five as Merrick was given a police escort to the private hospital where Jolene had delivered Teresa.

He thanked the officer as he raced toward the entrance to the hospital. "Grayslake," he shouted to the clerk at the reception desk.

"Labor room two."

Not waiting for the elevator, Merrick bounded up the staircase to the second floor. His heart was pounding, hands shaking uncontrollably when he came face-to-face with Michael.

"How is she?"

Michael patted his shoulder in a comforting gesture. "She's okay. They have her hooked up to monitors. Get yourself together before you go in there. If Alex sees you like this she's going to lose it."

Merrick patted his hair. "What do I look like?"

"You don't want to know. Go in the men's room and splash some water on your face. I'll wait here until you come out."

Merrick went into the men's room. He peered into the mirror, seeing the face of a stranger looking back at him. There was a look in his eyes he'd never seen before—fear.

Turning on the faucet, he washed his hands, then wet his face. His motions were mechanical when he dried his face on a paper towel, then combed his hair. Straightening his shoulders, he walked out of the restroom and into labor room two.

Michael stood in a corner watching an attending doctor

examine his cousin, reliving the scene when he'd waited for the birth of his child. He knew Alex wanted Tyler to deliver her child, but it was apparent Baby Grayslake had decided to ignore the calendar to make a premature debut.

He smiled when Merrick entered the room. He looked better.

Closing the distance between them, he nodded. "Nice. I'm going home to my girls. Call me later."

Merrick smiled. "Thanks for everything."

"No problema, primo."

A nurse approached Merrick. "Are you the father?"

"Yes, I am," he said proudly.

"You can put your jacket over in the locker. If you have a cell phone, please turn it off. I'm going to gown and mask you. We like to keep the room as sterile as possible."

Merrick turned off his cell phone and slipped out of his jacket, not seeing the nurse's stunned look when she saw the holstered automatic handgun tucked into the small of his back. It, too, went into the locker and she breathed a sigh.

Alex smothered a moan as a spasm of pain gripped her. She felt as if she were being split in two. The pain had begun mid-morning and had intensified with each passing hour. She'd been experiencing mild contractions since her eighth month, but these were different. By nightfall they were stronger and coming closer together.

The pressure on her bladder had also increased and when she sat on the commode and amniotic fluid flowed unchecked, she knew it was time to go the hospital. And for the first time since Merrick suggested she live with Michael she offered up a prayer of gratitude. If she'd been at the house in Alexandria she would've been alone—alone and frightened.

"Hey, Mama."

Alex opened her eyes to see a pair in clear gray smiling

down at her. "Hi…" she got out before catching her breath when another contraction seized her.

"How are you doing?"

"I am in pain, Merrick Grayslake."

"Do you want something to take the edge off?"

She shook her damp head. "No drugs."

The doctor completed his examination. "It's too late to give her anything. Your baby will be here in half an hour or less. I'm going to check on another patient. I'll be back in a few minutes."

Sitting on a chair at the head of the bed, Merrick held his wife's hand. He felt every contraction with her death grip on his fingers. It went on and on, him gently massaging her back.

He wondered who'd attended to Victoria Grayslake when she went into labor. Was there anyone to comfort her when she knew she would give up her life as soon as she delivered her baby? Had she been tortured before or after she gave birth? Had she made the treasonous videotape disclosure before or after she'd become a mother?

After his initial meeting with *the voice* there was no further communication. Merrick had traced the serial numbers on the disposable cell phones and discovered they'd been purchased in Anchorage, Alaska. He continued to carry the phones in the hope that the mysterious caller would offer another clue.

The doctor returned, checked the machines monitoring the baby's heartbeat, then checked to see how far Alex was dilated. He ripped off his gloves and lab coat. "She's ready. Let's move it, Nurse!"

Merrick stood up, completely helpless as the medical professionals sprang into action. Another nurse appeared as the obstetrician scrubbed his arms and hands. Moments before Alex's legs were encased in elastic stockings and placed in a pair of stirrups another doctor appeared, this one a resident.

"Dad, please stand at the end of the bed."

Moving in slow motion, Merrick moved to where he'd been ordered. A nurse tilted a large mirror to give him an unobstructed view of the birth and delivery. He watched in awe, transfixed as Alex labored to give birth. She pushed when told to push, the effort weakening her reserved strength.

"No puedo," she whispered hoarsely.

"Yes, you can. You have to do this, baby. Didn't we make plans to take little Vicky to the museum to look at all the pretty paintings?"

"You hate museums," she spat out.

Merrick kissed her forehead. "I don't hate them, darling."

"She's crowning." The doctor's eyes crinkled above his mask. "What do we have here? Somebody's a redhead."

Alex smiled through the sharp pains holding her prisoner. "She's a Grayslake."

The doctor rested a hand on his patient's belly. "One more push, Alexandra, and you'll get to see your beautiful baby."

She sucked in her breath and pushed. A soft gasp escaped her parched lips when she heard a weak cry. Her baby girl was here!

Peering up at the mirror she saw a tiny red-faced baby with red-gold hair. There was no trace of Cole in her daughter.

Tears filled Alex's eyes and spilled down her cheeks. "She's beautiful, Merrick."

Leaning over, Merrick kissed his wife's damp face. "Thank you, Ali."

"Check to see if she has all her fingers and toes."

"She's perfect."

"Check her, please."

The nurse tagged, suctioned, weighed, measured and cleaned a wailing Baby Grayslake. She handed the baby to Merrick, who kissed her head before handing her off to her mother. Instinctively, Victoria Grayslake sought out her mother's swollen breasts and began nursing greedily.

The intern took over from the attending doctor, who ripped off his gloves. He motioned to Merrick. "Your daughter is small, which means she'll have to stay in the hospital until she weighs at least five pounds."

"How much does she weigh?"

"Four pounds ten ounces."

Merrick smiled, attractive lines fanning out around his eyes. "Judging from her appetite, she'll gain that in a week." He sobered. "She wasn't due for another month. Will that present a problem?"

"There's no doubt that she's a full-term baby. What she may be is two weeks early, but not much more than that. Maybe your wife lifted something that brought on labor, but I wouldn't worry too much about mother and baby. She can stay until your daughter is medically cleared for discharge."

Merrick doubted whether Alex would agree to leave the hospital without her baby. He extended his hand. "Thanks, Doctor."

"Congratulations, Mr. Grayslake. You can see your wife once she's in her room. We have accommodations for new dads if you wish to spend the night."

"Thank you again."

Merrick left to find an area where he could use his cell phone to call David and Serena. Then he would call Michael and let him know he planned to spend the night in the hospital with his wife and new baby daughter.

Chapter 34

Chandler Duffy drove his fist into the granite countertop, ignoring the shooting pain racing up his arm. *When I kill them, they stay dead,* he fumed inwardly. The tall, elegant man with silver hair, known to his closest associates as the Silver Fox, literally had blood in his eye. When he'd received word that Merrick Grayslake was digging into his finances his blood pressure spiked dangerously. The result was a ruptured blood vessel in his right eye.

The Grayslake name had haunted him for years, and he still hadn't forgotten the face of the woman who'd insulted him, saying she found a wad of gum on the bottom of her shoe more appealing than sleeping with him. It took him a while, but she paid for the snub—with her life.

Reaching for one of five cell phones on a side table, he dialed a number. "It's a go," he said when hearing a familiar voice. He disconnected the call, put the phone back in its assigned order and walked out of his inner sanctum.

He would rid the world of any trace of Victoria Grayslake, once and for all.

Merrick sat on a cushioned love seat with Alex, watching her breast-feed their daughter. She was five days old and she'd gained one of the four ounces she'd lost. Alex's milk had come in and the tiny fingers clutched her breast as if it was a lifeline.

He smiled as Alex spoke Spanish to the baby. His wife had grown up with bilingual parents, while he'd learned the language from Mexican housekeepers. And if it were up to him, his daughter would speak as many languages as she could master.

Merrick leaned closer. "She keeps her eyes open longer."

Alex met her husband's proud gaze. "She only opens them for you. She must like your voice."

"That's because she's showing her daddy her beautiful hazel eyes." Victoria's eyes changed color from a light green to a grayish brown.

"I'm going to need you to go to the house and bring me something to wear. I'm embarrassed when people come see me and I'm in a nightgown and bathrobe."

Stretching his arm over the back of the love seat, Merrick played with her hair. It was long enough to cover the nape of her neck. "What do you want me to bring?"

"Sweatpants or anything with a drawstring waist. I doubt if I'll be able to fit in anything else."

"Your stomach looks pretty flat. It's your top that's outrageous."

Alex winked at him. "You like them, don't you?"

Merrick winked back. "I'm not above fighting a baby for Mama's *leche*."

Picking up a nursing pad, she swatted at him. "You're nasty."

"Hell, yeah," he countered. Moving closer, he kissed her cheek. "I'll be back with your clothes." Pushing to his feet, he headed for the door to her suite.

"Querido?"

He stopped and turned around. "What is it?"

"When will I be able to go home?"

Merrick knew she was talking about the house in Alexandria. "Soon," he said, hoping he hadn't lied to her. They were still going over the printout of the international banking transactions.

Alex offered him a tender smile before she lowered her head and stared at the baby in her arms, a little girl whose golden skin was the perfect complement for her golden hair.

Merrick punched in a code, deactivating the security system. Alex had outdone herself decorating the historic structure. She'd selected antique pieces and exquisite reproductions that rivaled the interiors of the homes in Williamsburg, Virginia.

The difference was their home wasn't a museum but one where they could live and entertain in elegant comfort. A home he wanted to come to every night to eat with his wife and children, a home filled with love and laughter from the other children he hoped to have with Alex. He climbed the staircase to the second floor, and hadn't gotten halfway when the doorbell rang.

A slight frown furrowed his forehead. He wasn't expecting anyone, because he'd just begun sleeping at the house. With Alex in the hospital he'd decided to give Michael and Jolene a break so they could enjoy their domicile with the presence of guests, even if the guests were family members. The bell chimed again.

Thinking perhaps it was one of his neighbors who saw the light on in the first story, he retraced his steps. Peering through the security eye, he saw the face of a woman with light-colored hair pulled back in a ponytail. Reaching around his back, he unsnapped the strap on his gun's holster. He opened the solid oak door and stared through the tempered glass on the storm door. The woman had pressed a photo ID against the glass. She was CIA. Maybe she'd come up with something on Duffy.

Merrick reached for the latch on the door, but before he could open it the familiar sound of a gunshot echoed in the quietness of the spring night. Dropping to a crouching position, he reached for his gun, holding it in a two-handed grip. The agent lay on the top step, her right arm in an awkward position, her government-issued automatic dangling from her fingers.

It was apparent no one heard the shot because none of the residents came out of their houses. They probably thought it was a car backfiring.

Merrick went completely still when he saw a tall shadowy figure move closer. The man had both hands raised above his head. There was something familiar about the man; he moved under a street lamp and Merrick recognized him. He was Cordero Birmingham, associate Bureau chief for the FBI's Northeast region.

Kicking the door open a fraction, Merrick trained the gun on the special agent. "State your name and your business."

"Special Agent Cordero Birmingham, FBI associate Bureau chief, Northeast," he drawled in a distinctive Southwest intonation. He climbed the front steps, kicking the gun away from the motionless hand. Leaning down, he pressed two fingers against the woman's neck. "She's alive." He straightened. "I'm going to reach into my jacket to get my cell phone to call 911."

"Don't," Merrick warned. "I'll make the call." Reaching into the breast pocket of his shirt, he took out the phone and dialed the three digits without taking his gaze off the special agent. The lamps framing the house highlighted silver hair with traces of red, a lean face with a pair of brilliant topaz-blue eyes. The call took less than twenty seconds.

"You didn't state your business."

"I came here to save your life."

"You call shooting one of my colleagues saving my life?"

"She's dirty."

"How do I know *you're* not dirty?"

"You don't. But if I were you I wouldn't be standing here talking to me. Your wife would be making arrangements to bury her husband. And she would raise a child who would never know her father. Just like you never knew your father *or* your mother."

Merrick's eyes fluttered but the gun never wavered. "What do you know about my mother?"

"I was her partner on one undercover mission, and I swore an oath that I would always protect her."

Merrick felt as if he'd been punched in the gut. Cordero Birmingham was *the voice.*

Lowering the gun, he secured it behind his back. He had questions, lots of questions he wanted the special agent to answer. But they would have to wait, as the sound of approaching sirens shattered the tranquillity of the night.

Chapter 35

Merrick sat across from Cordero Birmingham listening to the man reveal more than thirty-five years of secrets. When the EMTs arrived, along with the police, Cordero took charge when he identified himself.

The injured woman wasn't an employee of the CIA, but an impostor with counterfeit identification who'd been hired to murder a federal agent, and the Bureau would send a report backing up his course of action.

"You got Duffy?" he asked.

"We picked him up on a private airstrip as he was preparing to leave for parts unknown."

"How did you get him?" Merrick asked. "We've been burning the midnight oil going through hundreds of thousand of international banking transactions."

"And it paid off."

"What!"

"While you were at the hospital visiting your wife and baby, Justin Jefferson found what you'd been looking for. We got the call and we had agents watching Duffy's house, his vacation place in McLean and his private jet."

"How did you know about the hit?"

"We finally got a judge who wasn't in Duffy's pocket willing to approve a wiretap. We put a cleaning woman in and she placed transmitters in every one of his phones. He never used his house phone for his business. He had five cell phones, each with a direct connection to someone able and willing to do his bidding—for a price of course."

"How did he know we were investigating him?"

"You have a leak at Langley."

"Who?"

"William Reid."

"No!" Merrick groaned, shaking his head. He'd always liked Bill Reid. "Why?"

"Duffy was blackmailing him. He'd set Reid up with a hooker, and when your supervisor woke up the next day, the woman wasn't breathing. Reid thought he'd killed her when the cause of death was a food allergy. Duffy removed all evidence that Reid had ever been in the room. He convinced Reid to transfer from the Bureau to the Company because he needed a snitch inside Langley."

Merrick, sandwiching his hands between his knees, closed his eyes. "What is your stake in all of this?"

"I told you Victoria was my partner."

Merrick opened his eyes. "You said that before."

Cordero Birmingham looped one leg over the opposite knee, staring at the young man sitting less than three feet from him. He was so incredibly smart, yet he couldn't see what was so obvious.

"I was in love with her. It was my child Victoria was carrying when Duffy turned on her because she rejected his advances."

A tense silence enveloped the room as the two men regarded each other. It was as if Merrick could suddenly see the similarities that were so overtly apparent: height, the lean face, high cheekbones, aquiline nose and reddish hair.

"You're telling me that you are my father?"

Cordero nodded. "Yes."

"How long have you known about me?"

Cordero held his forehead. "I realized who you were when I signed off on your security clearance when you first applied to the CIA. I'd gone as high as I could at the DEA, so I requested a transfer to the Bureau." He lowered his hand, bright blue eyes flashing like lasers. "I wanted to contact you but you were always on some covert operation, so I decided it was better I keep my distance."

"Did you know I'd been shot?"

"Yes. I came to see you in the hospital, but you were heavily sedated. I wanted to tell you that you weren't alone. That you had family—you had a father."

"I have a family now."

Cordero smiled, flashing his perfect white teeth, teeth that Merrick had inherited. "I know that you're married and you have a little girl."

Merrick flashed a proud smile. "She has red hair."

Running a hair over his coarse silver hair, Cordero lifted his eyebrows. "I *had* red hair. My father's hair was a bright red—almost orange."

"Where did you learn Spanish?"

"My mother was half Mexican."

"Was the other half Yaqui?"

"Yes. How do you know that?"

"Someone told me I look Yaqui."

"You do. My father was a Brit who lost his heart to a young Mexican woman he met when he came to the States on holiday."

"Do you have any brothers or sisters?"

"I had a brother, but he died in Vietnam. His death devastated my parents."

"Tell me about my mother."

"She was very pretty and very, very smart. Victoria would read something once and she'd never forget it."

"Was she African-American?"

Cordero nodded. "Yes. Why?"

Merrick clasped his hands. "I didn't know what it was, but I've always felt African-American. Do you have a photograph of her?"

Reaching into his jacket, Cordero took out a wallet. He opened it and pulled out a small fading black-and-white photograph. "I've carried this close to my heart for longer than I can remember." He handed Merrick the photo. "When she told me she was pregnant, I told her to request a transfer back to the States so that we could marry, but Duffy was the agent-in-charge, so he stopped it."

Merrick stared at the photograph of the woman who'd given up her life for him. There was something about her face that reminded him of his daughter's. He handed the photograph to Cordero.

"Her granddaughter looks like her."

Overcome with emotion, Cordero willed the tears filling his eyes not to fall. "Do you think I can see her?"

Merrick averted his gaze. Too much had happened, too much had been said and too much had been revealed in a very short span of time. "I came home to get something for Alex to wear. I'm going back to the hospital. Would you like to come with me?"

Cordero let out an audible exhalation of breath. "Yes. It's

going to be strange meeting David Cole's daughter when I haven't seen her uncle in more than forty years."

Merrick froze. "You know Martin Cole?"

"No. Joshua Kirkland."

"How do you know Joshua?"

"We worked together on a joint task force operation that yielded the largest drug bust in Mexican history. I was new to the game and hadn't realized we had a leak in the operation until someone tried to gut Joshua. If it hadn't been for Mateo Arroyo, also known as Matthew Sterling, Joshua wouldn't have made it."

Merrick's head was spinning. What were the odds that his father knew Emily's father *and* her father-in-law? "Joshua's daughter is married to Matt's son."

Cordero's blue eyes sparkled with amusement. "You're kidding."

"No, I'm not. As soon as Alex and Victoria—"

"Victoria? You named your daughter Victoria?"

"Yes. It was Alex's decision. We're all going to Florida next month. I'd like you to come and see your old friends."

Cordero's smile was blinding. "I'd like that very much. Thank you."

A phone rang and both men reached for their cell phones. "It's mine," Merrick said. "Hello. Yes, baby. I know I should've been back hours ago. I'm coming, but I want to warn you that I'm bringing somebody. No, I can't tell you. I won't tell you. You'll see when we get there. Yes, you're going to like it. Hang up and I'll see you in a bit."

He disconnected the call, meeting Cordero's knowing gaze. "Women."

"I know, son. You can't live with them, and we definitely can't live without them."

Merrick stood up, Cordero following suit. "Did you ever marry? Have more children?"

"No. I wasn't the marrying kind, but Victoria changed my mind. By the time I was ready to settle down with a wife and child she was gone. I've had a few serious relationships, but nothing that would make me commit to marriage. One love in one lifetime is enough."

"Come upstairs with me and see where your grandbaby girl is going to hang out." ·

Cordero followed Merrick up the staircase, feeling the warmth in the historic old house even though his daughter-in-law and granddaughter weren't there.

He thought about Victoria and how she would react to becoming a grandmother. There was no doubt she would've been just a little crazy. He would wait awhile, get to know his son better, and then he intended to spoil his grandbaby girl rotten.

Epilogue

The Cole clan gathered in Boca Raton to welcome and introduce Victoria Cole-Grayslake to her many relatives.

Merrick carried his two-month-old daughter while Alex held the hand of her father-in-law. It was a perfect Florida late-spring day—warm, sunny, the temperatures in the low seventies.

Serena spied Alex first and took off running. She'd wanted to come to Virginia after her daughter had given birth, but David talked her out of it. That was the last time she swore she would listen to the man.

She held out her arms. "Let me see the precious angel." Merrick placed the sleeping infant in Serena's arms. Her eyes filled with tears. "Oh, she's so beautiful." Cradling her in one arm, she untied the satin ribbons on her linen cap. A slight breeze lifted strands of red-gold hair. "Oh, goodness! She's a redhead."

David came over and eased the baby from his wife's arms. "What a beauty." Victoria opened her eyes and smiled a crooked smile. "Hey, Merrick, you better keep a close eye on your daughter because you're going to have to beat the boys off with a stick."

Merrick smiled. "I'd rather use a gun. I'll sit on the roof and pop the little knuckleheads before they reach the front door."

"Who's shooting who?" asked a deep voice.

Merrick turned to find Joshua Kirkland behind him. "Joshua, there's someone here who thinks he knows you."

Joshua lifted his pale eyebrows. "Who?"

"My father."

Vertical lines marred Joshua's forehead. "Your father?" He'd been told Merrick was orphaned at birth.

"Don't tell me that you're so old you're now senile."

With light green eyes widening in shock, Joshua stared at a man to whom he owed his life. "Cord Birmingham?"

Cordero released Alex's hand, extending his arms to Joshua. "In the flesh." The two men embraced, slapped each other's backs and howled like coyotes.

Joshua turned and searched the crowd. "Matt, get over here and see who decided to join the family."

Matthew Sterling stood up, squinting slightly when he saw Joshua hugging someone who looked vaguely familiar. It wasn't until Cordero smiled that he recognized the toothpaste-ad grin.

"I'll be double damned! Cord! You old geezer!" He grabbed him in a bear hug, then kissed both his cheeks.

"Old!" Cordero spat out. "I'm younger than both you farts."

Matt rested an arm on the shoulder of the man who'd stood in as a witness for his wedding to Eve Blackwell. "What are you doing here?"

"I came to meet my granddaughter's family."

Matt looked from Cordero to Merrick, then back again. How had he missed the resemblance? "You've got a helluva son."

"I know that," Cordero said without a modicum of modesty.

Joshua rested his arm on Cordero's other shoulder. "This calls for a celebration. Let's go inside and start the celebration early."

"You know you can't drink like you used to," David said, teasing his brother.

Joshua shot him a look. "Speak for yourself, little brother."

David handed Victoria off to Alex. "Here, cookie, take my grandbaby girl. I'm going to have to prove to these punks that I still can drink them under the table."

Alex shook her head. "Daddy, you know that you're too old to play college-boy games."

David snorted. "From what I heard, the youngbloods couldn't hold their liquor the night before you got married. Am I not right, Merrick?"

Merrick stared up at the fronds of a sweeping palm tree. "No comment."

Alex moved over and stood next to her husband. She watched the old friends lock arms as they went off to where they would talk about the old days and the old times undisturbed.

"I like your dad."

Merrick wrapped an arm around her waist. "I like him, too."

"You know that he's spoiling Victoria."

"That's what grandparents are supposed to do. You'll do the same once we have grandbabies."

She rested her head against his shoulder. "But that's not going to be for a long time. Right now I want to have fun making babies."

He dropped a kiss on her hair. "When do you want to start making another one?"

"We can try again in two years."

He tightened his hold, bringing her closer to his side. "That sounds like a good deal."

Alex tilted her head, and she wasn't disappointed when he brushed a kiss over her parted lips.

Gabriel strolled over with his pregnant new wife. "Get a room."

"Bite me, Gabriel," she retorted.

Gabriel winked at his brother-in-law. "Is that what she tells you in the throes of passion? Bite me, bite me, baby," he said in a falsetto.

Merrick, his expression impassive, turned and looked at Alex. "How come you never tell me to bite you?"

She stomped her foot. "Merrick Grayslake, you're going to get it."

"I hope so, because it's been a while."

Her face burning in shame, Alex smiled at Summer. "Please come with me. I think Victoria needs to be changed." The two women walked while their men roared in laughter.

Laughter, shrieks, whispered words of passion set the stage for another reunion, this one more poignant than the other ones. Merrick found his father, and his father found old friends who were now his family.

There were a few new Coles on the way who would one day take their place and risk everything for love.

The fourth title in the
Forged by Steele miniseries...

USA TODAY bestselling author

BRENDA JACKSON

riskyPLEASURES

Unable to acquire Vanessa Steele's company, arrogant
millionaire Cameron Cody follows Vanessa to Jamaica,
determined to become the one temptation she can't resist.
But headstrong Vanessa is equally determined to prove that
she's immune to his seductive charm!

Only a special woman can win the heart of a brother—
Forged by Steele.

*Available the first week of April
wherever books are sold.*

KIMANI™
ROMANCE

www.kimanipress.com

KPBJ0120407

What a sister's gotta do!

At First
SIGHT

Favorite author

Tamara Sneed

Forced to live together to get their inheritance,
the Sibley sisters clash fiercely. But when financier
Kendra and TV megastar Quinn both set their sights on
wealthy Graham Forbes—sweet, shy Jamie's secret crush—
Jamie unleashes her inner diva.

*Available the first week of April
wherever books are sold.*

KIMANI
ROMANCE

www.kimanipress.com

KPTS0140407

Some promises were just made to be broken...

Other People's Business

Debut author

PAMELA YAYE

Stylist Autumn Nicholson looked like the kind of uppity,
city girl L. J. Saunders had sworn off. And Autumn wasn't
interested in casual flings, especially with a luscious hunk
who'd soon be leaving. But fate, well-meaning meddling
friends and a sizzling, sensual attraction all have other plans....

*Available the first week of April
wherever books are sold.*

KIMANI
ROMANCE

KPPY0150407

What happens when Prince Charming arrives...
but the shoe doesn't fit?

THE Glass SLIPPER PROJECT

Bestselling author

DARA GIRARD

Strapped for cash, Isabella Duvall is forced to sell the
family mansion. But when Alex Carlton wants to buy it,
her three sisters devise a plan to capture the handsome
bachelor's heart and keep their home in the family.
The question is...which of the Duvall sisters will
become the queen of Carlton's castle?

*Available the first week of April
wherever books are sold.*

"The people in Reeves' Jamison, South Carolina,
come alive on the pages."
—*The Romance Reader* on *Love's Promise*

Bestselling author

ADRIENNE ELLIS REEVES

SACRED GROUND

An inspirational romance

Gabriel Bell has just inherited fifteen acres and a house
from a great-grandfather he never knew existed—but the
will is anything but straightforward. What is the treasured
destiny that he has only three months to find? And what
does the intriguing Makima Gray have to do with it?

Coming the first week of April
wherever books are sold.

ARABESQUE®

www.kimanipress.com

KPAER0090407